A Tiger's Heart Wrapped in a Player's Hide

Book 2 of the Stone Chronicles

A novel

Written by S. G. Lee

Second Edition 2020

SB

An imprint of Shillelagh Books

London, Ontario, Canada

Acknowledgments:

Sincere thanks to Jodi and Sydney, without your constant support and encouragement, this book would not be possible. You are the best friends a writer could have. I dedicate this book to my daughters, my son-in law and my husband; who have supported my writing endeavours with encouragement and love. Special thanks to my beloved mother in heaven, who taught me dreams, can come true with hard work, perseverance and patience.

Table of Contents

Chapter 1 - A Tiger Wrapped in a Player's Hide

"There is an upstart crow, beautified with our feathers, that with his Tiger's heart wrapped in a player's hide, supposes he is as well able to bombast out a blank verse as the best of you."

Robert Greene 1592

In a room with old world feel, huge marble columns, and ornate wooden panels typically found in a gentlemen's club, a person addressed a huge crowd of men and women.

"He is an upstart. I tell you he presumes to speak for all of us of Magik!" the man asserted passionately.

"He is the head of the council," the other man argued.

"Who elected him the head of the council?" the person demanded of the room.

"His sponsor and teacher, Eric Redstone appointed him to council," answered a woman clearly sounding puzzled.

"Exactly appointed. Why isn't the council of Magiks, an elected position? Why is Le Custos in charge? Why must we suffer through governing men, who seize the power like Kings of old?" queried the person inciting the room.

"But Demetrious Blackstone comes from a long line of Magiks, who work for the good of all," defended another man. "His family has always protected all that is good."

"He is but a man, who puts on a cloak of goodness and altruism, but he is rich is he not? Did he not benefit, from his position of power?" questioned the person, "He holds down the Magiks and forbids them use their power for gain, yet he himself benefits from the same. He claims he protects us from the Vampires and the Werewolves. Yet the Vampires and the Werewolves have hurt no one. They just want to be their selves and he won't allow it. A little blood taken from the Normals would harm no one, but he doesn't allow it either. He keeps them hungry and weak, eating only of blood bank blood simply so he alone can control them, use them."

"The Werewolves? He keeps them penned in small villages, where they hunt game, but can never leave. Of course, these creatures are unhappy and on whom will they take spread their anger? Our children, and our children's, children; if we were to take over the council and rid ourselves of Le Custos, we could take back what is rightfully ours. Good people, I tell you, we deserve the Magiks positions, but we are denied the highest positions by those like Demetrious Blackstone. If we rid ourselves of him and Le Custos, we could make peace with the others and save the Magiks. What say you all in favour? Say Aye!"

A great cheer went up in the room, as most of those assembled in the hall shout "Aye." The few that don't agree, congregate in one small spot in the room near the door.

One of them said in whispers to a person standing nearby that holds a plate of food..., "I didn't see you before; were you behind a door?"

The person's body practically blocked the door.

"Of course, you didn't. I didn't want you to see me."

"What do you want from me?" asked the man feeling fear.

"Not a lot. I am a little peckish," the other person explained.

"Here take it. I'm suddenly not hungry."

The man then offered his plate of food.

"No thank you, that's not quite the snack I wanted," the other person explained.

"What do you want then? I'll go get any snack," the man replied, still afraid, but wanting to mollify the other person.

"I'm afraid food isn't what I want, it doesn't tempt my palate."

"I don't understand your Magik. You eat food," the man protested.

"But I don't eat, not anymore. I was a Magik, but now I am also a Vampire and I am so very hungry."

Within seconds the Magik/Vampire drained all three dissenters and disposed of their bodies, hiding them in a nearby closet. Only one person in the room even noticed. The person who opposed Demetrious looked well satisfied and addressed the crowd saying…, "All gathered here, you must now swear an oath of fidelity to me personally and to the new Magik Council. Draw blood and repeat after me.

"I swear allegiance to the house of Magiks, and to my new reign as your ruler. That's me by the way," the person said laughing, and then continued "Of this I give my loyalty freely, and if I break this oath, the punishment is death. It is done. You are now my sworn people; long may we prosper. And now we make our plans to take down the house of Blackstone."

~0~

Chapter 2 - Magik Vampires
Sarah and Aunt Iva

In the last year Sarah found herself first

frightened and then exhilarated, to find out
her family came from a long list of
distinguished people of Magiks. However,
she found not all of her family, were so
distinguished. In fact, the one member of her
family, who reached out to her (her then
unknown grandfather) had been a villain of
epic proportions. Bringing terror upon
countless of victims, that he either bent to
his will, or vampirized, by taking their will,
and their power; Grandfather Eccklestone
was a sought-after villain, by the magic
council. He had wanted whatever power
Sarah possessed for his own, and a willing
slave to fawn over him of his own bloodline.

Sarah used a new found gift to mesmerize, and get the guard, Charles Keystone to let her, and Alexander Blackstone, Darius' son, go free. Lord Eccklestone, however, met his end by his own bloodline, the son he sought to deny, William Tellstone (a willing accomplice) because of his need for father figure. Lord Eccklestone sought out one who was not even of his blood to claim as his son. William found out his father, not only was aware of him; but denied their connection of father and son, enraged he turned on him, battling Lord Eccklestone to the death. Sarah then escaped with Alexander, the boy her grandfather called son.

It hadn't been all fear last year, despite her grandfather. She met the love of her life in Demetrious who rescued from her grandfather's clutches. Most families of Magik schooled their children from their infancy on their usage of power. Sarah hadn't been aware of any abilities. She had grown to the age of twenty; without ever knowing she possessed power let alone how to control it. Demetrious understanding the abilities Sarah now wielded and couldn't understand, took her to his Great Aunt Iva to learn to control and wield the extent of her power.

Her deceased parents thought to protect her putting a cap on her abilities and it holding it fast until last year, when it started unwinding itself away from the power it held. Even Demetrious had been surprised to find Sarah held so much power. People of Magik usually held one power, but Sarah's own actions had revealed three distinct powers. This made Sarah as powerful as Demetrious in her own right. That made her practically royalty in Magik circles but Sarah wanted her abilities kept a secret she didn't want to be a target again. Alexander insisted that her abilities were still not allfound, but so far, he had been proven wrong.

Those who were multi-talented were revered among people of Magik, as long as they didn't flaunt their abilities among Normals. Sarah still worried, though that people of Magik would tar her with the brush of Eccklestone, since he had been her grandfather. So far though, the people of Magik had been accepting and she felt like one of them.

Demetrious and Sarah fell in love and become engaged. Demetrious' job as head of the Magik Council provided a true challenge, to their blooming relationship. Demetrious travelled around the world to do his job and Sarah continued her training with Aunt Iva, so they grew to value time spent together. Sarah wondered though if she rushed into her engagement. After all, she barely knew Demetrious when she agreed to marry him. She loved him, but they had so little time together, before he went away on council business.

The day after Darius' wedding, Demetrious had received a call from the council to convene another panel and to investigate mysterious attacks on the council members. Demetrious hadn't even the decency to confide this to Sarah; she overheard him telling Darius his brother. Not an auspicious start to their relationship after all. Sarah felt hurt that he didn't trust her enough to tell her what happened in the council of the Magik world, but she hid her anger and pain. She understood some secrecy came with his position, but he confided in Darius; so why didn't he share the same information with her?

He had been home only a day here, and a day there, in the last six months. Sarah missed Demetrious, but she also understood how important his job and how it stood to keep the families and their great powers in check around the world. She tried hard not to complain when he came home to her, for only a few hours, or a few days and left to do his job, but she was only human. She began to worry that she had been under a spell which had made her more subservient to people all her life and whether that had influenced her acceptance of all that had taken place the last year. She had to learn to be more self-sufficient and not give so much of what she wanted so that others could be happy. She had to be her own person instead of someone who had to be told what to do.

Sarah had relationships before high school boyfriend and a brief relationship from a guy in college; but none of them had grown past the kissing stage. Something had been missing and Sarah now knew what that was chemistry. She might have been attracted to those others, but none of them held the longing that she had for Demetrious. She ached when she couldn't be near him. The desire for physical interaction with him overwhelming, but despite that they hadn't consummated their relationship. Sarah's angry words had held Demetrious back and he wanted to make sure Sarah was sure of their love before he made love to her. Soon Sarah hoped this crisis would be over and Demetrious could come back to her side.

She had grown to love Aunt Iva and working with her at her clinic was rewarding, but she longed for the day when her lessons would end and she would travel with Demetrious.

Sarah also recognized she had a lot to learn to be able to harness her powers, but she wished she could be done with it all. She wanted to take her place beside Demetrious. They would marry and she would be with him, always. All his travels would take place with her by his side, even helping him out on council business. Not in an executive position, but her skills would help. Surely that would count, should count?

Aunt Iva appeared at Sarah's elbow in the kitchen as Sarah made a coffee.

"Sarah, woolgathering again?" Aunt Iva asked.

"Yes, I guess."

"I miss him too, but he's an important man. You understood when you became engaged to him that he worked constantly at this job," Aunt Iva insisted, "Now I need a cup of tea is there one there for me?"

"I understand that he had an important job, but it doesn't make me miss him any less. Now I'll make you a cup of tea."

"Thank you, Sarah."

"Demetrious said he'd be home yesterday, but the council called another special meeting, because of the troubles they've been having," Sarah explained sighing and putting the kettle on again.

"I married a councilman once. Wouldn't you love him less if he didn't help people so much? Turmoil exists right now; the vampires and the werewolves attack so many people. He saved scores of mortals and immortals none of them know how close they came to dying. Do you have an idea how many messes, he's handled?" Aunt Iva commented, "Of course my Roy, always found time for me."

"How would I know about any of this? Demetrious tells me nothing," Sarah complained. "How do you know these things Aunt Iva?"

"I have my sources. There's a new leader of the vampires. No one outside of their circle knows who he is, only that he is dangerous," Aunt Iva commented. "Demetrious and the council work hard to find out who he is and who he works with. The problem? Demetrious may have a traitor at the council. Of course, since he is so dictatorial, he should expect someone will oppose him."

"Demetrious isn't dictatorial. Where would you get such an idea?

"Well dear he has changed. Power will do that to a man. Demetrious can't even discuss them with you. They are so top secret and he isn't the type to share, not like my Roy."

"Oh, I get it. You try to make me see how judgemental I am being. You are correct, Aunt Iva. I wasn't being fair. No wonder poor Demetrious, looked so tired and worried, when he came home last week," Sarah voiced. "I do understand he has secrets, but I still wish he share some of his work with me."

"Demetrious is in a world of dreary council business, with varied opinions on a subject which should have been definitively decided fifty years ago. An alliance between the vampires and the werewolves would be such a huge headache for the council. The vampires believe we have kept them from their true nature and the werewolves believe the same. Some people believe if we gave into them, then maybe they would behave," Aunt Iva stated. "I of course, think those people spout nonsense. Demetrious has to be diplomatic and offer the Magik council opinion, without offending anyone; trying being in his position."

"I'm still having trouble believing such things exist. Demetrious told me there were such people as vampires, and werewolves, but I've never seen one," Sarah replied.

"And you didn't know about people of Magiks either, but here you are a year later, and you found you possess a lot more power yourself," Aunt Iva stated, as a matter of fact.

The kettle whistled and Sarah made the coffee exactly as Aunt Iva preferred it with two sugars and a little milk then handed it to Aunt Iva.

"Thank you dear."

"Have you ever met a vampire or a werewolf?" asked Sarah sipping her coffee.

"Once I knew a vampire, in all fact I barely got away from one. He mesmerised me. Usually they aren't able to do so to people of Magik, but he had the rare ability. He charmed me and I thought I loved him," Aunt Iva replied, looking sad.

"What happened?" Sarah asked.

"Young, and barely out of my teens, I met a young man and I fell in love."

"You thought yourself in love and you didn't know he was a vampire? What was his name?"

"It's not quite that simple. He wasn't a vampire when we met."

"What was his name?"

"His name was Peter Whetstone. A couple of years older than me, he appeared everything I thought I desired in a man," Aunt Iva recalled. "We were going to be married. I looked forward to the ceremony and the after party. I bought my dress, the flowers, and arranged the wedding details.

"But Peter disappeared without a trace, on the eve of our wedding."

Aunt Iva then gulped some of her tea as if trying to get her emotions under control.

"He disappeared the day, before your wedding? How did you find out he had disappeared?"

"I went to see him to give him a pre-wedding present, a tie I'd found with blue and gold stripes, that I knew he'd love. I entered his apartment with my key to find his place in shambles. I looked around saw signs of a struggle and went to my brother to get help, but they were unable to find out what had happened to Peter."

"Oh, Aunt Iva, I am so sorry," Sarah retorted.

"A year went by and I had decided he had died. Then he reappeared, looking gaunt, but more handsome than ever. Torn, I didn't want to see him. I thought I had moved on falling in love with my Roy, but the feelings were still there when I saw him again," Aunt Iva continued. "Peter and offered no explanation and laughed when I told him I thought he had been kidnapped."

"He laughed?"

"Yes, he laughed. My heart hardened against him at that moment, as he made light of my concerns and didn't even think of how I felt cancelling all the wedding plans."

"But you said he loved you. I don't understand."

"I thought so too. Peter thought he would waltz back into my life, and pick up where he stood before. But angry that Peter had deserted me, I wanted none of him."

"Demetrious isn't like him. He would tell me what happened. Now did you find out where Peter Whetstone hid for a year?" Sarah asked.

"Not right away. He was not happy about Roy either, and I think he planned something bad for Roy. But I'm getting ahead of the story... I had made a date with Roy, but I got a message that I was supposed to meet him at the restaurant. I went to the restaurant and the server escorted me to a table. Seated at the table was Peter. I wanted to walk away, but he compelled me to sit down and eat the dinner he ordered for me-all my favourite foods. Peter pretended to eat, but pushed the food around his plate. He

asked me to wait and excused himself, as if
going to the little boy's room. I don't know
what compelled me to follow, but follow I
did. I followed him right to the door, where I
saw him take the server and drain him dry.
He commented, "Did you enjoy the scene,
my dear Ida? We could do great things
together you and me. We would tour the
world loving and living forever. We could
conquer the world. What do you say
Iva...marry me and be my eternal bride?"
Peter asked me.

"Terrified I fled down the hall, but he
moved so fast. He was directly before me, in
the blink of an eye. Peter grabbed my neck
and was about to take me against my will,
when I spotted the broken cane. I grabbed it
and thrust it directly into his heart, saving
myself. He told me before he died... "I
wouldn't have harmed you against your will.
I love you."

Aunt Iva wiped her eyes and then continued,
"I felt sad and disgusted with myself; after
all I killed him taken his life. Before my
shocked eyes, the man I recognized as Peter
turned to dust."

"If he turned to dust, how did you know his
plans for Roy?" Sarah asked, seeking the

loophole of this story, if only to dispute there were vampires.

"I met with Roy after this occurred and we went to Peter's home, on behalf of the council. We were to erase his existence and hide the knowledge of his turning into a vampire."

"When we arrived at his apartment, we found his plans all detailed. Peter had ingratiated himself into the privy council of the Magiks and positioned himself to take over ruling the council. This would have made all revere him, as King of The Vampire Magiks. He hadn't planned to kill Roy, even though he felt he was a rival to my affections and a danger to him personal. He planned to reach out to Roy, not kill him. Poor dear, he still loved me and thought I'd leave Roy for him. Of course, I was much younger and beautiful then," Aunt Iva explained.

"But how did he hope to get you to leave Roy and take over the council? Wouldn't someone else have known he was a vampire and stop him, especially if he tried to take over the council?" Sarah enquired shocked.

"He planned on turning all those who were loyal to him into Magik /Vampires," Aunt Iva explained. "I found out later, he had been dating my younger sister Minerva or Minnie as we always called her. He deliberately threw her over for me."

"Wow, I didn't know you had a younger sister."

"Yes, I do, but we don't talk much since the falling out. She blames me for losing the love of her life."

"She blames you? But he was a vampire what else could you have done?"

"She wouldn't listen to me. We haven't spoken in nearly sixty years. I've tried but she won't speak to me."

Aunt Iva then wiped away tears.

"How foolish of her. You were brave, Aunt Iva. Do you think that could happen again? Someone who has power becomes a Vampire?" Sarah asked worried.

"I'm sure that is what the council is worried about in this case. A person who has Magik and is a vampire, would be an extremely deadly combination, and difficult to remain in control. Lack of control, can also cause insanity."

"Will Demetrious be okay?" Sarah asked greatly worried.

"Demetrious has been schooled since a boy, to take over the council. He has studied the art of war and the art of diplomacy. Demetrious can live up to the challenge. Not to worry my dear, he'll be fine," Aunt Iva responded.

"I certainly hope so Aunt Iva, if he's dealing with a person such as Peter Whetstone."

"Sarah, the thing you have to remember once they are vampires, they aren't people anymore."

"Of course, they are people. They are still people with feelings and emotions, even if they are changed."

"Sarah, you think everyone is like you with heightened emotions. Not everyone cares. It's unfortunate, but there are people who think only of themselves and when these people become vampires, their emotions are heightened. They become even more of the egotists they already were."

"You must think I'm naive, that you telling me this," Sarah complained. "I do understand people can be plain evil. I'm not stupid."

"Oh honey, I know you are not! You have a sweet innocent charm about you, which makes you believe everyone can change. I don't want you to be hurt, that's all."

"Thanks, I appreciate the thought."

"It will all work out in the end. I'm a firm believer in good triumphing over evil. Let's get started on your lessons Sarah. Today I think I'll teach you some T'ai chi."

"I thought T'ai chi was an exercise?"

"T'ai chi is a blend of mind and body. It is an internal Chinese martial art, practiced for both its defense training and health benefits. We teach children to feel their abilities as they get older. You never had the opportunity to learn that way, so this should help you to channel your abilities by making you more aware."

"I'm willing to try. You are my teacher after all."

"Well we have to get you a proper uniform. You can't possible learn any of the movements in those clothes."

"Will yoga pants and a tee-shirt work?" Sarah asked.

"Yes, so you know yoga?"

"No, I just like the clothing style."

"The youth of today." muttered Aunt Iva, "Come on go get changed and we will start, because I have the clinic today after one o'clock today."

~0~

Chapter 3 – Safety

"Sarah wake -up. We must leave,"

Aunt Iva cried shaking Sarah from a sound sleep.

"Leave? And go where?" Sarah asked.

"Demetrious has sent word that we need to go to safety."

"But if we are not safe, how can Demetrious be safe?"

"Sarah, Demetrious has many men guarding him, would you have him worry about you?"

"We're safe here though. Didn't you say these mountains and these hills held power that protected us?"

"Yes, the mountains shield us, and normally we would be safe here, but these are desperate times. There is a place that holds even more ability to protect us."

"There is?" Sarah asked surprised.

"Yes, now no more wasting time. We must be on the road by six a.m.to go to the place of power," Aunt Iva insisted.

"I still don't understand Demetrious said we would be safe here. What has happened? Why didn't he call me?" Sarah protested, but began to get out of bed and get dressed.

"A meeting took place in County Cork..."

"Ireland?"

"Yes, of course Ireland. It is where the council meets in crisis," explained Aunt Iva.

"Then what is the problem? Demetrious and his people met to discuss what to do about this Magik/Vampire and they found a solution," Sarah exclaimed.

"It wasn't Demetrious' council, so there was no solution, only more plotting against the council and more dead bodies. The Magik/Vampire's has seized allegiances from trusted persons of Magik. They pledged their alliance with their blood and dead townsfolk."

"But haven't most of Demetrious' people done the same? How can they betray Demetrious and live?"

"Demetrious may have made them swear in their blood, but he believes in the more tolerant way and does not bespell their blood."

"Bespell?"

"He doesn't bind their blood, so they will be instantly punished."

"Nonsense! He did that with Delilah."

"Did he? Or did he make her think, he did?" Aunt Iva asked.

"Doesn't that put Demetrious in danger?"

"Yes, if the person catches on. Didn't you tell me Delilah is dead? So, he won't have to worry about her."

"I don't remember telling you Delilah died," Sarah replied throwing on some clothes and then placing clothes in a suitcase.

"Sure, you did, don't you remember? Just before Janelle and Darius' wedding, you told me she wasn't seen again after Lord

Eccklestone was killed. I'm sure he killed her. He killed a lot of our people."

"My grandfather had much to answer for, but he did so with his life."

"I'm surprised at you Sarah; do you defend Lord Eccklestone?"

"No, of course not! I just don't wish anyone dead, even him."

"Your soft heart can be used against you. You'd be wise to remember that Sarah." Aunt Iva stated.

"I'm tired of people accusing me of having a soft heart. Being nice should be used against you."

"Sarah, please don't be difficult. You need to hurry."

"Do you expect me to change in front of you?"

"Really Sarah. How many times have I changed in front of you? Now hurry we have to go."

Sarah quickly threw on some clothes and then placed clothes in a suitcase.

"Good I'm glad you're ready, Charles will be here soon."

"Charles who?"

"Why, Charles Keystone, of course. Demetrious sent him to guard over us and keep us safe."

"Charles? I thought Charles was killed in Canada."

"So did Demetrious, until Charles came to him for a job," Aunt Iva explained.

"I don't know if I feel comfortable with Charles guarding us."

"Why? He seems like a nice enough man!"

"When we first met I my abilities weren't fine-tuned and I used too much charm on him."

"Oh dear, that can be bad, but if Demetrious trusts him you should too. Just make sure you set boundaries and you should be fine."

"I don't like this."

"Sarah really I didn't think you'd be the one to give me such a hard time. Just get ready to leave."

"Iva?" Charles voice cried out from the living room.

"We're coming out in a minute dear. Just be patient it takes a few minutes to pack all our things."

"Sarah and you are well worth the wait, but the flight takes off in an hour we must be to the airport by then," yelled Charles.

Sarah reluctantly picked up her suitcase and stepped into the other room. Charles stood in shadow and for a moment she thought her grandfather stood there. Fear took over and Sarah nearly ran out of the room. Then sanity returned. Her grandfather was dead; he couldn't be standing there. William and grandfather had been killed and all trace of their existence erased.

Sarah shook off the feeling and took another look at Charles. He was tall like her grandfather, but he had black hair. What had made her think he looked like her grandfather? The moustache, of course! Charles had grown a moustache reminiscent of her grandfather's and had affected her grandfather's English accent.

"Where do we go?" Sarah asked.

"Sarah, I am so glad to see you. I'll tell you when we get there. It's necessary to keep it a secret just in case someone tries to take you before we get there. Of course, they would have to kill me first," Charles explained.

"Thank you, Charles, for dropping everything and coming to guard us," Sarah replied politely.

"For you Sarah, anything," Charles answered.

Inwardly Sarah cringed and wondered why she acted so sweet to him. She shouldn't encourage him, but he was just so much like a puppy dog. She couldn't be cruel to him.

"So, you have everything?" Charles asked.

"Yes," Sarah answered, still thinking it felt strange that Demetrious trusted him with Aunt Iva and Sarah. Why couldn't he have dropped everything and come to them? What foolish, selfish thinking. Demetrious needed to be in his office surrounding himself with able people of Magik who could thwart the Magik/Vampire. He couldn't be expected to dismiss all his work and woes and make sure Sarah and Aunt Iva were safe.

"Sarah, listen to us," rebuked Aunt Iva.

"I'm so sorry what did you say?" Sarah enquired.

"It wasn't important."

"Not that you seem interested, Charles, dear; but my suitcase was also by the door."

"Sorry, Iva, I'll take it too," Charles apologized, picking up the two cases.

"Charles, dear, I'm sorry too. I thought you were related to that evil Eccklestone. I'm shocked, but pleased that you were instead related to my dear Roy."

"Charles is related to Roy?" Sarah asked shocked.

"Yes, dear some kind of cousin," Aunt Iva answered.

"How do you know that?"

"Always so suspicious Sarah! Demetrious sent the information and his Charles' birth certificate with Charles."

"I'm sorry you don't trust me, Sarah. I thought I'd earned your trust," Charles whined.

"It's not that I don't trust you. I haven't
known you that long."

"We can correct that; I'll be your bodyguard
for awhile," Charles said smiling.

"Wonderful," Sarah said under her breath
sarcastically, as they went out the door and
into a waiting car.

They were out the door and in Charles' car
in a just few minutes. The car continued
down a road and entered a private airstrip.

"Where are we headed?" Sarah asked.

"We're headed to an airplane, but I can't tell
you the final destination," Charles answered.

"Nonsense, you tell me right now, Charles,"
Sarah admonished.

"I can't Sarah. It's my job to protect you and
to do so, no one but Demetrious and I can
know where we end up."

"I'm mad at Demetrious, not you Charles.
Demetrious should treat me as an equal and
tell me to where he's having you spirit me
away."

"I'm sorry Sarah. I'd tell you if I could. Just
come with me now."

"Fine, but I object and I'm going to tell Demetrious my objections next time I see him."

"You do that Sarah," Charles answered helping Sarah and Iva out of the now parked car. Charles then took Sarah's hand and propelled Sarah and Aunt Iva into the airport and onto a waiting plane.

~0~

Chapter 4 - Protect Family at all costs
Six months later

Demetrious worked in his office with

ornate wooden panels. The office doors
however had lead and steel in them, nothing
could penetrate them when locked.
Demetrious was worried about his
administrative assistant, Petra Kaminski.
Petra had become rail thin and appeared
sickly and he worried about her health. Her
hair once blonde, when she first came to
work for Demetrious turned a light brown
and didn't suit her. This morning when she
had come to work her clothes were wrinkled
and mismatched, like she'd put them on in a
hurry. This had begun after he announced
his engagement to Sarah. He hadn't been
aware she felt that way about him. He
needed to replace Petra for both their sakes.

He should speak with her but he worried about saying the wrong thing. He had enough to contend with the Vampire/Magik. His office phone buzzed and he picked up the instrument.

"Your brother is here," the voice of his administrative assistant Petra Kaminski announced over the intercom.

"Please send Darius in to my office," Demetrious advised.

"Demetrious what has happened? This guy came for me and demanded I come and see you immediately," Darius complained, motioning to the man who stood nearby.

Caleb Gemstone was a man, often compared to a mountain. His arms legs and body were all oversized. He stood six foot six and although he appeared huge, not an ounce of fat was on him His two hundred and sixty pounds were all muscle. Some people marvelled at his muscle when he took off his jacket, which wasn't often. He was also Demetrious' main bodyguard, since the troubles with the vampires and werewolves started occurring.

"Thanks Caleb, I can take it from here if you'd like to wait outside, or take a quick lunch."

"Are you sure Lord Blackstone?" asked Caleb.

"Please Caleb, I've asked you a thousand times not to call me, Lord Blackstone again. Call me Demetrious, or if you must Mr. Blackstone, but don't call me Lord. It's like lumping me with The Worm and you know how I felt about him," Demetrious complained, "For goodness sake we grew up together."

"I would never want to insult you Lord Blackstone...I mean Demetrious. I know we grew up together. You are my friend but you're also my boss." Caleb answered, not sounding sure about calling his boss and the head of the council by his first name.

"You're one of my closest friends too, Caleb, that makes you able to use my first name."

"Thank you, Demetrious. Not to insult you again. but some of the family whisper you are not lordly and...," Caleb began, sounding hesitant to tell Demetrious this.

"Whispering what?"

"This is sensitive and only for Lord... er... Demetrious, not you, maybe I shouldn't be discussing this in front of you," Caleb explained starring hard at Darius.

"My brother is privy to any all information. Darius has the highest clearance of the council and I personally would trust him with my life," Demetrious replied in an authoritative voice.

"Very well, I will tell him. The people of Magik have been whispering about your familiarity. You are the head of council, yet you allow people to call you by your first name. There are people of Magik, who conspire with Vampires and Wolves, these people are weak and foolish. They look to the person they think is strong enough to lead them. They need someone who appears invulnerable, a strong leader to lead them and teach them the struggle that people of Magik made long ago, against the Vampires and Werewolves was valid," Caleb explained.

"And do you believe I am that leader?" Demetrious asked.

"I believe you are that leader, my Lord, and yes I address you as Lord, as an address of respect," Caleb commented.

"You have my permission to address me as Lord Blackstone, when in public, but in private Demetrious, please," Demetrious insisted.

"Thank you, sir, I mean Demetrious," Caleb responded, A beauteous smile filled his face and made him appear almost handsome for a moment.

"I would lay down my life for you and yours sir," Caleb avowed.

"My family has relied on your family for centuries to protect and serve. You are the strength of the council and we thank you for that service," Demetrious replied imperiously.

Caleb looked pleased and embarrassed at the same time. He bowed and turned to stop for a moment to comment, "Please be careful sir. Some do not judge you the way I do. They look at your duty and find it lacking."

"They find my duty lacking?" Demetrious asked shocked.

"Not I, Lord Demetrious, never would I doubt your attention to the council. I have defended you each time I heard such scurrilous talk."

"Thank you, Caleb. I will continue to do the work of the council and protect it with my life but I appreciate all your efforts."

"I will protect your life my Lord it is my sworn duty as long as you protect the council. Even now Frederick Fossilstone guards the door sir, until I come back from lunch." Caleb then bowed to Demetrious and left Demetrious' office.

"Talk about hero worship. The guy worships the ground you walk on and would follow you to the ends of the earth," Darius commented.

"He works for me. He guards me. That is all," Demetrious protested.

"Fine, if you say so. Demetrious, I worry about you, though. About Petra she looks sick. Has she taken your engagement to Sarah hard?"

"You recognized her crush on me?"

"Everyone saw it but you Demetrious. You'll have to find her another place to work, somewhere prestigious but also with someone who would appeal to her."

"You sound like a matchmaker Darius."

"I want her out of your orbit Demetrious. Scorned woman can be big trouble."

"Did you hear about Eloise?" Demetrious asked, changing the subject.

"Did I hear about Eloise? My son was the one who showed the doctors how to help her."

"Alexander helped her?"

"So, the great Demetrious doesn't know all?"

"Tell me how it happened, Darius."

"Alexander overheard me speaking of our cousin Eloise and of how she was damaged by the worm."

"You can say his name, Lord Eccklestone now. He is dead, so he can do us no harm."

"Fine, Lord Eccklestone! Alexander read some of the tomes from his teacher and some ancient texts from the council library. He told me he thought he had seen a way to help Eloise come out of her akinetic mutism."

"Talk English, would you?" Demetrious complained.

"I'm not a shrink."

"I believe they prefer to be called psychiatrists. But I'm speaking of the fact, in which she sat there, didn't move and didn't speak."

"Now she's speaking? Yes and no? How did Alexander get her to speak?" Demetrious asked.

"The way he explained it to me and the doctors there was a damaged part in her brain and he rewired some of it. The doctors believe the rest will regenerate and we may yet get Eloise back the way she used to be."

"I would be so happy if that were to happen."

"Me too, but she's she has always had a crush on you Demetrious. That could be a problem for you."

"It's only because she said I reminded her of someone she once loved," Demetrious explained. "She's over that now. She thinks of me only as a brother."

"Might be true, but you seemed to have a lot of women who like you, Demetrious."

"There's only one woman I care about and her name is Sarah Maidenstone, soon to be Sarah Maidenstone-Blackstone."

"This isn't why you called me here though is it Demetrious?"

Demetrious sounded weary and let out a sigh. Darius looked over at him worried, wondering what had happened. Darius then looked around Demetrious' office as if to see through walls at all that went into the building.

"Why do you have heavy artillery guarding you? Why did you summon me?" Darius demanded.

"I have word of a disaster. A secret meeting of the Irish council of Magik took place a few months ago in Ireland, in County Cork...," Demetrious uttered.

"What? But you called no meeting! Insurrection? Tell me quick don't hold back," Darius commanded.

"One who is a Vampire of Magik opposes me. He demands followers and has declared himself ruler. Those who will not follow and oppose him are drained and never seen again," Demetrious explained. "They take an unbreakable oath allegiance to his house of Magiks and to their new ruler. Punishment is death. They are told they give their loyalty freely, but it has been coerced with a show of killing with Vampire powers. They plan to bring down the house of Blackstone and Le Custos," Demetrious related.

"Then they come after Alexander and Janelle, I must get to them," Darius replied panicked.

"I've already sent and a team and Alexander with Janelle to Aunt Iva's. They should be arriving any moment now; but I need you to go protect them all. Aunt Iva, Sarah Janelle and Alexander need protection. I can't trust anyone else with this, and I can't leave. Please tell me, you'll do this."

"Of course, I will. But Sarah can protect herself," Darius offered.

"She can't right now. She's extremely vulnerable right now in ways she doesn't even comprehend," Demetrious explained.

"I don't understand, Sarah's, ill?" asked Darius.

"No, she's not ill, but I've seen her in a dream. She is in grave danger from a trickster," Demetrious admitted.

"You dreamt a seer dream? This must be serious then. You believe it's a trickster? I can't believe there is still a person of Magik powerful enough to project realities? I thought all that powerful, had died with Eccklestone."

"I have seen this, and I do not dream the future often. I just can't get a bead on to who it is though," Demetrious explained. "I need Sarah protected."

"I will protect her you can count on me," Darius promised. "I will guard her and our entire family, brother with my life. No harm shall come to them. I call on the angels to protect my family and help me do the same. Angelus custodio prosapia meus, angelo contego familiam meam," Darius chanted in Latin, weaving a spell of protection until he can arrive.

"Protect family at all costs," Demetrious repeated in English as a vow.

"I will Demetrious. Hold strong fight the Vampire/Magik and understand we will keep them safe. Do you have a name yet?"

"No, I don't have a name. But I will find him. He will not escape the council's wrath. He's crafty hiding behind others. I suspect he may also being working with Vampires and Werewolves so be wary of any of them. We have lost so many men and women and I blame myself I should have seen this coming. Cunning and skillful he hides in plain sight."

"Demetrious you are not omnipotent. You don't have my seer abilities either and even I didn't see this coming, so how were you to see this coming?"

"I should have but now I must act with no worries that some near to me could be harmed."

"I'll protect Sarah and the rest of our family. None shall come to harm."

"Darius, you don't know how much this means to me. Thank you for taking on the responsibility to keep our loved ones safe, it relieves my mind," Demetrious thanked Darius.

"I think I do brother. You'd do the same for me."

"Your flight awaits. See you soon Darius, hopefully with news of the vampire Magiks defeat," Demetrious avowed.

"Godspeed, Demetrious."

Darius departed and Demetrious breathed a sigh of relief. His brother would guard their family like gold, but most of all they all be safe. Demetrious would concentrate on finding the Vampire Magik and put an end to his reign before any more people die. Darius wondered how to help his brother, besides guarding their families. Perhaps he could network from Aunt Iva's? He had a global phone thanks to Demetrious' pull and an excellent connection for access to the internet.

He wouldn't just sit around guarding the loved ones. Even if it was important, he could be doing more. He'd pay back Demetrious for all he had done for him. He would help them nail the Magik responsible for these attacks. Janelle would also see the man she married held Blackstone blood and was as bold and powerful as Demetrious. It wouldn't hurt for Alexander to see his old man was as powerful as his Uncle either. Sometimes he thought Alexander hero worshipped his Uncle and looked up to him a lot more than he did his own Dad. He would shoe them all he was strong and powerful just like Demetrious, after all he produced strong Magik abilities of his own.

Darius was a seer, granted it had been failing him recently, but he was pretty sure when he used too much of his other abilities it syphoned from his seer abilities. He was a Blackstone. He would be proud and show everyone he was made of the stuff that made Blackstone's leaders. He could do more for the Magik council and he would.

~0~

Chapter 5 - Rowen of the Werewolves

Rowen Pentagan felt overwhelmed and exhausted. Rowen should be on her honeymoon; instead her she oversaw werewolf council matters. Dragomir, her husband of two days, was incredibly patient with her job as Alpha of the werewolves. He hadn't even balked when asked to take her last name, instead of Rowen taking his. Rowen didn't even have to explain. Dragomir seem to understand immediately why it was necessary to retain the prestigious name of Pentagan and how it would cement her position as Queen and Alpha of the werewolves.

It couldn't be easy for him to be consort to the Queen of the werewolves. Dragomir however was a alpha werewolf, amongst the werewolves subservient in their eyes only to her. He was amazingly patient and kind. He had been her truest friend and instructor when she first came to the werewolf camp.

Three years ago, Rowen hadn't even comprehended that she was a werewolf. One bit of meat after being a life- long vegetarian, mix in a full moon and bingo she had fur and teeth. She was alone scared, hiding from humans she could harm and trying to fend for herself when Dragomir and his brother came to see her. She joined their werewolf camp and found out she was the long-lost tribe of the Pentagan.

She was Queen, because of her bloodline, but the council of the Alexandre tribe really hadn't respected woman werewolves and they tried to marry her off the first chance they got to obtain her bloodline and power for their tribe. They told her that she would remain Queen, in name only. She would marry and Petru the King's forty something brother, would be her mate and ruler. Rowen not only balked at this she fought Petru for her right not to mate and won.

Her first taste of the evil power contained in the blood of her enemy would do what her bloodline couldn't earn, give her the respect she was due. Petru had died at her hand to obtain her freedom. There had been three others she had killed since then. All of them challenging her to the death and Rowen had not been able to refuse the challenge, as it would endanger herself and others around her. She would not have gotten through any of this without Dragomir by her side, listening to her complain about her new life and responsibilities and difficulties that she faced. Some werewolves still tried to deny her place, as head of the Werewolves and there were always assassination plots.

Many werewolf clans still held to archaic traditions, which involved keeping werewolf women barefoot and pregnant. They believed no women fit to lead. Rowen had worked three years herself, on her own clan to convert their beliefs and still encountered some dissenters who clung to the past. One whole branch of werewolves (almost have the country of the United States and parts of Canada), just ignored her completely, even go as far to appoint their own Alpha werewolf. Of course, this was male werewolf.

His name was Damocles Scourby, the second. Damocles was the son of the scourge of the werewolves, the first Damocles Scourby whom Rowen had killed two years ago. Rowen thought back to that time. Dragomir and Voda, Elena Dalakis and Rowen had all searched for Damocles, but instead of finding Damocles, Rowen had been found by Demetrious Blackstone who questioned her sudden reign. Demetrious had wanted them to stop looking for Damocles. Demetrious claimed he would handle Damocles and stop his killing of innocents.

Rowen had ignored him and kept searching. Unfortunately, Damocles found Rowen first. He had taken her prisoner. Rowen had tried to escape been caught and fought him almost to the death. Demetrious had found her standing over Damocles broken body. Damocles was beaten but not dead.

Demetrious irate had threatened to bring her in front of the Magik council. Rowen standing on sheer will power, did not appreciate being yelled at. Demetrious told her she was a foolish woman. Rowen had finally angrily showed Demetrious where she had been held for two days. Where she had been tortured and threatened that unless she became Damocles mate, she would die. He had done some kind of mojo on some of Damocles people. Demetrious then started believing her that Damocles was the aggressor.

Rowen exonerated; Demetrious had let her return to her position. Rowen thought it would now be a problem of the past, but Demetrious Blackstone had overruled that. Demetrious edict had made her so angry. Rowen couldn't understand why he granted Damocles Scourby rule of all of his father's werewolves. Damocles had been proven an aggressor. He had after all kidnapped Rowen and killed at will.

Rowen argued to no avail that she was ruler of all and that Damocles was a usurper, but Demetrious claimed that that was too much territory for on werewolf. Rowen contended and Demetrious conceded that she, Rowen could reign as Queen over all the werewolves; but that each werewolf clan need a separate ruler as well and underling to Rowen.

Rowen felt that Demetrious Blackstone interfered in her business and her governance. Demetrious Blackstone maintained he was the head of Magik and therefore controlled all. Rowen had been perplexed why this man wouldn't listen to her arguments. What right did he have to dictate their nature and their governance?

Dragomir had pulled her aside to tell her just how much power the man held and how she risked not only her own but the life of her werewolves by fighting with him. Rowen heard Dragomir out and felt she had no other choice then to capitulate to Demetrious edicts. Her people's safety always came before her own wishes and needs.

Demetrious had further stipulated that she, Rowen, must also check on them once yearly to make sure they weren't breaking Magik rules or plotting against her. Rowen felt that this edict was unnecessary as she had already planned to spy on them; but not just once a year. Rowen decided she had better place a spy there in the Scourby camp to protect her and her clan's interests.

Rowen felt guilty for possibly sending the spy to his doom, for if he were found Damocles would kill him and possibly this Demetrious Blackstone because he didn't like her interference. It was that same spy that had gotten word to Rowen about the

plot against the Magik council. Rowen
hadn't heard from him in weeks and feared
him dead, when word had come from
someone else. Her spy had passed his
message onto her. The information was dire
Damocles Scourby the second, by all
accounts he was a powerful werewolf. He
had now aligned himself (as her spy had told
her) with a bunch of Vampires who opposed
the Magik council making him an enemy of
the Pentagan-Alexandre Clan and all other
who were aligned with Rowen. If Rowen
didn't act Scourby would threaten both the
werewolves and Demetrious' Magik council
and while she didn't like some of
Demetrious' edicts it was better to support
the enemy you knew rather than the enemy
you didn't know or maybe knew too well.

This is what created the huge headache for
Rowen, which precipitated her cutting her
honeymoon short. Rowen's responsibilities
weighed heavy on her, but she would not let
her werewolves down. Rowen was the
queen by destiny; she must do her duty to
the werewolves and keep them safe. She
deserved a honeymoon but that was neither
here or there now she had a job to do. They
were at war with those werewolves.

They had affiliated themselves with a vampire, which was bad enough, but now they sought to end such powerful people as the Magik council. That would be suicide and Rowen would not allow her clans to suffer for the actions of a few rogue werewolves. Demetrious Blackstone would not be able to point a finger at her or her clan members and declare them traitors.

She had even heard that Damocles declared there was no other Alpha, only he. Rowen had left these clans to their own devices feeling that did not have the time, or energy to bring them under control, but now with them openly opposing her she had to take action. Rowen was Alpha by blood and she would demand their allegiance to her and her reign; or it would be out and out war on those who choice to align themselves with the pretender Damocles. If Damocles fought back, she would rip out his throat herself, as she had done to his father. None were allowed to put the fate of all werewolves in jeopardy as long as Pentagan blood ran in her veins. The council awaited her judgement and she stewing over this for an hour, with only Dragomir quietly reading for company.

"Is that your latest novel?" asked Rowen
"I'm sorry what a terrible wife I am. I
haven't even had a chance yet to read it yet,"
Rowen retorted suddenly noting the title of
the book Dragomir read.

As he sets down his e-reader and turned it
off, the cover came up as a screensaver.

"Yes, don't you love the cover? I found this
wonderful graphic artist in London, Ontario,
Canada. She created this cover just as I
wanted it."

"I'm glad Dragomir. You write so
beautifully," Rowen commented

"My first try writing about werewolves, I
hope my readers enjoy it."

"You are very talented Dragomir. Look at
all your other titles you've published under
the pseudonym of Derek Kiss. It's funny
how people think they are just stories."

"The readers seem to like the stories. They
like to be scared."

"Of course, they do and people like to read
about werewolves not knowing that they
really exist."

"Rowen, its war isn't it?" her mate Dragomir sighed seeing her face and realizing she avoided the inevitable decision.

"Yes, they've started the war. But first I have to send word to Demetrious Blackstone that we had nothing to do with any of these crimes. He can't think that we would ever move against the council," Rowen responded. "We must report in person as I trust no one to give him the message."

"I don't like him," Dragomir blurted out angrily. "He's too friendly with you. I don't want you to see him."

"Dragomir are you jealous? He's engaged now and even if he wasn't, I'm married to you. Forever! Liking him has nothing to do with this. Jealousy is a foolish emotion we don't have time for ;if we don't get word to him, he'll think our people are behind this and make them pay. I have to go in person and let him know who is behind this."

"Then I'm going too," Dragomir avowed.

"I wouldn't have it any other way," Rowen responded smiling.

Chapter 6 - Tangled Webs
Petra

P etra Kaminski sat at her desk waiting

for Demetrious to leave. His stupid brother, Darius, had left. Why hadn't he? She needed to report in, but Demetrious had become suspicious. Intelligent and hard to fool him, but Petra succeeded and what she was did was for his own good. She had to separate him from Sarah Maidenstone-Dexler, before she destroyed Demetrious' ability to govern. He couldn't see how Sarah had used her abilities to bewitch and beguile him, but she, Petra, could. She seen how he had changed and had let a few things slide, that he would have normally have acted on. It was a shame she had to agree with his enemy but she wouldn't let his enemy harm Demetrious. That is where she drew the line. The Magik-Vampire might think Petra would continue to do his or her bidding, but Petra wanted Demetrious. That was the only reason she had agreed to let them know where to find Sarah, Aunt Iva, Janelle and the retched Alexander.

Demetrious had so far attempted to keep all of Alexander's abilities from Petra; but she had overheard part of conversation with the boy's tutor. Alexander was a phenomenon, a once in a millennium person of Magik. He held great power and most likely had great untapped abilities that would manifest as he grew older. It was then that Petra knew in order to carry out her plan to save Demetrious; she had to have Alexander taken as well. Alexander would be able to see right through her deception with his abilities and spoil everything.

Didn't he see he could come to harm and all because of that retched Sarah. So, what if she came from the Maidenstone line? They weren't a great bunch. She also had Eccklestone blood. The lineage of evil ran in her, Petra would not allow her to also taint Demetrious and blend her wickedness with Demetrious' virtuousness. If anyone would blend their blood with Demetrious it would be Petra. She would carry his child.

Demetrious thought Sarah hung the moon
and stars, but she was a foolish child
compared to Petra. Petra could give him
everything he hungered for and more. She
was after all trained as a Kaminski. She
could be the wife of someone high up in the
council, and she had picked Demetrious out
years ago to be that someone. Hadn't she
learned all his interests and studied them so
she could talk intelligently about them.
She'd taken this job to be near him. She
would never allow Sarah to ruin him.

Demetrious needed a spouse that he could
share his burdens as the supreme leader of
the council of Magik not a smug idiot who
needed to be rescued constantly. Sarah was
easily deceived and swayed so she was all
wrong to be Demetrious spouse. He needed
a woman who could withstand torture if
need be. Demetrious needed someone who
would stand by his side, offering
suggestions to aid him in his reign. Petra
knew she could be Demetrious' equal, not
that simpering Sarah Dexler. Sarah must
have used Demetrious leftover feelings for
her mother to get him to love her. Why
everyone fell for her innocent sweet act
Petra couldn't fathom. Petra had never hated
anyone as much she hated Sarah for taking

advantage of Demetrious. After all she had been with Demetrious for years and before Demetrious had saved the deceitful Sarah, he had shown signs of appreciating her. If Sarah hadn't used her abilities on Demetrious, he would be engaged to her, not Sarah. The phone rang interrupting Petra's thoughts.

"Demetrious Blackstone's office; just a moment, and I will see if he's available to take your call," Petra said into the phone, then put the call on hold she called Demetrious' phone.

"Demetrious, Rowen Pentagan is on line one. Will you take the call?" Petra asked into the phone.

"Certainly, put her on Petra," Demetrious answered.

Petra listened intently into the call this would be more information for the Magik /Vampire. As long as this information didn't harm Demetrious, Petra would share it. Petra hated that bitch werewolf, Rowen anyway. Rowen had tried and failed to snag Demetrious a few years ago. If Rowen thought to get on Demetrious' good side she could think again. Petra had defeated her once before telling Demetrious of Rowen's plot against him.

Petra had lied of course, but Demetrious trusted Petra. So, he had believed her and had awarded half of the werewolf leadership to Rowen's rival. Rowen thought she was a tough woman, but she never come up against the likes of Petra, Petra was sure she could keep this bitch in her place. She would stick to her plan it would all work out and she could comfort a grieving Demetrious and then her dream of being Mrs. Blackstone would come true.

~0~

Chapter 7 - Mirror, Mirror

T here also had been a lot of changes,

and odd things happening the last few months for Sarah. First Aunt Iva had spirited her way to a different cabin in the woods in the middle of the night. Aunt Iva had said they would be both be safer there, as her cabin was too well known.

Sarah understood the vampires would love nothing better than to get their hands-on Demetrious girlfriend, meaning her and Aunt Iva. Sarah protested though when Aunt Iva wanted to start a clinic again. Aunt Iva talked her into it though. Aunt Iva insisted that the people needed help and she would see that they had it. Besides she had said idle hands were the devil's work.

Aunt Iva seemed scared and distant. Sarah must do everything to help her, so Aunt Iva

could feel safe. Someone as old as Aunt Iva
and under such stress could be at risk for
stroke or heart attack. They were safe
Demetrious had made them so.

Demetrious had even sent someone to
protect them. Though at first Sarah was
surprised he sent Charles Keystone. After all
Charles had been aligned with Grandfather
Eccklestone. It was truly odd that he was
related to Aunt Iva, but maybe that would
help him to adjust to be on the side of good
now. Yes, Sarah had been surprised about
that too. She had no idea he was related to
Aunt Iva.

It was along drawn out story, but the gist of
the story was that Iva had not been aware of
his existence. She had been overjoyed to
welcome to her home. Aunt Iva loved
having family with her. Aunt Iva felt that
Charles' appeared like a godsend when all
other the men were too busy fighting the
enemy to protect Sarah and her.

But Sarah had been distrustful at least at first
then she has become comfortable in his
presence almost to the point where he was a
beloved brother. She refused to think it
could be anything else. She would not be
attracted to him. She would not be one of

those women they talked about who quoted the saying 'absence made the heart grow fonder' and then added 'for someone else'.

Sarah loved Demetrious. Every time she was near him her heart beat a little faster and she felt the need to reach out and touch him. He made her feel whole and happy. She would stay true.

Sarah walked through the forest and was soon walking into Aunt Iva's new clinic once again. Every day the clinic was full. She had once thought Aunt Iva only had a clinic three times a week, but these people kept coming and coming with their health issues. She watched as a young woman holding a young boy of three years old entered the clinic. The boy seemed to have whooping cough. Hadn't he been vaccinated? Wasn't there a doctor or hospital in these parts? Aunt Iva took charge and took the boy into a cubicle. Aunt Iva would do what she could with her abilities then send him home with medicines.

Wasn't this announcing their presence to Demetrious enemies? And if all that wasn't enough Sarah felt under so much pressure, almost as if someone drained her abilities. But that was impossible wasn't it? After all she had a protection spell from Aunt Iva. Maybe it was all the use of her abilities? Thank goodness for Charles. He convinced her that feeling drained was nonsense.

Sarah recalled a conversation with Aunt Iva..., "We needed a man in residence especially now that Darius helps Demetrious. Janelle and Alexander are safe with them, but someone is threatens our family, which means you and I are in danger Sarah," Aunt Iva had said "Besides the boy is family he needs us."

"I know Demetrious wouldn't mind Charles staying with us...,"Aunt Iva continued trying hard to convince Sarah.

"I understand Aunt Iva. You don't have to give me the hard sell. He's your family and he needs to stay somewhere, besides I like Charles," Sarah agreed readily.

Pulling herself into the present, Sarah realized how good that really was they weren't been harassed by anyone and they were safe from harm. They also had been able to continue with their clinic, something they couldn't have done if Charles wasn't around. Yet why did she always feel conflicted about her feelings when she was around him?

The only real problem as she could see it was that she hadn't heard from Demetrious in so long. Had something happened to him? Or was it he had just lost interest in her? Could the spell that Aunt Iva cast be the only thing that held them together? No, that was foolish.

Although Sarah kept hoping to hear from Demetrious that call just never came. Was he really that busy? Why couldn't he find two minutes to speak with her.? Were they in that much peril? Sarah let out aloud sigh.

"What is the matter Sarah? I heard you sigh," Aunt Iva exclaimed.

"I'm missing Demetrious I wish he'd call." Sarah answered.

"Demetrious, Demetrious, all you talk about is Demetrious," Aunt Iva uncharacteristically sniped.

"I don't think I talk of Demetrious all that much," Sarah replied surprised.

"I guess I'm taking out my anger at the boy on you. Sorry Sarah. I believe time with your partner is important. I don't understand why that boy isn't making time for you. Maybe he doesn't love you as much as he says? Now let's hurry and get to the clinic it's going to be a busy day I just know it," Iva replied, looking like she wanted to say something else, but holding back for her own reasons.

"I don't understand why you are so hard on Demetrious. I wish he'd come home," Sarah replied.

"He'll come home with his tail between his legs before you know it. He'll have a lot of making up to you when he does."

"He has a lot of responsibilities and this person makes his life difficult."

"Well I just hope that women werewolf...what was her name? Oh, yes Rowen. I hope she doesn't torment him again."

"Torment him?"

"Yes, she was like a cat in heat for him. She wouldn't leave him alone."

"He has a fiancée now, surely that will change things?"

"Not for her kind. Those werewolves are very predatory. She won't leave him alone she'll be cloying all over him."

"I'm not worried Demetrious loves me," Sarah said biting her lip.

"Of course he does dear. He'll just push her away, no matter how lovely she is. And she is incredibly lovely."

"Do you actually think that he won't be able to resist her? Because I don't believe that!" Sarah insisted shaken.

"Oh no, of course not dear, although Demetrious has had a number of girlfriends you are his first fiancée. Now let's go make short work of that list of patients and help them all," Aunt Iva said changing the subject.

Sarah thought about all that had happened since they had arrived here months ago. Walking with Charles in the woods everyday had been fun. No, not fun... disarming in some ways. Sarah had let down her guard with him was that foolish? Sarah considered Charles a friend even if she knew he had feelings for her. It felt right walking with Charles by her side to protect her. After all Demetrious had sent him to guard her so she did nothing wrong in enjoying his company, if it went no further.

Sarah was pleased about how much she had learned and how she was able to control her gifts that much easier. She had developed so many more abilities to help those who needed health care. She could also better control the use of her ability to lift objects and control air flow. The one odd thing though, was her ability to see the future which she had developed had suddenly faded.

Sarah couldn't seem to feel the tingles like she could before, when people who harboured bad intentions were near. Just the other day a man had come up to her, and almost struck her. If Charles hadn't stopped him he would have because Sarah had neither seen, nor felt him. She didn't understand why that ability had stopped working did someone block it. Should she be afraid?

Sarah was dismayed to realize Aunt Iva had made some good points about Demetrious. She knew Demetrious was busy, but why wasn't he making time for her? Why hadn't she seen him in so long? When was the last time he called her? Could he be moving away from her emotionally, before their life together had even begun?

No! She wouldn't doubt Demetrious. She loved him and he loved her, she would have to quit being selfish and realize that other people also come first. She knew that coming into this relationship, so she would put these foolish fears away and support him.

"Well look here, there's a letter from your Demetrious."

Demetrious letter was full of his love and she held it close to her heart. Demetrious told her to sit tight that he was onto the Vampire Magik and trusted that Charles would keep them safe. Demetrious letter reassured her. So Charles had been cleared by the Magik council after Billy and Grandfather had destroyed each other. He really had come to visit his Great Aunt Iva. Demetrious too, thought it would be the making of Charles. She just wished she could hear Demetrious' voice. A letter was nice, but she needed to see him maybe on a Spacetime call. That would at least make her feel less alone.

Demetrious thought Aunt Iva's love could save almost anyone. So, Sarah would be safe here. But somehow deep inside she felt something was wrong. She just couldn't put her finger on what it was.

~0~

Chapter 8 - Charles

Sarah felt uncomfortable as she walked through the cottage, Charles eyes always seemed to rake over her where ever she went. The cottage should have been large enough to avoid his eyes, as it was a six-bedroom, old fashion wooden structure, but she felt them all the same. It had the hall vaulted ceilings that she had noted and loved in White Christmas as a common room and a large kitchen. The kitchen made her feel even more uneasy, though she didn't know quite why. Maybe it was the pea soup colour on the walls and the darkened spots where there should be windows? Hmm, the walls of the kitchen now seemed to be yellow. Maybe her mood had made her think the walls were pea soup green?

Sarah came to breakfast table to find Charles sitting at Aunt Iva's table.

"Hello Sarah, don't you look beautiful this morning."

Sarah felt slightly uncomfortable, by his continued affection and over the top comments, but she didn't quite know how to break him of this habit; other than to constantly remind him she was engaged. It looked like she would have to remind him again.

"Thank you your very kind Charles, but you do know I'm engaged?"

"Of course I know you're engaged, but like a fine painting, I can enjoy the view can't I? Your golden hair and your cat-eyed brown with yellow streaks are just so captivating."

Maybe she really had put too much of a spell on him. After all when Sarah first met him she had used a new ability that she didn't have a handle on. Charles just didn't show any signs of realizing that she just wasn't available. Sometimes she worried that his affection boarded on obsession, but that wasn't true was it?

"Charles, I love Demetrious. His raven hair and blue eyes appeal to me in a way your appearance can't."

"But I have dark brown hair too."

"Charles..."

"Do you like the kitchen now?" Charles asked changing the subject.

"Like it?" Sarah asked, wondering what the devil Charles spoke of.

"Yes, do you like it?"

"I'm sorry Charles. I don't know quite what you speak about."

"You said you didn't like the kitchen being so dark; that it should be bright and cheery. So I painted last night. It took me until four a.m. and it's just dried what do you think?"

"It is a very lovely yellow."

"I knew you'd love it."

"I still don't understand why there isn't a window in this kitchen."

"A design flaw obviously, but see what I did. I painted window here for you and even hung some blue curtains. See you can see trees and blue sky just like you would if there was a window here. Your favourite colour is blue isn't it?"

"It's actually red, but blue is my second favourite colour," Sarah said thinking of Demetrious' eyes.

"My eyes are blue. Coincidence, I think not," Charles waxed.

"So are Demetrious' eyes, remember I told you," Sarah stated softly.

"My eyes are bluer and brighter," Charles cried kissing Sarah full on the lips.

"How dare you?" Sarah cried.

"Please Sarah, you know that Demetrious is not right for you."

"I'm sorry. I don't want to hurt you. Charles, but as I love told you repeatedly, I love Demetrious and his blue eyes."

"What does that guy have that I don't have? Is it that he met you first?"

"Charles, I've tried to be gentle with you, but I love Demetrious. I will never love you. I'm sorry."

"He's probably using a spell on you," Charles said under his breath.

"What did you say?"

"I said he probably use magic on you. Or his aunt did ...my aunt did. She means well, but I've caught her trying to get other people together. So why wouldn't she use her powers on you and Demetrious?"

"How dare you? I thought you admired Demetrious and respected him."

"I do, Sarah. You take things out of context. Don't you think you are a little overwrought?"

"No, I'm not. You have overstepped your bounds Charles. I love Demetrious and I'm marrying him."

"Sarah, Demetrious is not who you think he is. He and his aunt would stoop to anything to win," insisted Charles in a soft voice.

"A gentle, kind, considerate, loving man, of peace, Demetrious would never stoop to win me with magic, nor would Aunt Iva," Sarah denied, but she worried that maybe he was right.

Aunt Iva had used magic to bring them together was their feelings real? Sarah searched her mind and heart. Her feelings weren't artificial or contrived. She loved

Demetrious and he loved her so why did she doubt that even for moment?

Charles must have sensed some of her feelings for he continued speaking..., "I'm sorry Sarah; it's just that you've been here for months and he never calls or comes to visit. If I had a woman like you, I treat her like the jewel she was."

"Charles, I blame myself. I've obviously encouraged you in some way and for that I'm sorry. But you have to realize once in for all I love Demetrious. I'm marrying him," Sarah firmly, but gently.

"Yes I know but...,"Charles said breaking off and kissing her.

Sarah felt his lips on her and it felt like she kissed Demetrious. He started to deepen the kiss and it was then that she started to resist. She pulled her lips away from Charles and wiped the back of her hand across her mouth. How could she have cheated on Demetrious this way? What was wrong with her? This was ridiculous. Sarah didn't have feelings for Charles. He was attractive, but he wasn't half the man Demetrious was.

"Keep away from me Charles," Sarah demanded. "I'm going to have to tell Demetrious, that I kissed you now."

"Please don't tell him. He'll hate me. I'm sorry. You told me, I should have listened. But if you ever change your mind, or need someone else to hold your hand, I'm your man," Charles pleaded. "And if he ever treats you badly Magik council, or no head of the Magik council, he'll be sorry."

"Okay, I guess we can drop the matter then. Just don't ever kiss me again," Sarah said hoping that this would end this mistake.

"I won't unless you ask me too."

Sarah thought about maybe she just needed to find a great lady for Charles. Good looking, almost as good looking as Demetrious, Charles had shoulder length dark brown hair, not quite as dark as Demetrious' raven coloured hair and blue eyes. Sarah noted that Charles' blue eyes weren't quite as blue, or as luminous as Demetrious' eyes either. Sometimes when Sarah looked at Demetrious' eyes she felt herself the only thing in his view and she lost herself completely in his eyes.

Why, oh why, had she kissed Charles? What
was wrong with her? She couldn't seem to
think straight. Would Demetrious forgive
her when she told him she'd kissed Charles?
Maybe she should keep this to herself.

Charles needed someone to feel that way
about him. Someone who could be his soul
mate the way Demetrious was Sarah's. Yes,
Sarah decided that was her new plan to deal
with Charles. He just needed someone and
Sarah was handy so she put someone else in
his way but whom? Mercedes Nocciolo
seemed to really like him and she was of the
Italian stone families. Sarah had met her
some time ago through Janelle. Now how to
get her in Charles' sphere? It couldn't be too
hard. After she went home to Kentucky, she
work on it, but until then she'd keep her
distance from Charles.

Chapter 9 - Where Is Sarah?

Demetrious sat at his desk worried. He had to do something the situation couldn't continue. He had neglected Sarah and now she had gone missing. He reached for his phone and spoke to Petra.

"I haven't been able to get in touch with my Aunt Iva, or my brother Darius, Petra. Could you send Caleb Gemstone to me?"

"Certainly, I will do that Demetrious," Petra answered.

Petra worried this could be very serious. Demetrious hadn't guessed her part in this, had he? Petra waved her hand feeling the chain of the spell. No, she was protected. The spell she weaved still held Demetrious could not find out any of what she had done.

She wouldn't lose him. Not when she neared achieving her goal of an end to Sarah and herself comforting Demetrious finally winning his love.

Petra stepped outside the offices to the outer sanctum and motioned to Caleb Gemstone.

"You've been summoned, Caleb."

"Thanks Pet," Caleb said flashing his hundred-watt smile.

"How many times must I tell you not to call me Pet? To you I'm Ms. Kaminski. Is that clear, Mr. Gemstone?"

Sorry, Ms. Kaminski."

"I should tell Demetrious of your disrespect."

"You do that."

"Oh, just follow me," Petra cried irritated.

Petra then took Caleb into the office and knocked on Demetrious inner sanctuary door, then opened it.

"Demetrious, Caleb's here."

"Thanks, Petra. Close the door on your way out."

Petra then closed the door.

Caleb Gemstone strode into Demetrious' office. Caleb felt a great kinship to Demetrious. Demetrious had helped Caleb, when he was young and troubled by his size and lack of abilities. The council had not looked kindly on an out of control teen with anger issues in the family. Demetrious had found another teacher for Caleb who could help him with his anger and channel it into abilities that protected others. Demetrious had helped him find his true purpose in life and offered a friendship that Caleb needed. Caleb would defend Demetrious with his life if need be.

"What is up boss?"

"We can't talk yet," Demetrious said pushing a button that opened a secret room. Caleb followed him into the room and the door sprang shut.

"Boss, where did this room come from?"

"I had in installed in the middle of the night three weeks ago. Only four of us will know it's here. I'm about to show it to Rowen Pentagan and her husband later today when she arrives. This room is completely soundproof and the walls are lined with lead.

No one, not even a person of Magik can spy on me here. No spells but mine work here."

"Way to go boss. Now tell me what you want done and it will be done."

"The situation that I told you brewed has arrived. I had hoped Darius would be able to keep them safe, but Darius was waylaid before he ever got to Sarah."

"Your brother has been seized? How do you know?"

"I haven't heard from him in weeks. My brother would have found a way to check in with me. Once more I can't find his wife and son Alexander either. I think they probably grabbed the boy first, his mother went to save him and then my brother was taken too. Now they have them all."

"So you want me to find them boss?"

"Yes but I also need help finding Sarah and Aunt Iva I think someone has them too."

"I thought you installed tracking devices on them."

"Caleb that was only a temporary device, which sent messages. I gave them tracking devices that last a mere three months and then are absorbed by the body and eliminated. The devices have long ago been expelled."

"Do you know they're last known locations?"

"Sarah and Aunt Iva were in Aunt Iva's home, outside of Four Miles Kentucky. Alexander was at the academy and Janelle was in their home nearby. I'm not sure where Darius was grabbed," Demetrious explained, trying not to sound worried.

"We will find them safe and sound. These people won't dare harm them. They know to do so would mean their lives."

"Do they think grabbing your family will make you weak? They don't know you well, do they boss?"

"I am a strong man, but even to man such as I; my family would always be considered a weakness."

"Do you know who this Magik/Vampire is?"

"I have suspicions but I have no definitive proof .The man I suspected is presumed dead and has always been loyal to the Magik council. And yet all signs point to him."

"So, who do you think it is?"

"I think it is Alfred Pennstone," Demetrious claimed.

"The Pennstone's are one of the inner circle. Even if he were alive, why would he betray you?"

"Maybe he blames Sarah and I for Delilah's death at Lord Eccklestone's hands."

"Boss, he was supposed to have died at Lord Eccklestone's hands. If you suspect he is alive, how do you know that Delilah isn't also alive?"

"I don't but I trust you to ferret out all this information for me."

"Boss what you've told me could change everything," Caleb commented.

"Yes, it does; this means war," Demetrious answered breaking a pen in anger. "I shall find the person who did this and they shall rue the day they touched any member of my family."

~0~

Chapter 10 - Traitors Amongst Us
Rowen

Rowen waited in the outer office. Why hadn't Demetrious' administrative assistant let her see Demetrious yet? When Rowen had visited before Petra had been here. Apparently, she had been on holiday. Rowen didn't like this woman and she certainly didn't like the way she stared at her husband Dragomir.

"You insult me woman. Do not feast on my husband with your eyes," Rowen exploded.

Raven's her teeth extended and only with great restraint did she not let her wolf side take over.

"I beg your pardon!?" Petra replied frostily.

"Rowen, this is not like you," Dragomir whispered urgently. "You must control your temper. She's baiting you."

"Dragomir this is an insult to our clan, my leadership and to me as your wife. I cannot let this go," Rowen replied.

"I'm sorry if you misunderstood. Any look I might give your husband was curiosity, nothing more. I didn't even know you had married," Petra apologised.

"We are still in the honeymoon stage but my wife is my life. Do not misunderstand that," Dragomir explained.

Rowen glared at him for explaining to this bitch. Then steeling herself and setting aside her anger she demanded with only a hint of anger, "I have waited long enough Petra, I will see Demetrious now."

"Do not dictate to me wolf. Demetrious is a busy man. He will see you when it is possible, and not before."

"Do not try your mind games with me. Demetrious needs to see me. I have vital information for him."

"Lord Blackstone, Rowen of the Werewolves is here," Petra said speaking into an intercom.

"Send her in," Demetrious instructed.

"Not you, only her," Petra insisted baring Dragomir.

"You will let my equal in command, my husband, Dragomir, pass."

Rowen again bared her teeth and looked scarily angry.

"No," Petra insisted.

"Let them in Petra," Demetrious demanded, opening his door and hearing the conversation.

"You can go in now both of you," Petra exclaimed, like it was her idea.

"Demetrious, is it safe to speak here?" Dragomir asked softly.

Demetrious didn't hear his soft voice and continued to move in his office ushering them to a seat.

"Demetrious, I had believed Damocles Scourby the second, had been plotting against you with the vampire leader Mihai Du Inconue, and came here to tell you. However I have been since informed that though Scourby is aligned with the Vampire in charge, Mihai Du Inconue is not the vampire in charge of this revolution. I just can't get a handle on his position in this battle or even if he is a part of this."

"You sound as confused as I am about this," Demetrious replied, "I had heard rumblings of a Magik/Vampire operating, but not that Scourby had aligned himself with him."

"Mihai Du Inconue has gone to ground and maybe recruiting vampires to fight whoever is against us all. I know there are vampires aligned with Mihai Du Inconue. No one speaks the name of the vampire who fights against us, but they say he is one of yours. A Magik/Vampire," Rowen explained.

"You have great sources then for I have heard none of this. With your history with Scourby you could have read into this. Did you?"

"I treat you with respect, do not insult my honour with this foolish question Demetrious Blackstone," Rowen exclaimed angrily. "Damocles Scourby the second, may be my enemy, but the safety of my clan and all the clans of the werewolves come before petty disputes. I would never bring information to you based on lies for my own gain."

"Forgive me, Rowen and Dragomir. I have not been a good host; you are on your honeymoon. Are you not? I have a fine champagne in my inner office that would be perfect to toast. That is if you can still drink, if not I have a lovely cider," Demetrious placated.

Demetrious indicated with his hands that he believed that bugs had appeared in his office and he believed someone could be listening to their conversation. He popped a cork of champagne for the listener then put on a recording that sounded like their voices. Rowen was amazed even with his strange abilities this shocked her.

Demetrious motioned for them to follow him and escorted them into his inner sanctum, his secret room closing the door so quietly no one would hear it.

Demetrious then commented, "I am sorry I had to question or make you feel I impugned your honour Rowen. I needed to know that you were still the same werewolf I met two years ago. Tell me quick we can't be in here long, do you have any more information for me?"

"Actually we do Demetrious. Tell him Rowen," Dragomir exclaimed.

"You have traitors in your organization Demetrious," Rowen began. "But before we tell you to prove what I am about to tell you, I must take the blood oath."

"I, Rowen Pentagan of the Werewolf Clan Pentagan do hereby pledge my fealty and my clan's fealty to Demetrious Blackstone and his clan for as long as he lives. I do so swear by the blood oath. I say this in Latin to make it true and binding. Ego, Rowen Pentagoni de werewolf Clan Pentagoni dont hoc sponderem fidem fidelitatem Demetrious Blackstone et eius familia nam quamdiu vivit. Id faciam iurare per sanguinem iuramentum."

Rowen then sliced her thumb with a knife and touched it to Demetrious' thumb.

"You do not swear allegiance to the Magik Council?"

"No, I do not know all the traitors that have infiltrated your council. I would not be allied with them," Rowen answered.

"Very sensible, now you know the names of the traitors?" Demetrious asked.

"Actually I do, and the first one on the list is Petra Kaminski, your administrative assistant."

"What that's impossible. I vetted her myself she's worked for me for years," Demetrious protested.

"I have a text and recordings of telephone conversations she made to someone who works for the Magik/ Vampire. See here are the documents and the recorded voices," Rowen exclaimed, pulling them out of the briefcase she held.

"That can be faked."

"It wasn't. Listen to the recordings," Dragomir protested.

Demetrious waved his hand over the recordings after a few minutes processing the information as his features changed and he looked devastated.

"Petra what have you done?"

Demetrious scanned the other documents and stated "I think I know who this Magik/Vampire could be and it is not who I thought it was. I know it is not Mihai Du Inconue. I thought this person dead, but they shall fool me no longer. You will take on a chore for me. I need you to approach this Magik/Vampire and offer your clan. You will tell the Magik/Vampire that you are angry with me. I have mistrusted you for the last time and you weary of my governance. You want to rule all the werewolf clans like you were destined to lead."

"They won't believe me. Petra will tell them I came here," Rowen protested.

"Ah, but they will. The speech you give outside this room will convince them."

"I don't understand."

"We're going to go into the other room. I will dismiss what you just told me making it sound like I don't believe you. I will insist that Mihai Du Inconue is behind all of this along with a Magik/Vampire I do not know but suspect. Now, remember protest, sound outraged. Don't let on I know about Petra either, she must be given the rope to hang herself. You know what the Sun-Tzu Chinese general & military strategist who lived in four hundred B.C. said "Keep your friends close, and your enemies closer."

"Done! That traitorous bitch won't know what hit her," Rowen explained.

A Tiger's Heart Wrapped in a Player's Hide

~0~

Chapter 11 - Illusion and Trickery

Sarah went into the woods with Aunt Iva for her morning ritual of T'ai chi. If Aunt Iva really thought that this could channel her abilities then she would learn it. Maybe it could afford her some protection from those who would harm her as well. She didn't always want to use her abilities on people martial arts training could help. Couldn't it?

The slowness of the movements puzzled her and she ventured to ask Aunt Iva. "Why is this so slow? I thought was defensive as well as healthy?"

"Sarah it is a defensive art as well but it also helps the mind focus. There are five different styles each with a different master."

"What are the styles?"

"The styles? Chen style of Chen-Wangting and Yang style of yang-Lu-ch'an, Wu Hao style of WuHu-hsiang, Wu-style of Wu Ch'uan-yu and finally Sun style of Sun Le."

"So many styles, you're sure this is really necessary Aunt Iva?" Sarah asked her eyes glazing over.

"Sarah really you have to learn to focus. Of course, this is important. The T'ai chi we practice comes from the master Yang-Lu-ch'an or Yang family style. It is important to open your mind about new things Sarah and this is what our master teaches us."

"I'm listening. I promise."

"A person who is not well, or like you has had their power in such flux for a number of years needs to learn a state of calmness. So T'ai chi teaches one to concentrate on what could be wrong with the body relieving that, and all stress. It also helps with physical effects they place on the body which causes disharmony in the body. It does focus on defense as you asked, but none of this can be achieved without physical fitness. I believe in a running regiment as well, so we will begin to run starting today covering a mile a day until we reach being able to run ten miles easily."

"Run ten miles? I hope you're joking. I hate running. I have no intention of running a mile, let alone ten miles."

"Really Sarah, must you be difficult? Do you, or do you not, want Demetrious to be proud of you? Must he always look after you?"

"Demetrious doesn't look after me. I look after myself. I saved myself from grandfather. Alexander and I were ready to leave when Demetrious came. You know this, so why would you say that."

"Sarah, don't deceive yourself, Demetrious was there to save you. Could you really have gotten away without him?"

"Why do you say these things? Yes, Demetrious helped, but Alexander and I could have escaped," Sarah insisted.

"Maybe I don't know the whole story, why don't you fill me in?" Aunt Iva asked.

Sarah felt something off about Aunt Iva for weeks now, and she had put it down to stress and worry; but this conversation had set off warning bells in Sarah. Aunt Iva knew all that had happened with Grandfather Eccklestone. So why did she ask this now? Aunt Iva had become senile?

Sarah thought back to that time, remembering it all. She remembered how Demetrious, Alexander and Sarah had explained to Aunt Iva how it all had happened. Grandfather Eccklestone had kidnapped Sarah. He had kept her and Alexander prisoner using his strong abilities against them. He convinced Sarah that she was fat and that he, Grandfather Eccklestone was a maligned leader that people were extremely jealous of. Sarah knew she had been extremely lucky Alexander had been able to lift the spell, Grandfather had held her under. That child Alexander was amazing, and the power he held was actually pretty scary. But the child seemed to have wisdom beyond his years. Alexander wielded his power sparingly and harmed no one. They had watched as Lord Eccklestone was defeated by his own unknown son William, who he had denied with his last breath.

After his wedding to Janelle, Darius found a great teacher for Alexander The teacher,

Dabir Ḥajar al-Aswad was an older man and
a distant cousin of Demetrious. Dabir was
one of the Arabian Blackstones. He had a
vision when he was young; that he would be
needed to teach a member of the council and
so he joined the inner circle at a young age.
Dabir had sworn his allegiance to the leader
of the council and when Demetrious came
along, he said this was the child of his
vision.

Dabir said he had seen that Demetrious
would be the great leader that they had all
waited for. He and Abraham had taken over
the training of Demetrious as a youth. Dabir
loved Demetrious like a father would, but he
also loved Darius who he too had trained.
When Darius had looked for someone
powerful and ethical to train his son in his
abilities, Dabir was the first-person
Demetrious and Darius had thought of. At
least this was what Demetrious had
explained to her. Aunt Iva knew all of this,
so why did she question Sarah? Either she
had gotten very old before Sarah's eyes or...
It couldn't, be could it? That this woman
standing in front of her wasn't Aunt Iva?

But how could she appear so convincing and
just how long had this person been able to

convince her that she was Aunt Iva? How
could Sarah have been so foolish? How
could she not have seen that Aunt Iva didn't
stand before her. But what was the real
motive for this? Who or what was behind
this? Why had this fake Aunt Iva tried to
teach her T'ai chi? It didn't make any sense,
perhaps she'd imagined it?

"You're going to be difficult and not speak
to me?"

"Of course not, Aunt Iva. I thought we'd
start running," Sarah covered.

Maybe after her run she'd be able to tell if
this wasn't Aunt Iva, because for now she
couldn't tell the difference. Could running
would help her get out of this? Sarah could
think of what to do next.

~0~

Chapter 12- Family Ties

Sarah ended her run and felt exhausted.

She'd actually run a mile and felt proud of herself; but was she wrong about Aunt Iva being someone else? Aunt Iva couldn't be someone else. She had to be imagining danger where there was none.

"Finished already? I don't think you finished ten miles. Catch your breath and start again," Aunt Iva commanded.

Sarah looked hard at the woman in front of her, again. Oh no, she had been correct. She looked like Aunt Iva, but there were subtle differences in her movements and actions. If you looked close enough. It wasn't Aunt Iva. Sarah could tell that now.

How could Sarah not have seen this before? Was she so wrapped up in her own needs and wants, that she hadn't seen the metamorphosis of Aunt Iva, into this woman? This deception had to be on a grand scale, as it had fooled her so easily. And yet wasn't Sarah easy to fool? Sarah wanted to scream why did she always trust so easily?

No wonder, she hadn't heard from Demetrious in so long. But if they had tricked her could someone trick Demetrious this way? No, Demetrious wasn't as easily deceived. He had been chosen to lead the council because he was shrewd. Yet he hadn't found Sarah. Did he even know she had been taken? Demetrious could take action of the council was threatened, but if they were so skilled at deception then someone could be infiltrating the very office of the council. That would put Demetrious in grave danger.

Sarah wanted to kick herself. How could she not have realized that they were deceiving her sooner? Could it have been something in the water, the food as well, as a spell they cast? She should have been safe from their spell; after all she had renewed the spell Aunt Iva had taught her. Maybe she needed to invoke the chant again?

"Petitio Principii! Ominous spirtus invocāre praesidium servo atum Seraphina. Of this I solemnly ask. Evil or ominous spirit, be gone. I invoke a protection spell to protect to guard me, Seraphina, S.E.R.A.P.H.I.N.A."

Hopefully that would help. Sarah thought. She needed all the help she could get to defeat these imposters and escape. But how could she do that without alerting them that she was on to them. Could they be drugging her food? If the drugs were in the food, then two could pay at that game. Sarah would pretend to eat their food and pick up her own food at the variety store near the clinic. Sarah also had access to drugs at the clinic, so she'd take them and use the drugs on them. She would compel them to let her go.

No, that wasn't a good plan. They could be harming Aunt Iva. She needed to take charge find out who this woman was and find out where they had Aunt Iva.

Sarah grew angry and before she even knew it, she had willed the power inside her to hold this woman in mid-air above a tree. Power surged from hill and dale; deep within the earth she felt the power surge. Then realizing her anger had grown expediently, she calmed herself controlling the power.

Pushing some of the anger away, Sarah brought the fake Aunt Iva down, so she was now suspended only six feet above the ground. The fake Aunt Iva was now against a tree, instead of the hundred feet Sarah's anger had taken the woman. Something emitted from the woman forcing Sarah back. Sarah felt a force tingling in her own limbs which she fought back against. This fake Aunt Iva had defended herself; she'd tipped her hand. She couldn't continue to pretend she was Aunt Iva.

"Sarah dear, what do you do to me?" asked the fake Aunt Iva.

"Don't speak to me. I don't want to hear from you, until you are ready to admit what you've done."

"Sarah, have you lost your mind? You could have killed me. Let me down at once. Come on now you can do it dear."

"No, I will not let you down."

"Sarah, are you possessed? Quit using the ley lines, they are too powerful for a novice like you."

Ley lines what was she talking about? If Sarah had somehow accessed these ley lines then that was a good thing. She would continue to hold the evil bitch before her. What had this woman done to Aunt Iva?

Sarah continued to hold her fast against the tree, but demanded from the woman. "I'll use what power I choose. Now you will answer my questions truthfully. Do you understand?"

"What the devil is wrong with you?" queried the fake Aunt Iva.

"You will answer my questions truthfully, or answer immediately for your crime of impersonation and kidnap and/ or murder. Do you understand?"

"No, I don't understand. Sarah what has come over you? You act very strange. Why do you do this to me?"

"Did you think you could deceive me forever? Where is the real Aunt Iva?" Sarah exclaimed ice in her voice.

Sarah stood in front of the woman her arms raised a surge of unbelievable strong power filling her body as she held the spell.

"I am the real Aunt Iva. You're confused. It's understandable you've been under a considerable strain; Demetrious still loves you hold onto that. Don't lose sight of reality and now to tap into ley lines unprepared well...it will be okay. I can help you, my dear," the fake Aunt Iva claimed.

The fake Aunt Iva then reached out and grab Sarah's arm scratching Sarah with long fingernails.

"You scratched me. Have you tried to harm me and failed?"

"It was an accident. You moved just as I tried to touch you to comfort you," protested the woman.

"Drop the act that you care. Aunt Iva wouldn't scratch me, not even by accident. Her nails are clipped short to protect the patients she treats. I don't know who you are, but you can drop the veil or whatever you use to appear as Demetrious', Aunt Iva. I know you are not Aunt Iva," Sarah demanded, still holding the fake Aunt Iva suspended in mid-air.

"Fine, but you better hope they don't hurt Iva," the woman stated still whispering under her breath.

"No, you better hope they don't harm her or you won't live to see tomorrow," threatened Sarah surprising herself.

Feeling weakness, she attributed to the anger inside her Sarah sat on the ground to gain some strength and continue securing the fake Aunt Iva. The fake Aunt Iva still whispered faintly in words Sarah couldn't understand.

"You don't care about Aunt Iva. And quit your whispering. I know you're trying to harm me and if you don't stop. I won't just threaten you; I will silence you for good," Sarah cried.

"You dare to threaten me? How could you think I don't care? She's my sister," cried the fake Aunt Iva.

"Then you are?"

"In for a penny, in for a pound, if I must tell you, I am Minerva, Iva's sister. People call me Minnie though."

"Aunt Iva told me you hadn't spoken to her in sixty years? Why should I believe you are worried about your sister?"

"Yes, stubbornly I haven't spoken to her in sixty years; but I had my reasons and I still love her."

"Then how could you do this to your sister?" Sarah asked.

"They have her. I don't know where is, but they hold her prisoner. They said if I didn't pretend to be her and convince you, they'd kill her and then me."

"Nice story. Do you expect me to believe that you didn't do this willingly? You hated your sister for taking Peter from you," Sarah said still not believing in the truth telling spell she used on Minerva.

Minerva still struggled, but she smiled at Sarah trying to convince her she was harmless.

"I didn't do this willingly, and I forgave my sister long ago for something that wasn't her fault, but Peter's. Peter told me he loved me but I was just a substitute for Iva. Peter was a weak man."

"But you still loved him."

"Yes, I loved him at one time. But my love was extinguished with his betrayal and death. The reason why I didn't speak to Iva for sixty years is that I didn't want her to learn of my grandchild."

"You have a child? How? Peter Whetstone was a vampire."

"I had a child and his father was Peter Whetstone. We were intimate before he got turned. My son, like his father was a wastrel and a liar."

"You speak as if it is the past tense when you talk about your child," Sarah noted.

"Of course, I do, Peter Andrew is dead. I don't believe in telling lies about the dead."

"I am sorry for your loss then... to lose a child in your lifetime, how devastating."

"I thank you for your sympathy. I did treat you well. I taught you T'ai chi, would someone who was evil do that? Let me tell you the whole story."

"Fine, tell me, but I don't have to believe you."

"My Peter Andrew was too much like his father, so though I loved him, he was a great disappointment. He abandoned his child and didn't marry the mother. She went on to marry another man who raised the child as his own. This denied me my grandchild. I see her but she doesn't even think of me as her grandmother and now they've threatened her and her child as well. Please for the sake of my sister and my grandchild, don't let on you know."

"Where do you hold Aunt Iva?" demanded Sarah not committing to the promise.

"Here. I've seen her but I can't get the bonds off that Charles placed on her."

"Charles?"

"Of course, Charles. He's one of them. He's a vampire. Why else do you think he keeps the windows covered?"

The fake Aunt Iva then laughed.

"He's a vampire? But he goes out in daytime. How does he do that?"

"He uses a special spell to go out in daylight, but he still worries about the light coming in. He is very high in the upper echelon of the Magik/Vampires, so of course I obeyed. I don't want to become one of them."

Charles was a Magik /Vampire? Why had she trusted him? She should have known he lied; after all he worked for Grandfather. But no, she went for long walks in the woods with him, smiled at him every day. Sarah had treated him like he was her best friend. She'd almost kissed him. She had betrayed Demetrious even thinking about kissing Charles. What had been wrong with her? She wouldn't betray anyone she loved this way, and yet for a moment there she had leaned in for kiss with Charles before she'd pulled away. Okay, so Charles was cute and if she didn't care about Demetrious so much, she would have been tempted, but it had to be a compulsion? Yes, that must be it. Vampires could compel and he undoubtedly held tremendous power being one of Magik. No, she couldn't excuse herself, she was to blame and now Sarah had put everyone she loved in danger.

"Did I lose you girlie? Did he suck you in with those woo-woo abilities of his? Them damn Vamps are some powerful."

"How would you know?"

"I know Peter Whetstone was. I would have done almost anything for him...until he scorned me and his child. When he came back, I was full of joy. I told him about the baby I carried and he would even acknowledge it was his. He just kept saying he was in love with my sister. My sister! Poor innocent Iva, it looked like she'd be happy after he died. How could I tell her I had his baby? And it wasn't just her. They might have treated my child differently, if they knew who his Daddy was."

"You felt sorry for Aunt Iva," Sarah questioned suspiciously.

"Of course, I did. Iva didn't have a clue. She thought I had gotten fat; despite them powers of hers. She didn't want to know I carried Peter's baby and I decided I wouldn't tell her. So, I told her she stolen my man and I never wanted to speak to her again. Not a day goes by, that I didn't miss my sister."

"Then I can trust you to take me to her and help me save her?" Sarah asked.

"I'll help you if you'll help me save my granddaughter, from those Magik/Vampires. I only hope they haven't turned her already."

"Me too," Sarah replied under her breath.

Sarah let Minerva down, but kept a compulsion spell on her so she had to obey Sarah.

A tree moved near Sarah and she became frightened, someone was there. Even if she couldn't see them the hairs on her arm told her so. She then held Minerva up to a tree tightly so she couldn't flee.

"Iubeo audio loqui,"Sarah commanded silencing Minerva's voice and hearing.

Sarah glanced around she was sure someone hid there.

"Show yourself," Sarah demanded in her fiercest voice.

"Is that truly you Sarah? You haven't been harmed? Why do you sit down?" asked a voice she recognized as Alexander, Darius' son.

"Alexander? How did you get here? Is your Dad with you, or Demetrious?"

"No, I came alone. I found where you were and I came to rescue you, but you seem to have rescued yourself again," Alexander explained.

"I'm fine. I 'm just sitting down resting, while keeping her suspended. How did you know I went missing? Demetrious doesn't know or he would have found me as well."

"Demetrious has no idea, and quite frankly they can keep the secrets from everyone, including Uncle Demetrious but not me."

"There isn't a lot of time. We have to rescue Aunt Iva and fast before the villain comes out of the woods."

"You know where they hold Aunt Iva?"

"Yes, I know where she is and I know that woman is not Aunt Iva's, but her sister. Her name is Minerva Touchstone," Alexander explained.

"I already found out her name. I just made her tell me that, Alexander."

"Really? Did she tell you they captured my mother and me and that we escaped?"

"No, where is Janelle?"

"Don't worry she's somewhere safe, where they can't find her," Alexander explained.

"Darius hid her?"

"No, I found a hiding place for her. Dad has been taken."

"They took your Dad?" Sarah asked.

"Yes, I heard his voice and then it was gone."

"So, we have to find him too."

"Yes, I have to find him before they use him to harm Demetrious. I have to save Aunt Iva first. With her abilities and mine we will be able to find out where they took my dad."

"Let's go get Aunt Iva, now," Sarah exclaimed.

"I don't think you could get in there. Can you make yourself invisible?" Alexander enquired looking into her face.

"No, I haven't been able to master that."

"That is probably because she sabotaged you."

"That could be. She wouldn't want me to learn how to get away from them, now would she?"

"I'm sorry Sarah, but if you can't do the spell, then it's my job to rescue Aunt Iva."

"You're only eight years old. I can't let you risk yourself like that."

"Geesh Sarah, I'm almost nine."

"Alexander this isn't an insult to you, though you may find it so. You are young and you have much to learn."

"Adults always say that. The truth is I am the one better able to save Aunt Iva. I have more abilities then you."

"You do, but I can control my abilities and I can access and use them a lot easier, since I last saw you."

"Can you become invisible?"

"No, I can't. I can make tornado winds and move objects and I can control minds and make them like me (though I still haven't quite got a handle on the after effects.) I can heal and sometimes I get flashes of the future. Once I made lightening come out of my fingertips, but I haven't been able to do that again. Why do I tell you everything? Alexander did you do something to me?"

"No," Alexander replied, but Sarah was sure he lied.

"Alexander, you know you aren't supposed to do that."

"Sorry, it wasn't me. But I'm going and you're staying here and resting while I rescue Aunt Iva."

"I don't need to rest. Alexander what have you done to me?" Sarah asked, as she realized she couldn't move.

"Like I said I'm sorry that happened to you, Sarah. Hopefully you'll be able to move in about a half an hour. I'll be back soon. I promise," Alexander explained, and then walked away leaving Sarah in the woods with Minerva.

Sarah was angry at Alexander, but also scared. Why had Alexander made it so she couldn't move? She could have helped him. Alexander went up against these people and they didn't even know who they were. There was Charles of course, but who else was in on this deception? Alexander could be facing an army and Sarah wasn't there to help him.

Sarah looked over at Minnie and relieved to see that Minnie still held by the bonds Sarah had placed on her. Sarah relinquished the control of Minnie's seeing and hearing by stating, "Precipio tibi quod loquor et audio etiam. Sed ne me malum facere tibi ~ I command you to speak and hear again, but I prevent you from harming me."

"Was someone here? I feel like someone was here. What did you do to me? Don't you trust me Sarah?"

"Let's see... you were masquerading as your sister, a woman I care about, while they held her prisoner. They could have been torturing her all this time. Did you care?" Sarah asked.

"I did care, but I couldn't let them harm my granddaughter and my great granddaughter, now could I?"

"If you tell me the truth, then I will see what Demetrious can do to rescue your granddaughter and great-granddaughter. But know this, I have learned well over this year. I am not the same Sarah Maidenstone who could be so easily tricked. Those who I love, those whom I am loyal to, I give leniency to. You are not one of those, so I do not expect anything but treachery from you. If you endanger anyone I care about, I will let Demetrious deal with you. If anything, you do endangers Demetrious I will see you punished. Personally! Remember who my Grandfather was, and do not cross me, or you shall rue the day that you met me."

"I won't cross you. I promise you Sarah, on my life," Minnie replied hiding her face as she hid a laugh.

"You laugh at me, but you better realize I am serious."

To prove it Sarah hit Minerva across the face with a tree branch.

"That hurt. I'm sorry Sarah for doubting you. Will you let me down now?"

"In a while, we're waiting for someone."

"You can trust me tell me who. I didn't scream when you gave me back my voice."

"I'm not going to tell you, so quit pressuring me."

"What is that? Is that who you waited for?"

Sarah looked where Minnie pointed and was amazed to at first see a shimmer, then a glimmer, an outline of a person in the woods. It wasn't like the person was visible.

She saw a chalk outline of a person standing upwards. Like a paint- by- numbers picture coming to life in front of her, little squares came together and became the shape of a person. It was all very peculiar, and when it came to peculiar things happening, she thought of Demetrious. Was he here? The gift of invisibility must come in really handy, she wished she knew how to use that skill. Could it be that Demetrious had stopped time again? But why would he do that, unless he knew she was in danger?

Time had not stopped Sarah thought, as she looked at her watch. So, who was this? Friend or foe? Who or what caused this ripple in reality?

A man materialized he appeared to be about forty with dark hair and warm brown eyes. It puzzled her that he looked so familiar, but she couldn't place him right away. He glanced at her almost as if his eyes memorized her and a memory that Sarah didn't even know she had sprung forth.

Sarah remembered being small, playing with toy horses and Barbie's and the man before her now came into her view. He offered her another Barbie in a box. She remembered opening the box excitedly and crying,

"Uncle Ink, thank you. I wanted this Barbie so much, but Mommy said they were sold out."

"You are welcome Sarah."

Sarah remembered complete memories with this man, not just this one. She remembered times when he had visited her in foster care when she was first taken into care. She didn't have an Uncle that lived. How was it possible to have these memories? If he knew her in foster care, why hadn't she lived with him? Then that it all came rushing back to her. In fact, so many memories come back to Sarah that she fainted dead away.

~0~

Chapter 13 - Reunion

Sarah slowly became aware and wondered whose arms held her? She searched her mind and remembering what had happened, just before she had fainted.

A flash of memories so numerous flooded her mind that they threatened to overwhelm her once again. She remembered how the man had always made a fuss over her, when he had visited her parents. He was her beloved Uncle Ink, as close as a blood relative to her. Uncle Ink had once had a son and a daughter but they had died. There was still a hole there and she didn't remember how or why. He had found Daddy and treated Daddy as his son and Sarah as his granddaughter. He had protected them time and time again, from Grandfather's reach. When Grandfather's men had shown up looking for them time after time Uncle Ink was able to chase them away and make them forget. He had his own men protect them when he couldn't.

Sarah had once been fearful of the men and from changing home, after home to flee ahead of the men, but Daddy had said Uncle Ink would protect them all with his life. Sarah felt safe then with Uncle Ink and she did now as well. A sense of wellbeing came over her, as she realized he carried her in his arms like one would a beloved child.

Sarah opened her eyes wider clearing the cobwebs in her brain and stared into his face. She remembered him looking just the same as he did now. How was that even possible? She thought as he set her down on a sofa. Ink then say down beside her.

"Hello my little Seraphina. It's been awhile since I saw you. Do you remember me now?"

Sarah nodded, suddenly speechless. Maybe these were planted memories? She had been tricked already once. No, he was her Uncle Ink, these memories were real.

Her Uncle Ink starred at her and Sarah realized he read her mind when he said,

"You remember who I am, but not what I am?"

"You can read minds?"

"Yes. Do you remember my condition?" Uncle Ink asked probing.

Sarah searched her memories and suddenly it came to her "You are a vampire."

She should be frightened but instead it made her feel safe. How odd.

"I am not just a vampire, my dear Seraphina, but a Magik/Vampire."

"If you are a vampire how can you be in the woods?" asked Sarah.

"It's overcast and I have my magic to keep the sun from me," Uncle Ink answered.

"Wait a minute, where have you been all these years? You left me."

"I had to. I had no choice."

"No choice! You always have a choice. How could you have done this? How could you leave a child who had no one to strangers?"

Sarah pulled her knees up to her chest with her hand and lay her head down to hide her tears. She had been abandoned to foster care, when she could have been in a warm loving home. Angry enough to spit, Sarah wanted to hit him. How could he have done this to her?

"Seraphina, I love you like you were my own daughter. I was there the day you were born and your mother and father made me your godfather. I wouldn't hurt you for the world."

"You left me to protect me, you expect me to believe that?" Sarah asked.

"I did."

"I'll take that with a grain of salt."

"Seraphina, I wouldn't have left you if I didn't have any other choice," protested Ink.

"No choice? Then let's hear the reason. It figures. You won't even answer and I'm supposed to just believe you? Tell me how is that I didn't remember you? Especially if you were the closest thing I had left to a relative," Sarah asked.

Sarah sat up tall and glared at this man who called himself her Uncle Ink, when she realized the answer to her question.

"You glamoured me! You made me forget you. How do I know you didn't plant all those other memories?"

"I didn't."

Sarah looked at him and wanted to believe him.

"I'm so confused I don't know whether I'm coming, or going," Sarah complained.

"Maybe this isn't the time to discuss this," Ink exclaimed.

"You've taken me to the house away from Minerva, but I don't even know if I trust you..."

"Sarah, you should remember I know when you're lying."

"More probing? I'm sick of everyone trying to take advantage of me."

"I'm sorry Sarah, that wasn't my intention."

"Then why did you do that?"

"Do what?"

"Leave me alone. I was bereft and I needed you. You left me in the foster home and went away! I could have died and you didn't care," Sarah complained.

Sarah tried to pull herself together. She wiped her eyes backhandedly then crossed her arms in anger and glared at Uncle Ink.

"I left you there because it was the safest place for you. Your grandfather had a very long reach and he would have found you," Uncle Ink explained.

Ink tried to hug her, but Sarah pushed him away.

"He did find me and he killed my foster parents. Where were you then?" Sarah asked wiping away more angry tears.

"I was his prisoner. He had me encased in cement and bound with silver chains. If I hadn't been rescued, I would still be there."

Sarah gasped in horror. She wanted to stay angry, but Uncle Ink had been silvered and chained encased in cement. What a horrific thing for Uncle Ink to go through. How could she remain angry? If he hadn't let her be taken into foster care, she'd have been either a mindless drone of grandfather's, or dead. Had she misjudged him? Should she hear more, before she made any more snap judgements?

"How long did grandfather have you a prisoner?" Sarah asked softly.

"He had me encased in cement and silver chains for seventeen years. I was released last year, after his death."

"You were encased in cement? Oh, Uncle Ink, I've misinterpreted a lot of things. You led them away from me and even gave up yourself to save me. Didn't you?"

"Nothing any godfather wouldn't do," Ink replied.

Sarah reached out to Uncle Ink trying to just touch his hand but Uncle Ink folded her into his arms and held her close kissing the top of her head and letting her cry it all out. Sarah allowed herself to fill his arms like a child in a parent's embrace. For that is how it felt to her, like she had reached safety and home. After a few minutes Sarah looked up and into Uncle Ink's face.

"That evil man, my grandfather Lord Eccklestone has much to answer for. I can't believe his blood runs in my veins. I hope he's roasting in hell."

"Most people cannot choose their relatives. I want you to remember that even though he was your grandfather by blood, your blood was also your mother and father. Good people both of them the salt of the earth," Uncle Ink soothed.

"And I have you too my chosen relative, my beloved uncle. How could I have doubt you? I should have known you never leave me without the best of reasons," Sarah cried. "How did you survive?"

"Let's not talk about that. It's the past. I would have done anything to protect you my child. I'm just sorry I wasn't able to keep Eccklestone from taking you from Demetrious."

"You know about Demetrious?"

"I do know of him. He's a fine man. I couldn't have picked better for you, myself. I only hope he will be safe."

Sarah pulled herself away from Uncle Ink and looked at him again much alarmed, "What do you mean you hope he'll be safe?"

Ink looked at Sarah his eyes soft and his voice gentle, he said, "There are a number of moles in his organization. I haven't quite figured out who they are, but one of the traitors I'm sure of is his secretary Petra Kaminski."

"Petra? No, you are mistaken. She adores Demetrious. She wouldn't harm him," Sarah protested.

"Petra's love for Demetrious is unrequited. You know what they say about a woman scorned," Uncle Ink explained.

"I knew she had feelings for Demetrious, but to betray him?"

"You always want to see the best in people Sarah. Trust me, I have the proof she has leaked information about Demetrious council and his doings. She is a threat to all people of Magik."

"If Demetrious appears to be in danger, we must do something to help him that is after we make sure Alexander has rescued Aunt Iva safely. We must notify Demetrious and let him know about Petra. Demetrious trusts her completely. He can't continue to work in the dark. We can't sit here chatting!"

Sarah then tried to get up, but Alexander's spell must be still in force for she couldn't get her legs to move.

"Alexander was here...in the house? Is he safe? He is only a boy!!He shouldn't be taking on this bunch by himself," Uncle Ink cried alarmed.

"Alexander seemed to think he knew where they were keeping Aunt Iva. Alexander is a boy, but well able to take care of himself with his abilities. Alexander can get in and out without being seen. Besides I couldn't stop him, he is too much like his uncles. In any case, he alone knew where they were keeping Aunt Iva. Now where is Minerva?"

"I left her behind she tried to kill me, when I took you."

"What did you do to her?"

"I didn't kill her, but I did erase all memory of today. I also erased all memory of you. But I don't know how successful I was. Come we have to go now."

"But we need to go to Alexander and Aunt Iva," protested Sarah, "Wait a minute, this isn't the house they kept me in. Where are we?"

"Once you are sheltered, I will go to them."

"That will take too long. I need to get back there, and save Alexander. Then go to Demetrious and warn him," Sarah complained.

Sarah tried to get up again, but did not succeed. When would this stupid spell of Alexander's wear off? Sarah hoped Alexander hadn't messed it up, but surely once she got to Demetrious; she could get him to fix the spell. Until then she'd pretend it wasn't happening. She could still move the rest of her body though moving her limbs, felt decidedly odd.

"Vampires can fly, my dear. Remember? I can move at superhuman speed and have you there in minutes, only to return in minutes," Ink explained.

"You're sure it isn't far? We need to rescue Alexander."

"Trust me dear. I need you safe and then I will help young Alexander."

"I am tired, maybe after a nap. I can help you."

"That's it just relax, my beloved Seraphina. Close your eyes while we soar to safety."

Sarah obediently closed her eyes. Ink then
proved his point by scooping her up in his
arms and soaring into the sky. Sarah felt the
sensation of flying as air rushed through her
body. A blur went by her eyes. Dizzy from
the heights, sounds and view Sarah closed
her eyes again. In minutes she felt herself
being set down a sofa, in an unknown
building. Sarah then felt herself drawn into a
deep sleep; she couldn't respond from.

~0~

Sarah awoke sometime later not feeling much better than when she went to sleep. Sarah looked around the room in which she slept on a sofa and opened her eyes to the past. The room seemed familiar somehow. She realized with shock it was the apartment that she and her parents had lived in. She looked around and spotted Uncle Ink on a nearby chair watching her.

"Why have you brought me here and why haven't you taken me back to help Alexander."

"I wanted you to feel at home and remember Sarah."

"Remember what? That I was once happy?"

"Close your eyes and think about the past and drink in the smell," bade Uncle Ink.

Sarah breathed in deeply and found the sights and smells invoked happy memories of her parents and playing with her Barbie's. Sarah recalled playing cars with a young boy and superheroes.

What was the little friend's name? It was odd that she didn't recall this child before. Michael... the boy's name was Michael. She felt like there was more to this boy though, like he was related somehow to her. But how was that possible? She had no relatives. She popped her eyes open and looked over at Uncle Ink in shock.

Uncle Ink noting her discomfort cautioned, "The memories come back to you, my sweet. Take your time, close your eyes again, and let the reminiscences come to you."

Sarah obediently closed her eyes again. Who was Michael? She thought trying to compel the remembrance. Memories of playing with a small boy with eyes the same colour as hers flowed into her mind. He called her Fee. She remembered playing Batman and Robin. She recalled Michael insisting that she play Robin and herself protesting, that she was Batman or Batwoman as she preferred to be called. They ended compromising, Michael was Batman and she was Batwoman. Together as one, they would save the world. She remembered Uncle Ink giving Michael cars and trucks. Sarah begged for the same thing for herself. She heard voices talking, one of them Uncle Ink, but didn't understand what they were saying. She opened her eyes, and there before her was an adult Michael.

Michael was tall six-foot- three and had the same curly gold hair as hers. His hair hung to his shoulders like a mane. His eyes were cat eyed brown with yellow streaks, but they shone with wonderment looking at Sarah.

"Michael?"

"Fee?" Michael asked like he couldn't quite believe his eyes.

"It is, Seraphina, Michael. I've found her," Ink commented, nodding.

"Fee, I can't believe it. I've searched for you for years."

"You have?" Sarah asked puzzled.

"Of course, don't you remember me?"

"You are Michael," Sarah answered sounding sure but still puzzled.

"Yes, my name is Michael; but do you remember who I am to you?"

Michael reached out with his hand to grab Sarah's; but Sarah pulled back.

"I don't know. Are you some kind of relative, a childhood playmate?"

"Uncle Ink, help Fee remember. Please," Michael pleaded.

Ink placed his hands on Sarah's forehead and Sarah gasped in surprise. She now knew who Michael was. He was her own dear brother, her twin. Sarah felt overwhelmed and then felt all the blood drained from her face as she fainted.

~0~

Chapter 14 - Brotherly Love

Sarah opened her eyes seconds later to

Michael peering into her eyes. She felt all kind of overwhelming emotions, joy and sorrow, intermingled with such tremendous love.

"Michael? I can't believe I was made to forget you!" Sarah cried holding her arms wide open.

Michael flew into Sarah's open arms and Sarah hugged Michael like she would never let him go. After a few minutes, Sarah let go and Michael sat beside her on the sofa. She then turned to Uncle Ink and with angry fury asked him.

"How could you do this? I thought it bad that you abandoned me, but separating twins? You're not much better than Eccklestone. He is my brother, from the same womb, my closet living relative. You tore my right arm away, and yet you took him away from me. No wonder I've felt all alone for years," Sarah tore into Uncle Ink.

"That's not fair, Fee," Michael protested, "You don't know all the facts."

"Really? He left me and took you, my twin brother."

"I had no choice Seraphina. Do you remember that Michael was kidnapped?" Uncle Ink asked.

"Michael was kidnapped? When? I don't recall this!" Sarah protested.

"I was taken by grandfather's men. They thought I was one of Ink's children that he used for blood donations. They didn't know I was a relative of grandfather's. They...," Michael broke off here as if what he had to say was difficult.

"What did they do to you?"

"They threw me in with some tigers. I thought they would tear me limb, from limb. One of them a tigress, sheltered me. She saved me. I was broken, bruised, and fevered, from their bites. I didn't understand what had happened to me. I thought I had survived and nothing else could go wrong, Uncle Ink would come and take me home to you, but I started to change."

"Change? Change into what? Are you a Vampire too?"

"Close your eyes and I'll show you."

Sarah obediently closed her eyes. When she opened them, she stared at a tiger...a huge tiger with Michael's eyes. She watched again his body changed, the tigers body compressing and molding into a human body. Sarah looked on in awe his body was the six-foot- three male Michael again.

"What are you now, Michael?"

"I am a weretiger, an endangered species it seems. The man who bit me and made me is dead. I killed him, his mate who sheltered me tried to keep me safe and teach me at least until they came. When they came, she died."

"Until they came? Who?"

"The vampires that thought they could make me one of them. But I escaped. Can you accept me as your brother, the weretiger or must we part again?"

"Do you joke? Do you know how much I've longed for family since mom and dad died? And now to remember that I have a brother and not only a brother but my twin...if you think I'll let you go again you can think again."

"I'm sorry I doubted you, but I've lost other people from this change in my circumstances."

"Oh, Michael, how do you deal with this? Does it happen all the time? Or do you have control over this? And who raised you?"

"It took me time, but I learned to control when I become a tiger. After all I had years to do so," Michael answered, trying to pass it off as nothing.

"But I asked who you were raised with Michael and you didn't answer me."

"Some people found me and took care of me."

Uncle Ink touched Michael's arm and insisted, "People? Michael, you can tell your sister the truth," admonished Uncle Ink.

"Hush, they might not like everyone to know," Michael responded.

"Michael, tell your sister," Uncle Ink commanded.

Michael looked pensive and leery of opening up even to Sarah, but he took a breath and began, "Kate and Angelus Svartsten took me in. Kate is not one of the people of Magik, but Angelus is. They are both however vampires."

"Vampires? Vampires saved you? And one of them was a Magik/Vampire. But why wouldn't you be an abomination to them? Demetrious told me that werewolves and vampires don't like each other, add in that you are a different species and they wouldn't help."

"They are very enlightened vampires."

"Enlightened vampires, you mean like Uncle Ink, who cares for us and considers us family?"

"Yes, Fee, they were good to me. It wasn't until I was older than I found out they were born at least two centuries ago, maybe even more. Of course, they won't discuss how long they've been on this earth," Michael explained.

"There are vampires that old?"

"Yes, my dear child. They also rescued me from my maker, when I was first turned. They nurtured me taught me to value human life. They basically adopted me," Uncle Ink explained.

"They knew you, is that is why they helped Michael?"

"Yes," answered Ink.

"I believe that is true. They took me in and treated me like their grandchild. Angelus sees the future and he said I and my family were important to the future. They were good to me and they have been helping me to try to find Uncle Ink and you," Michael answered, "Angelus, rescued me broke the cement and pulled me from the silver chains that held me."

"How could he touch the chains?" Sarah asked.

"Michael told you he is of Magik. He is not only a vampire, but is one of Demetrious' bunch."

"You are sure he is not the one that opposes Demetrious?"

"Angelus is light and goodness. You do a great injustice to him. He would never harm the innocent the way this devil that opposes Demetrious had," Uncle Ink exclaimed.

"I am sorry Uncle Ink. You always seemed to be a good judge of character and since he helped both Michael and you, I guess I can trust them too."

"Seraphina, I need to go save young Alexander. He is the future of all your people. He is very powerful and if taken into the wrong hands..."

"Let us go save Alexander then," Sarah insisted.

"But Sarah, you need medical attention...," Michael insisted.

"Nonsense, I'm fine. Let's go Uncle Ink."

Ink looked at Michael as if to say let it go. Michael then nodded his agreement. Ink then he grabbed Sarah in his arms and without even looking lifted off and sailed through the front door. Sarah saw nothing but a blur, as they moved so fast through space. In minutes they were back at the cottage.

A pile of dust near the door gave Sarah
pause. Despite the fact that Charles had
helped kidnap her, she hoped it wasn't him.
It was probably her fault Charles had gone
alone with whoever's plan this was. The
ability that she had used to get away must
still be imprinted on him. It was obvious he
still loved her. Maybe she was as bad as
Aunt Iva, because she was tempted to
glamour him again in favour of Mercedes
Nocciolo. Mercedes would be perfect for
him and she would treat him well. Charles
problem was that he was very needy and he
looked for a woman who would mother him.
Mercedes loved to mother everyone. If he
had someone by his side he wouldn't be
tempted by the dark side. She only hoped
Demetrious wouldn't punish Charles too
severely. She suspected that the Magik
Vampire had glamoured Charles and
enhanced his already compromised psyche.
Yes, it was definitely her fault.

"I'll check faster for young Alexander if I
leave you here by the door, but please watch
for others and be my look out Sarah," Ink
instructed.

Ink seemed to be gone for seconds and then
came back saying "Someone has killed a lot

of vampires, but Alexander isn't here. Neither is Aunt Iva. Was Charles Keystone here? I think I had a whiff of his scent."

"You know Charles' scent?" Sarah asked suspiciously.

"I met Charles months ago. He floundered in his new state. I tried to offering him sound advice, but he wouldn't listen."

"New state? Oh, I forgot that woman, Minerva, explained how he was turned."

"Charles is a vampire like me."

"But how did that happen?"

"In the aftermath of Lord Eccklestone's killing by his son William, the vampires he held in a pit escaped. Charles was overtaken by one who had already fed on some of Lord Eccklestone's men and they made him like them."

"Poor, Charles."

"Poor, Charles? The man held you prisoner here, did he not?"

"He never treated me badly and I think it's my fault he is so obsessed with me. When Alexander and I were escaping Lord

Eccklestone's custody I used a gift on him. I had never thought or even knew it was a gift I had, or really how to use it. I bonded him to me like glue. I tried to take off the spell but it seems I was unsuccessful."

"So, Charles loves you?"

"He thinks he does."

"That is unfortunate, but maybe we can use that to our advantage. I still think he may have glamoured you. I believe I can follow his scent and that he is in possession of Aunt Iva. When I find him, he will remove the command for you to trust him and feel sorry for him. I'm going to drop you with your brother then go look for the young scamp, Alexander. I won't let anything bad happen to him. I promise Seraphina."

"I want to come with you," Sarah demanded.

"I can fly faster without you."

"Fine, drop me with Michael, I'll wait for you to come back, but I don't like this."

"I promised your mother I would keep you and your brother safe and I will. Come now child, I will bring home Alexander and then find Aunt Iva."

~0~

Chapter 15 - A Tiny Little Scratch

S arah was deposited on the sofa once

again and Ink flew away. She looked around and called out for Michael, but there was no answer. She tried to get up from the sofa, but her legs didn't seem to want to work, instead she tumbled to the floor. Pulling herself along the floor until she got near the kitchen, she looked through the open door. With disbelief she realized her brother, Michael, lay on the floor unconscious. She was scared and went to him to make sure she was not mistaken and he had been slain. She crawled pulling her legs, which felt numb and not entirely there. Reaching him she touched Michael's neck. He was alive.

Who could be powerful enough to take down Michael? Then stepping out of the shadows was the figure of Alexander.

"Oh, thank goodness, you are all right Sarah. I tried to get by this weretiger, but he wouldn't let me. See, I subdued him, I think. I couldn't find Aunt Iva, but I wasn't about to let you get kidnapped by these people and let Uncle Demetrious down. Wait until my Dad and Demetrious find out I was the one to save you. They'll be so proud of me."

"But Alexander, I didn't need saving except from you. You should have stayed with your mother. If something happened to you and you were kidnapped; they would be forced to do anything to get you back!"

"But I saved you Sarah," Alexander protested.

"I really didn't need saving Alexander. I did fine on my own. You really don't even know the strength of your abilities. You used something too powerful to immobilize me. My legs won't work now. What did you subdue my brother with? Why do you men always think I need saving? I saved myself from Minerva and Charles. Then Uncle Ink comes along, and takes me to my brother, saying I'm still in danger. I wanted to call Demetrious and tell him Petra works for the Magik Vampire. But Uncle Ink will get word to Demetrious about my safety. Wait a minute, why do I babble?"

"Sarah, I didn't immobilize you. Minerva did. Then that vampire kidnapped you and brought you to her. You can't trust them. You couldn't have fallen for their lies; you don't even have a brother," Alexander protested.

"You are mistaken Alexander, about a lot of things. The weretiger, is my twin brother Michael. Now something you did immobilized me. Fix that."

"He's a weretiger, they're dangerous beasts. I didn't even know they existed anymore except in books. Maybe he's not even a weretiger, maybe it's an illusion and they are tricking you."

"Don't be ridiculous, weretigers exist and this one is my brother."

You're the one mistaken. Those two have mesmerized you. I accessed Demetrious' files. You don't have a brother. You are an only child."

"You didn't access Demetrious files? You couldn't."

Alexander smirked and then commented, "When you went missing, I overheard Dad talking to Uncle Demetrious on the phone. So, I accessed his files to find you."

"How could you overhear any of the conversation? Your Dad had a satellite phone Demetrious gave him. You wouldn't be able to overhear any of the conversation. You shouldn't be able to do any of this."

"Well...,"Alexander looked sheepish here.

"What did you do Alexander?"

"There are only two common types of encryption used in the two types of satellite phone standards used around the world. I just reversed engineered them with my mind and then ran the program through my computer and presto I could tap into any phone calls Dad got. Dad had some access to Uncle Demetrious' files, so I used that to access information stored about you," Alexander explained.

"How do you know this stuff? You're only a child. You really shouldn't be taking in your head to do these things. What is your father to do with you Alexander? Don't you see that doing that was wrong and now that it has been done others will be able to do this too? Wait! That explains the mole in Demetrious office. Someone else taps his satellite phone. Of course, that's it. It couldn't be Petra."

"Maybe that's true. It is easy to tap into them if you know how. The files about you said you were an only child, so there is no way you have a brother. That guy must be lying," Alexander explained. "Wait a minute, you mentioned, an Uncle Ink too. Where is he? You don't have an uncle living either."

Uncle Ink suddenly materialized in front of them.

"Ah, but young Alexander, she does, and before you use your powerful abilities on me, let me introduce myself, I am Mihai Du Inconue," Ink explained.

"Sarah step away from him he's dangerous. This is the Magik/Vampire Demetrious seeks. He plotted against Demetrious."

"I am not your enemy Alexander, nor am I Demetrious'. In fact, I think of the Blackstones as family. I admit, young Alexander, that I am a vampire (but a more powerful vampire than I) has become a Magik vampire. That vampire must have been made by a very old vampire who has since died because I cannot ferret him."

"Nonsense, Uncle Demetrious has excellent sources. He would know all this and I pretty sure you are at the top of his list."

"I thought at first it was Alfred Pennstone, but I was mistaken. Although Lord Eccklestone threw Alfred into a pit of hungry vampires, one took pity on him giving him blood then turning him. Alfred, weak and easily controlled, someone used him to front them. They killed him, staking him, when he was no longer needed. I'm not sure who the leader is. The vampire who has opposed Demetrious is clever. They have been able to keep their identity secret, even from me, but I shall find them out. They shall rue the day they pitted themselves against those who align with the Blackstones. I haven't been able to peg who it is, but I'm starting to suspect it is a woman. Why I'm explaining this to an eight-year-old, I don't know."

"Alexander, do you use a truth spell on Uncle Ink? How did you do that? I didn't even see you chant it," Sarah asked.

"I don't have to say anything out loud. I just think it and it happens. I have to be really careful what I think now. The other day I got angry at my tutor and wished him away and he disappeared. Luckily I got him back from where ever he went."

Sarah frowned at Alexander. This development sounded scary.

"Now don't look at me like that Sarah. He put a small leash on my powers. He said I needed to control them better, before he'll take it off. I can still use them though just at much smaller ability. I was mad at first, but then I realized he was probably right. I don't want to hurt anyone who doesn't deserve it," Alexander explained then glared at Ink.

"Alexander!" Sarah admonished.

"I will let this intrusion stand for now. Young Alexander, you really need someone more powerful to teach you that truth spells can backfire and sometimes harm you," Ink commented.

"I don't have to listen to you. I only listen to Sarah," Alexander shouted stepping further away from Ink.

"Alexander, please listen to him. He is my honorary Uncle."

"And you believe his story? He probably planted memories in your brain," scoffed Alexander.

"Alexander it isn't a story or implanted memories. I remember this clearly. He knew my parents well and they respected him they trusted him to safe guard me. When my parents were searching for a new city to live in, he hid me from my Grandfather Eccklestone. My parents had hired a woman to babysit us. Her name was Kara Jones. She was dependable steady and would keep us safe. My parents decided she would watch over myself and Michael during the day and keep me safe while Uncle Ink slept. Kara had met Uncle Ink, and she knew he was a vampire, but as long as we were safe, she didn't worry about Uncle Ink. At night Uncle Ink would watch over us until she returned in the morning. My parents had promised to return soon. Lord Eccklestone had other plans for them though and he found my parents and had them killed in a car accident. When Kara was informed that my parents had died, it was like she was under a spell. She became scared that Uncle Ink had committed the murder to obtain me and Michael's existence was wiped from her mind."

"That is a boomerang spell," Ink commented.

"A boomerang spell?" Sarah asked.

"Yes, in a boomerang spell. Someone uses the blood of a murdered victim to find the child progeny of the person and have the person who minds them hide them," explained Alexander.

"Progeny how do you even know these words?"

"Geesh Sarah, I'm in advance classes. I read at a university level. I need to so I can learn new techniques for my abilities."

"Sorry Alexander, it has to be hard being so intelligent and so young."

"Yeah, people always think I can't possibly do what I can do. I read books, old ones that tell me about spells no one has used in years."

"Your tutor lets you read those."

"Like he knows?"

"Alexander!" admonished Sarah.

"Now about this boomerang spell, it was probably one of the last spells your mother, or father did to protect you. I've read about these. Given their state it may have contained an error that made Kara forget Michael."

"You're saying with their dying breath my parents sought to protect Michael and me?"

"Yes," Alexander stated"

"Tell me more of this story Sarah," Alexander begged.

"My brother had to hide and run to Uncle Ink, when they came to get me so they didn't know about him. Kara turned me over to social services. Uncle Ink thought about getting me back, but he was a single man. He wasn't a relative; he knew the social services might put up barriers. Probably none he couldn't overcome with his abilities, but he slept during the day and grandfather still looked for me. Grandfather didn't seem to know about Michael at all. Uncle Ink thought I would be safer, maybe being adopted. I remember crying out for Uncle Ink in the foster home and for Michael and my parents. I made myself sick with the longing for them. Uncle Ink snuck

in one night and hypnotised me to forget
about them, in seconds I didn't remember
Uncle Ink, Michael and barely anything
about my parents. He truly thought he did
the best thing for me."

"You made her forget her family?"
Alexander replied shocked.

"Sarah is a sensitive; the longing for her
family could have killed her. I thought I
could get back to her in a few years when
they weren't looking for her anymore; but
Lord Eccklestone's people captured me and
encased me in silver chains and cement,"
Ink commented.

"If you were encased in cement, how did
you get out?" Alexander asked skeptically,
pacing in front of Ink.

"I was rescued by a great man who searched
high and low until he found me."

"But why did Michael look for you then? I
assume you, Mihai Du Inconue, wiped his
memory too?" Alexander asked.

"Call me Ink please."

"No, I don't want to. I won't be swayed with
an informal name; you are out to harm my

Uncle Demetrious. You cannot fool me," Alexander insisted, his arm raised to thwart Ink.

"He's not trying to harm Demetrious. Alexander, don't be difficult. Uncle Ink is trying to be friendly. Michael remembered me even with the suggestion Uncle Ink gave him and cried for me. They took him to a foster home too, only grandfather's people found him. They thought he was a child that Uncle Ink loved and adopted. Eccklestone took pleasure in throwing him into a pit containing beasts. Michael escaped and he searched high and low for me for years, only finding me because he heard the gossip that a Magik vampire had taken me prisoner," Sarah exclaimed.

"So, if he's your brother, how come he's a weretiger?"

"When grandfather's people found him, he was thrown in with weretigers. One of them took pity on him and turned him. Did you use a spell on me Michael to get me to tell you everything so frankly?"

"I needed to know all the facts as you understood them Sarah, without the dumbing down that adults always do when they speak to me."

"Listen kid, you might have a good right hand when I'm surprised, but I can take care of my sister now, so you should leave," Michael insisted rubbing his head and sitting up.

"If you think for one minute, I'm leaving my Aunt Sarah with you two, you can think again. My family appears under siege from an unknown person, for all I know you two oppose Demetrious and lie to me. You might be able to trick Aunt Sarah but you won't me. If you seek to harm, the house of Blackstone I will will stop you. Angelus custodio prosapia meus, angelo contego familiam meam."

"Don't chant that at me. I too protect family at all costs. We do not try to harm the house of Blackstone. We value it above all others, except our own," Ink answered.

"You say you value Blackstones above all others except your own. So how am I to trust you? Why would you value a Blackstone over your own family?"

"I owe a great debt to Blackstones that can never be repaid."

"Sarah is my family. I already consider her my aunt so that makes her my family. I will not allow anyone to harm Aunt Sarah. She is a Blackstone remember that if you claim to be so loyal."

"Neither would we. Sarah is my beloved sister," Michael insisted.

"I'm supposed to trust you two? Minerva did something to her. If you love her so much, why haven't you called a doctor?"

"I'm fine Alexander. Once you take off, whatever you did I'll be even better."

Alexander grabbed Sarah's hand and tried to pull her to her feet but nothing happened.

"Sarah, you've been spelled to deny this is happening, but it's more than that. I read about a virus that starts this way from a scratch. You weren't scratched, were you?"

"Minerva scratched my arm, but it's nothing."

"She scratched you?" Uncle Ink exclaimed alarmed.

Sarah looked at her arm. A tiny scratch already healing appeared to be there; why did they worry?

"It's nothing see," Sarah replied holding out her arm.

Ink examined the reddened scratch. The scratch now inflamed with yellow pus now coming from it had a red streaked line now shot up Sarah's arm. Ink looked alarmed, clasped Sarah to his breast and without a word flew away. Sarah still didn't see anything, but a tiny scratch.

"Where has he taken her?" Alexander asked, "Stop him."

"You're a little late Alexander. He's gone."

"You should have stopped him. I'll fix you then I'll find Sarah."

"Alexander, he had to take her. He has realized the seriousness of this. I should have seen this. Why didn't I see this?" Michael muttered.

"I don't understand what you're talking about. I'm leaving, now to find them," Alexander proclaimed.

"No, you're not. If this disease is what I think it is we are now under quarantine."

"Quarantine? If this is a just to keep me here..."

"Alexander, I'm sorry I know you are only eight, or is it nine years old?"

"I'm nine next week and what are you sorry about?"

"This is a plague. It was engineered centuries ago by a man named Luka Kalderaš who hated the Magik council."

"Plague, I think I read about the virus that caused it. Is it the one called Endocholemiaplegia?"

"Kid that's it. It starts with a scratch which contains the virus. But where would Minerva get a sample? They were all destroyed when the disease was eradicated."

"You're saying Sarah has endocholemiaplegia?" Alexander asked. "But that's impossible."

"A deadly disease to those who are of the family Magik kid, I don't want to scare you but we have been exposed. Like I said we're under quarantine."

"Then we can't leave?"

"Not if we don't want to infect everyone we know."

Alexander looked like a scared little boy for a moment then he asked, "So do you have X-box?"

"Name your poison," Michael cried opening a cabinet under the television to reveal an X-box and games.

~0~

Chapter 16 - Desperate Times, Desperate Measures

Demetrious sat at his desk when his intercom buzzed.

"Caleb Gemstone is here," his new secretary Eloise stated.

"Demetrious, Nice to see your cousin looking well."

"Eloise has come a long way and now she can have a full life."

"Eloise is a beautiful woman. She'll have lots of suitors."

"Suitors? Sometimes you talk just like the rest of your family."

"Don't remind me Demetrious. I get along with them better now but I still feel like that square peg in a round hole. "Caleb admitted hugging the wall, then realizing he looked too casual he straightened up.

Changing the subject Caleb asked, "Now what did you do with Petra?"

"Petra Kaminski is at Stonehenge Prison."

"Has she been tried then?"

"She offered no evidence to commute her sentence. Hopefully they will be able to re-educate her. She wouldn't give up her boss Alfred Pennstone."

"Demetrious, Alfred Pennstone was made into a vampire, but he was killed. He couldn't be her boss."

"Who killed him?"

"I was unable to find that out. I was lucky they even told me he was killed. They are very afraid of this Magik/Vampire. They say those who talk die."

"We still may find out who this is. I sent Aristotle Bluestone to search her mind."

"Demetrious, must you? This is Petra."

"Petra, knew the consequences of her actions. It pains me, but I must put the all the people of Magik before her. I can't let emotions dictate my governance of Magik peoples and the other unnaturals."

"I'm sorry Demetrious, maybe I'm overstepping my bounds by cautioning you, but I'm worried her family will go after you, and then we will have another war on our hands," Caleb said regretfully.

"You need have no worries on that score. I have done what is necessary to protect all our peoples. I reached out and spoke to her father. He was deeply distressed by her indiscretions. He begged her to tell the Magik council all she knew, sadly she refused. Her family has now disowned her. I have also secured written permission from her father to search her mind for any and all threats to the people of Magik from the Magik/Vampire. Her family name will formally be taken away from her in a ceremony Friday.

"I hope he is able to find the information easily then."

"Me, too. Enough people have been harmed," Demetrious admitted.

"Demetrious we will find your family. I promise on my life." Caleb exclaimed, "I'm going back out into the field and I will find the Magik/Vampire."

"I have every confidence in you Caleb. I would trust you with my life."

"I'll call in regularly Demetrious."

Caleb then turned on his heel and left the office.

Demetrious hoped Caleb was correct but he was really heart sick. He had still had no idea where Sarah or Aunt Iva could be. With all his resources they still had no information. They had been unable to determine where they had been taken... and now, no word from Darius, Janelle and Alexander. He was supposed to remain calm and cool but how do you do that when your entire family was under siege.

The Magik vampire had almost succeeded. He, or she, knew all Demetrious' weaknesses and zeroed in on them. He thought he knew who had been behind this all but so far, he had not found them or any proof that Alfred Pennstone was behind all of this. It certainly felt like someone who knew Demetrious family and knew Demetrious well. He trusted Petra and they had laid a trap, but somehow Petra had also ferreted out where his family really was. He felt that he had let Aunt Iva, Darius, Janelle, Alexander and Sarah all down.

Why hadn't Rowen checked back in? He would have to leave his ivory tower despite the other council members' edict against it. They had rallied against Demetrious leaving his office or his guarded apartment to even go to Sarah. He shouldn't have listened why had he? Had someone used their ability to keep him here away from Sarah? Who could have such strong abilities?

Alexander! Had they used Alexander playing on his need to help Demetrious and the council stay ahead of this dire threat? When he spoke with Alexander next, he'd find out that is if he ever found Alexander again. No, he wouldn't think that way he'd get his family back safe all of them. He was Demetrious Blackstone and he could and would save them and all the people of Magik from this threat.

Aristotle Bluestone could still relay any information by satellite phone. He would find and save his family himself, but first he needed to appoint an interim leader in case something happened to him but who?

His cousin, Cormac McCarthy-Peters was the man? He could take over in the interim and if something should happen then he would take care of all the people of Magik. Cormac would take care to find and save his family. Demetrious picked up his cellphone and dialled.

"Cormac?" Demetrious asked as the cellphone was answered. "It's Demetrious. You know why I'm calling?"

Demetrious chuckled, then continued, "I forgot you too were a seer. I do need you here. When can you be here? What? You're kidding me! You're outside in my outer office?"

Demetrious pressed the buttons for an outside line then said into the intercom, "Eloise send in Cormac."

Demetrious turned his head as he heard a voice but saw no one.

"She's not there Demetrious. She's gone to her doctor's appointment. I told you, I'm at your office now," Cormac replied laughing as he became visual. He then turned into a raven then turned back into human form again.

"I know of your abilities Cormac. But going through doors and walls without being seen that's a new one."

"I wanted to sneak up on you. Sometimes when I turn invisible as I materialize, I become a raven. My brother, Aodh becomes a hawk."

"But you can both handle it. Right? You still both return to your physical form?"

Cormac nodded. Cormac strapping and over six feet tall was also very wide. Oddly enough he had no fat on him. He was just big. His hair was fiery red and curled and clipped tight to his head. His twin brother Aodh also was built the same being identical except for his hair part which favoured the right side, instead of the left as Cormac's did. He was just as Demetrious remembered a perpetual smile always on Cormac's face, Aodh had a perpetual frown.

"You know what I need you to do?"

"Of course, I'll take over temporarily, so you can save your family. We are family, after all," Cormac answered.

"Are you prepared to take over then?" demanded Demetrious holding out a document to sign.

"As long as it is only temporary, I never wanted to be a leader. There, now go find Alexander, Darius, Aunt Iva and Sarah. I really want to attend the wedding I've seen with both of them." laughed Cormac signing on the dotted line.

Demetrious then sighed in relief all would be well. Cormac had foreseen a wedding, surely that meant he seen Demetrious' and Sarah's wedding. All of his family would be safe. He would defeat this evil person and all would be all right in his world.

~0~

Chapter 17 - Familia Praevalebit

Ink landed; worried for it would soon be

sunrise. His arms were heavy and he worried that he wasn't quick enough but time would tell. He needed to go to ground, but he also needed Sarah cared for.

A woman appeared dressed in nurses' scrubs, with teddy bears on them.

"Kate?" asked Ink.

"Like my attire? This is Sarah is it not? Angelus heard your pleas for help. He has fetched the doctor. See, there he is," Kate pointed to a doctor, who placed Sarah on a stretcher and took her into the other room.

"Angelus must not be around her. She has the plague."

"Fear not, Angelus has had this plague and survived. The doctor is of Magik, who has also survived the plague," Kate answered.

"But how did you convince him?"

"Angelus tested his blood against Demetrious and Doctor Palmstone was convinced to come help Sarah."

"I always suspected you were distantly related to Demetrious."

"I'll explain shortly."

"I must know how Sarah is. She is like my own daughter."

"All will be well Mihai."

"Thanks, but don't sugar-coat this for me. I know Sarah is in danger and you know I prefer to be called Ink."

"We must wait to find out Sarah's fate. Come I have a story to tell you that will keep your mind busy."

"A story?"

"Yes, a story. Angleus and I would like to take back our real names. We are after all Demetrious' family."

"But will Demetrious believe you won't harm him and his family? That you are distant family?"

"We are his family. He is more open minded then the rest of his relatives before him. He will accept us."

"And what if Sarah dies?"

"She will not die. Angelus saw this."

"Seers visions are not always finite, Kate."

"Fear not Ink, my son. She shall be well again and she will bear my grandchildren."

"Grandchildren? I don't understand."

"Angelus and I were born before the great plague that swept across Europe."

"I knew you were old, but that old?

"Please Ink from now on call me my real name Ekaterina."

"And what is Angelus real name?"

"Before I tell you that I must tell you the story of how we met. I was born Ekaterina Seneslav. I was sixteen and very ill. I had contracted the plague. Bled regularly by the doctor, I grew weaker. I was dying, when I believed that my sister had come to pluck my blood from me."

"But it wasn't her?"

"No, it wasn't."

"Who was it then Angelus?"

"No, it was not Angelus, but Luka Kalderaš. He was my beau, but he had died. He couldn't bear to see me die, so he turned me. I awoke in the grave earlier, than he expected and I clawed my way out. It was then that he came to me and told me that I was a vampire. I didn't care because to me it meant I was alive and with him."

"You loved him? But you are not still with him?"

"No, he betrayed me. It's a very long story."

"Explain the story to me please Kate... er Ekaterina."

"Just call me Kate as usual."

"Luka was a very old fashion man. He even found a priest to marry me as a vampire. He seemed indulgent, but he expected obedience from his wife his chattel. I was his property and had to obey his every command. If I didn't understand or know the rules well then...," Kate broke off here, remembering her ordeal.

"What did he do to you? How did he betray you?" Ink demanded to know.

"He said he loved me. I was a newborn child, left alone He left me to hunger, changed into Strigoli, and no understanding of any of it."

"Why would he leave you alone? You don't leave fledglings alone."

"He didn't have permission to turn me, so he tried to hide me from his clan. His father summoned him and he went forbidden me to drink of humans. There were no animals, the plague had silenced even them. His twin brother Lucius came and showed me a new world. What could I say? New and the craving so strong, to drink of humans invigorating."

"You drained humans?" Ink asked shocked.

Kate nodded, but seemed ashamed.

"I confess I enjoyed being bad. I drank of human blood, but I didn't kill my victims. I've moved on since then. 1 saw how wrong that was," Kate replied defending herself.

"I'm sorry Kate. I have no right to judge you."

"It's okay, I've judged myself since then and found that Ekaterina, a very selfish spoiled little girl. I've grown up since then."

"Please continue, Kate," Ink begged.

"Lucius was the bad boy type. He encouraged me to go against his brother's wishes. He told me I could never see my family again, but I couldn't resist looking in on my sister Katrina."

"Your sister's name was Katrina? Your parents weren't very original," Ink commented.

"My sister was named after my maternal grandmother; I was named after my paternal grandmother."

"Oh, okay."

"Anyway, I went to visit Katrina. I wasn't going to let her see me, but I found her dying of the plague. I couldn't leave my sister to die. Lucius followed me and it turned out he knew my sister. He loved her, or at least had some feeling for her. He turned her as she lay dying."

"Lucius made Katrina a vampire?"

"He did, but Katrina was different somehow. It was like every nasty part of her was accentuated."

"We've seen that happened especially in those who were too close to death," Ink agreed.

"I was close to death and I didn't change," protested Kate

"Didn't you? Were you always this strong woman?"

"No, but my strength didn't come until much later. Anyway, Katrina became forward and fawned herself on other male vampires. At least that is what Lucius told me."

"Where is Katrina now?"

"I have no idea she ran off with Luka's Uncle Stansilov. She may be dead, so many of us were killed in the dark time. Luka chased away his brother Lucius. Luka told him never to darken our door. He blamed Lucius for me standing up to him."

"He sounds like a tyrant."

"He was a tyrant. He kept me in the dark cool earth and hungry to punish me."

"How cruel."

"I was cruel in kind. I silvered him and
escaped, leaving Lucius to free him. For
nine long years I lived in England, without
him censoring my every move. I knew I had
to move on before they noticed I did not
age; so, I moved to the wilds of Scotland."

Ink shook his head like he couldn't believe
what he heard then commented "Scotland?
You in Scotland? You must have been bored
to tears."

"No, I wasn't bored, at least not for long. I
found Angelus only then his name was
Aengus. Luka was the dark to Aengus' light.
Aengus told me he was a part of the Magik
council."

"Angelus was part of the council?" Ink
asked shocked.

"Aengus, as he was known then, was one of
the great ones in the council. I must admit I
didn't even know who Le Custos were until
he explained it to me."

"Luka really had much to answer for. He
didn't tell you of Le Custos either?"

"No, and then when I met Aengus, I fell in love with him, but I was a married woman, I could not break my vows. At least I thought I could not, but passion overtook me and Aengus made me his."

"And then what happened?"

"Luka happened. He found me again."

"Oh, no. I'm surprised you lived. This Luka sounds the type to kill in that instance."

"Luka begged me to forgive him. I felt torn and guilty. I had said vows before God and I had broken them by sleeping with Aengus. I tried once again to be his wife. I said my goodbyes to Aengus and cleaved myself to my husband Luka.

"Then how did you see Aengus again and end up with him?

"Aengus heard that Luka's Uncle Stansilov and his father were coming to kill Luka and I. They found out that Luka had broken the law in making me. His Uncle Stansilov decide that to eliminate the troublemaker and his progeny would satisfy Le Custos if they found out. The truth was though he hated Luka. Aengus risked all to come and warn me."

"Was Luka grateful?"

"How could Luka be grateful? After Aengus told me I felt the connection that had drawn us together. Luka found his wife in another man's arms naked."

"Oh..."

"Luka called me a faithless whore. Then he attacked Aengus and I was shocked to find Luka knew him."

"Aengus knew your husband?" Ink enquired.

"Aengus knew my husband and there was bad blood between them. Aengus' deceased wife Elizabet was Luka's sister and Luka blamed Aengus for her demise."

"Oh, dear, and you were caught in the midst of these two powerful men?"

"I was. Luka of course had other ideas. He had decided to kill Aengus. I pretended to care about Luka and convince him that Aengus death would only bring harm to Luka. I tried so hard to save them both."

"And did he listen?"

"No, Luka did not! Luka tried to wind silver chains around me and condemn me to the earth until he came back.

"So, what did you do?"

"Before I met Aengus, I had fled Luka's home for binding me with silver chains and condemning to the earth until Luka chose to release me. I spoke to Aengus about this and he spelled brass chains to appear to be silver, lest Luka condemn me again. So, the chains that Luka wound around me were the fake silver ones. I waited pretending to be thus trapped and then I broke off the table leg making a stake. I then flew back to where Aengus was. I begged Luka to let Aengus go promising never to see him again. I promised eternal devotion, but Luka would not hear me. He drained Aengus almost dry and would not let me go to him."

"But Aengus lived."

"He lived, no thanks to me," Kate stated sadly.

"What did you do?"

"I killed my husband. Do you hate and revile me now?"

"No, obviously you had no choice. You saved Aengus the only way you could. Didn't you?"

"I did. I poured my blood into his mouth. I expected Aengus to condemn me and be angry. Instead he was tender and sweet. He told me that Luka had murdered many people of Magik and had been condemned to die. He had been told to kill Luka, but for my sake, he'd let him go. Only my love for Luka had kept Aengus from killing him."

"Wow, so that is how you and Aengus met?"

"Yes. The story doesn't end there however Aengus' brother Broderick came and wanted to stake us. Aengus convinced him not to and promised we would go to the New World. There we would eat only of the flesh of animals and never use the last name so associated with Le Custos."

"What was their surname?"

"I'll tell you in due time, Ink. Let me finish the story first so you can understand. We took the names Kate and Angelus Svartsten. Broderick married us and saw us safely to a boat that took us to Norway. We took a number of boats to Newfoundland and there a miracle happened. I gave birth to our son Andreas."

"You had a child; but that is impossible. You are a vampire."

"Impossible maybe, but God gave me my dearest wish."

"Your dearest wish?"

"A child of our union."

"A child? That makes no sense-vampires can't reproduce," muttered Ink.

"I told you I was granted a gift. Maybe it was because of Aengus' powerful magic? All I know is that Andreas was born. Andreas was headstrong like the rest of his noble family. He knew from the time he was very young that we were vampires."

"It must have been hard to raise a child."

"Like any parent we strived to raise him. It was difficult. Andreas was curious, he found out that we had been forced to take another last name and never stopped hounding us for the information. When Andreas was eighteen, we felt we must tell him what our real names were. He began calling himself a

Blackstone, once again." Kate continued ignoring Ink.

"Blackstone? Your real last name is Blackstone, just like Demetrious? Well of course you are related to Demetrious."

"Angelus, is Aengus Blackstone."

But I don't understand how could you have a child? No vampire in all of history has given birth."

"Aw, but she has. It was a miracle; possibly because Angelus was a person of Magik God performed the impossible and gave me my son."

"So, are you related to Demetrious?"

"I am."

"You are some kind of great-great-great-great whatever aunt to Demetrious?"

"No, I am his...what...18th great-grandmother. My children and my grandchildren have all passed away except for my dear Demetrious and Darius Blackstone. When we became an oddity to the community endangering Andreas, Aengus and I pretended to die and moved on. We still watched over them keeping them safe."

"You've kept the family as safe as you could, all these years. Haven't you?"

"We have and we will continue to do so as long as we still exist. God gave us the gift of a continuing family line it must continue."

"That's why you have the motto, 'Circumspice tecum cor et anima pro fide conservantur ditet familia.' Look within your heart and soul for loyalty preserved enriches family.

"But you have never seen the other hidden part of our crest that says Familia praevalebit ? It means the family Blackstone shall prevail. Sarah must live. If anyone can save her Doctor Palmstone can."

"We wait and see and then we will tell Demetrious."

"You don't think we should tell Demetrious now?" asked Kate.

"No, he needs all his wits about him to find his aunt Iva and his brother Darius. We shouldn't distract him right now. When the time is right, you can come forward."

"I hate to do this, but I believe you are correct. This may have been his enemies' plan to distract him." Kate admitted, "Come I have some fresh cow blood in the fridge and a coffin awaiting your sleep."

~0~

Chapter 18 - What Big Teeth You Have Granny

Minerva sat in the kitchen drinking her tea. That little bitch, Sarah had got exactly what she deserved. Sick of all the fawning over that girl, Minerva had acted and where had it got her? What was so precious about her anyway? So, she was pretty, lots of women were pretty.

Charles-the coward- had disappeared shortly after that nasty Blackstone kid, Alexander, had arrived. That rotten kid had held her prisoner and demanded to know where Iva was. She had pointed him in the right direction and he had gone leaving her with Sarah. He hadn't even realized Minnie had already infected Sarah with the plague. Ha, ha, so much for Alexander being the next great Blackstone.

Sarah had suspected Minerva, so Minerva had placed some plague serum in her ring.

One twist of her ring and a simple scratch from it and Sarah was infected. Too delicious, Sarah had fallen for Minnie's innocent act and by now she lay dying. This would take down the house of Blackstone and finally make Iva pay for killing the only man she'd ever loved. Sarah would infect Alexander, Demetrious and his other family members. The Magik /Vampire would surely reward her for helping them take down the family Blackstone as an added bonus.

Minerva heard noises and looked around but saw no one. She was frightened could that dreadful Blackstone child become invisible? She looked all around her tiny house but saw no one and no hint of power. She sat down to drink her tea again but felt uneasy.

"Who is there?" Minerva asked and then jumped when a hand grabbed her.

"Hello, grandmother," the voice said sweetly.

A dark figure glided into the kitchen and sat down.

"Oh, it's you then," Minerva responded.

"It's me. You've moved from my house in the woods I had to come find you."

"Sorry dear, those dreadful Blackstone's came. I had to fight for my life to get away."

"And where is Sarah Maidenstone?"

"I suspect Alexander took her. As I said I had to fight back with my life."

"Yet dear grandmother, there isn't a scratch on you." the voice responded, with icy coolness.

The voice dug her painted long red fingernails into the wooden tabletop in an angry manner.

"I did use my magic to protect me," Minerva responded.

"Funny, that isn't the story I heard."

"It isn't? Whoever told you different, they lied!"

"Were they lying? What big teeth you have Granny," the voice commented, with a long sharp fingernail rolling across Minerva's neck.

"Teeth I don't understand."

"Really granny, don't you read your fairy tales?"

"I have never read fairy tales."

"That is right. You weren't there to read your child, or grandchild fairy tales. It's from 'Red Riding', it goes like this the little girl in the fairy tale says "[1]Grandmother, what big arms you have! It goes on and on listing body parts until she says, "All the better to hug you with, my dear," the grandmother answers.

"Grandmother, what big legs you have!" Red Riding Hood continued.

"All the better to run with, my child," grandmother replied.

"Grandmother, what big ears you have!"

"All the better to hear with, my child".

"Grandmother, what big eyes you have"

"All the better to see with, my child."

"Grandmother, what big teeth you have got!"

---

[1] ("Quotes from Red Riding Hood by the Brother's Grimm")

"All the better to eat you up with."

"I still don't understand. That's not the grandmother, but a wolf."

"Ah, but you have to look beyond that. I think the grandmother appeared to be a wolf in sheep's clothing. Basically, it means you lied."

"I'm not lying. Sarah got away."

"Just like your son got away?"

"Why do you bring that information up about my son again? You know how I suffered. Ask Charles what happened to Sarah. He'll vouch for me," lied Minerva.

"I can't ask Charles. Charles, the dear boy, met an unfortunate end. You gave my grandfather away. I know you did. Don't think because you are my great-grandmother that you can lie and cheat me."

"I haven't; I swear I haven't. We are family. Don't listen to the family lore. I loved your grandfather, but my family took and gave him away."

"You know it's a funny thing, I wanted to believe your story was true. I think you've even convinced yourself over the years that it was true. But the truth is somewhere in between. I've come to realization; you didn't want my grandfather. He was an obstacle to your ambitions."

"That is simply not true. I loved Peter Andrew, my darling boy was all that I had left from his father."

"You lie even to yourself. So why should I expect you to tell me the truth?"

"I don't lie. I love you dear child. You are the only family I have left. If I had known about you, I would never have left you with those people, your step-father's family."

"Wouldn't you have? Am I supposed to dry unshed tears of joy at your declaration? You sent Peter Whetstone to his doom with Iva. You knew Iva would kill him, yet now you tell yourself he was the love of your life and Iva must pay. Yet she is family. Isn't that right, granny?

"She killed him. I didn't tell her to. How dare you?"

"Don't speak that way to me. If you tell me the truth, I might let you live for family's sake."

"I'm sorry of course I'll tell you what you wanted to know. We're kinfolk after all," Minerva responded frightened by her great-grandchild's threats.

The woman's eyes narrowed and her nostrils flared as she asked, "Where is Sarah and what did you do to her?"

"Do? I did nothing to her. She discovered the ruse and attacked me. Is it my fault I had to defend myself cleverly?" Minerva simpered.

"Exactly what clever thing did you do to defend yourself?" her voice low and deadly soft.

"I filled a ring with a disease and when Sarah grabbed me, I scratched her so she became infected."

"I heard Sarah was ill; what did you infect her with?" asked the voice nonchalant, while inwardly seething.

"I infected her with endocholemiaplegia. She'll be dead by sunrise. No need to thank me, dear," Minerva exclaimed happily.

"Thank you? You stupid evil old hag! I love Sarah. She is like family to me. More family then you have ever been. Why do you think I saw to her every comfort, and now you've sentenced her to death? And not just any death, a painful clawing death! You shall pay dearly for this," the voice screeched and moved Minerva six feet off the floor.

"What do you do to me? Please, stop! You are my family."

"Family? You have no idea what family should mean! See this? This is a neat trick I learned from Eccklestone." the lord vampire exclaimed, choking the life out of Minerva from a distance.

"Please stop," begged Minerva.

"I will but only because this is too good for you though. You deserve a slow agonizing death and I have one for you... in the pit of despair. You see I lived through the pit of despair, but you won't. The vampires there are under my command and they will have no pity for the likes of you," the lord vampire, then kissed Minerva's cheek, "Goodbye, great-grandmother, dear."

"Please, dear we're family. You won't really harm me, will you?" Minerva whined.

"Take her quickly to the pit, I will hear no more of her pleading," the voice commanded to another vampire near them.

"Yes, my lord," the other vampire responded.

"Please dear Sarah, fight this illness so I may see you another day," the voice prayed aloud.

"Where shall we look for Sarah, lord?" a vampire asked.

"We must access records for a Doctor in the Magik council who has survived the plague and find out where he/or she is. Wherever they are we will find Sarah," Lord Vampire commanded.

"I'll contact Petra right away Lord. She can access the information we need and save your Sarah," the other vampire soothed.

"You are my loyal servant and I always remember I reward such loyalty. If Sarah doesn't survive Demetrious Blackstone will pay. It is his entire fault. I should never have trusted my great-grandmother to look after her."

"And what of Charles?" asked one vampire

"Charles is a most loyal member of our group. He informed me of Minerva's treachery and how she allowed Sarah to be taken. He loves Sarah almost as much as I do. Charles will be rewarded."

"Then you didn't kill him, my lord?"

"Of course not, only those who betray me die," Lord Vampire stated menacingly.

"I would never do so my lord."

You better not. You have all sworn the blood oath and if you break it you die. It is as simple as that. Now let's go find my dear Sarah."

"Yes lord." agreed both of the vampire minions.

~0~

Chapter 19 - A Waste of Life

Petra paced her cell. How could she escape her fate? They would come and her life would be over. Demetrious would never forgive her. She had seen how he viewed this behaviour. He considered it treachery, a form of treason. How could she have believed this would have made him love her? Damn that Sarah Dexler- Maidenstone. Damn her to the bowels of hell.

"Hello, Petra." a voice said interrupting her thoughts.

"I knew you'd come. Aristotle Bluestone will come to extract my memories. You can help me get away. I don't want to be re-educated. I just want Demetrious to forgive me."

"Demetrious loves Sarah."

"I know and you love her too, don't you?"

"Yes, but she doesn't even know I exist."

"You can still make her love you. Just don't harm Demetrious. If you do, she'll never love you."

"I respect the man even though I hate him. If he dies it won't be by my hand."

"You are very good to him. I appreciate it."

"I'm glad you do Petra, but you know why I'm really here."

"I don't understand."

"Come on Petra, let's not be coy."

"You're going to kill me?"

"Yes, I'm sorry Petra. You are a waste of life."

"I'm sorry, please forgive me. I did try to help," Petra muttered.

"You couldn't complete the simple task I gave you. You are too much in love with Demetrious to be of any help. It grieves me to do so, but you have information that I don't want Demetrious to have."

"Can you do it painlessly?"

"Of course, you shouldn't suffer, you were a loyal subject."

"May I, write a goodbye note to Demetrious?"

"I guess I could do let you do that, being the generous person I am."

"Thank you. I'm sorry it came to this; I had hoped to break her hold on him; so you could be with her."

"I know you did Petra."

Petra wrote the letter and then signed it,

Love Petra.

"That letter will do. You don't give anything, but your love away."

"I didn't give my love away. Demetrious made it worthwhile."

"Aw, poor Petra. No one to call to call you their Pet. you're amply named."

"Must you make fun of me now?"

"Sorry Petra. When she is with me; he will be with you."

"But you promised..."

"Did I?"

"You did. You said you wouldn't harm Demetrious. Please keep your promise."

"I wish I didn't have to do this Petra. This has been an enlightening chat, but Petra, it's time," the killer replied.

The killer spoke a chant and Petra began to choke.

"Forgive me Demetrious," were the last words on her lips as she died.

The killer then set a spell to contain the fire to only the cell and then it wouldn't go beyond into the prison. Then left hurriedly, the killer didn't want to be there for the answering call of the fires being extinguished.

~0~

Chapter 20- Ball of Confusion

Sarah tossed and turned in her bed. She was so hot. Why was she hot? She had to get up and turn the air conditioning on in her apartment. She had an important test in the morning and she had to get her sleep. Then why wouldn't her legs work so she could get up and turn on the air conditioning? She remembered she had slipped on the ice and broke her leg. That couldn't be right; if she had broken her leg, then why was it so hot? Was the thermostat broken on her furnace?

Sarah went back to sleep only to awake an hour. It was so cold now. Had she got up and turned on the air conditioning after all? But hadn't she decided that it was winter? Her brain was fuzzy, like cotton wool had filled it up. Why couldn't she think, or even open her eyes? Something had happened and she couldn't seem to put it together.

What could she remember? She had broken her leg when? It was the day her foster parents the Dexler had died.

They were dead... the Dexlers were dead. Then she wasn't in school anymore and she needed to find a job tomorrow or she'd be out on her ear. Something was wrong with this idea. This information didn't seem correct. That was a while ago what had happened since then? What was wrong with her? Why couldn't she think? She would open her eyes and then she'd understand what had happened.

Sarah tried to open her eyes. Demetrious! She had met Demetrious. He was her world now even when she wasn't with him, she thought of him. Dreamed of him!

So why had she forgotten him? She had planned to marry him in the spring. What had happened to her? Why couldn't she open her eyes? Something was wrong with her it was obvious. But what?

Sarah heard a voice she didn't recognize say. "Sarah it is okay, lie still. We'll make you better."

Who was this? She had to try harder to open her eyes. Sarah felt like she was in danger.

Something had happened to her, something bad. But what was it?

Her eyes popped open. Uncle Ink had come to her and taken her to Michael. It was wonderful to see them both again. How could she have forgotten them?

Was that it? Had someone wiped her mind again?

She had to keep thinking but her mind was so foggy. Wait a minute. Alexander had said she had been cut. Had she become infected with something from Minerva's scratch?

Sarah stared down examining her hands and arm for the cut. She realized with growing horror her long fingers were now nothing but long bones without flesh. She examined her hands they too were skeletal. She pulled back the blanket over her legs and saw legs that were not covered by skin. That is when she lost it. Sarah began to scream. She couldn't be dead. She was alive, wasn't she? If there were such things as vampires, werewolves and other creatures, had Minerva turned her into a zombie?

"Sarah, dear it's okay. You're very ill but Doctor Palmstone is here and he will make you well."

"The flesh falls off my hands. I'm not wasting away? I'm not a zombie?"

"The flesh is still there Sarah, covering your bones. This is all in your imagination. You are not a zombie. There are no such things. Look again. See you have skin. You are very sick and have a high fever. You haven't died my child," Kate answered.

"You are sure?"

"Of course, I am," Kate answered.

"Who are you, my nurse?"

"Something like that."

Sarah looked around and saw a tall dresser. She noted there were no mirrors in the room. A closet left opened revealed clothes from other eras.

"How very odd," Sarah thought, as she peered at the woman who said she was her nurse. It was odd, but she knew somehow this was a vampire. Were they holding Sarah prisoner? Would they turn her into a vampire?

"It seems very dark. How long have I been here?" Sarah asked trying not to sound afraid.

"Ink brought you here a week ago."

"Oh, so you know Uncle Ink."

"I do."

"Where's Demetrious?" Sarah asked.

"Demetrious can't come to you."

"He loves me, he would be here. How do I know you aren't lying to me and you aren't with them?" Sarah demanded, dropping any pretence.

"I am not lying," Kate answered sounding offended.

"And yet Demetrious isn't here."

"Fine, since I think you can handle this information, I'll tell you. You have a disease that can infect others of Magik. It can kill them. We couldn't risk Demetrious being exposed," Kate explained.

"Demetrious wasn't exposed. Was he?"

"No, he wasn't exposed, but if he came to your side he would be. A lot of people with Magik die from this disease."

"Then I'm going to die?"

"Not if I or Dr. Palmstone can prevent it. Dr. Palmstone has had the disease. He knows how to treat this disease."

"Why would you care? I know you're a vampire."

"You know I'm a vampire? You can see this?"

"I know that you are a vampire. So why would you care, why wouldn't you align yourself with other vampires like the one who opposes Demetrious?"

"Does Ink align himself with the evil one? I care whether you live, or die, because I love a man of magic, whom I married many years ago."

"You're married? Vampires marry?"

"Yes, not many, but a few of us choose to follow our human ways."

"What is your name?"

"My name is Ekaterina but people call me Kate."

"You already know I'm Sarah," Sarah said yawning.

"Sarah, dear, we will talk more later. You need to rest."

"But we have more to talk about."

"Sarah you've been through a lot and there are many people who care about you."

"What if Demetrious comes here?"

"Demetrious won't come here. We haven't told him about you for his own protection. He can't be distracted right now either. He has found her, the Magik/Vampire that opposes him."

"Who is this person? Is it someone we know? Demetrious needs help he can't take her on all by himself."

"Ink has gone to help him along with many other vampires who oppose her. Ink has also found Darius and he can help Demetrious."

"Oh no, I can't believe I didn't think of Alexander and Michael they were exposed to this disease."

"They will be okay. Doctor Palmstone has sent a vaccine for them. With a little luck they won't ever have any symptoms."

"Then he gave this vaccine to me?"

"He made this vaccine from your blood
Sarah. It can't help you."

"But I'll get better?"

"You will child now just rest. Now forget
you ever saw me and concentrate on getting
well. Remember only that Demetrious loves
you," Kate soothed.

Sarah knew this vampire compelled her to
sleep and she tried to fight, but she was
weary and she gave in.

~0~

Chapter 21 - The Magik Vampire

D emetrious flew to the site in which

they had held Sarah. He hoped to find a clue
to where they had taken her by the time he
arrived.

Cormac held down the fort acting as head of
council and completing council business, so
he was free to find Sarah, Aunt Iva and this
Magik Vampire and defeat him, or her.
Aristotle Bluestone had sent no word so
apparently Petra could be a hard nut to
crack. If anyone could get the information
Aristotle could. Demetrious could almost
have felt sorry for her, but for Sarah and
Aunt Iva's kidnapping. Petra knew how
much he loved Sarah and Aunt Iva and yet
she had betrayed them. Not only that, but
she also told them Darius's whereabouts.
Those things he could never forgive!

He had received a weird telepathic message
from Alexander. It was choppy and hard to
understand; but Alexander said he and his
mother were safe. He also said something

about Sarah and something that sounded like
Sarah's family. Alexander must have been
talking about how they were Sarah's family,
obviously, Alexander must have been too far
way for the message to arrive clear.
Alexander had only recently come into this
ability and obviously like all his other gifts it
was extraordinary, but still had limits.

Demetrious searched the barn beside the
property. Someone had been here recently.

 "Aunt Iva?"

 Demetrious felt Aunt Iva's presence. He put
his hands out to find the silver cord and
follow it to Aunt Iva. He followed it into the
woods and there in a cluster of bushes, lay
Aunt Iva. Demetrious' heart leapt into his
mouth.

Was she dead? He touched her neck. Her
heart still beat, but she was unconscious, and
she needed immediately medical treatment.
He called Doctor Tempstone. The phone
rang and rang. Aunt Iva needed a doctor
now who could he call? Doctor Trippstone,
Father Trippstone's brother of course. He
had started his practice a year ago, but he
was good. He could help Aunt Iva.

He flipped open his cell phone and called. Doctor Trippstone promised to be here within the hour.

As Demetrious waited, he worried about Aunt Iva. The poor woman had been attacked twice in the last year simply because she loved him, and now Sarah could not be found. The people around him suffered for his leadership. Was he the right leader? Should he continue to lead? Where were these qualms coming from? Maybe a spell lingered here giving him doubts? That must be it.

Demetrious would succeed because he was trained to be a leader. His grandfather long ago had told him that he was picked as a boy because of his strong moral fibers and his analytical mind. At times like this though he felt ill equipped for the job. His family meant everything to him and obviously the opposition knew that. They had struck where he was most vulnerable. But he couldn't let them win. All the people of Magik were his family except those who would oppose a just council. Many of his people had been converted to vampire without their consent. These were the people who needed his help. Their lives were irreparably changed. He must find this Magik/Vampire and help those people.

Demetrious checked again to make sure Aunt Iva still breathed. Yes, she breathed. He hoped that the air ambulance would arrive soon to take her to Doctor Trippstone. He heard the whirling of the helicopter before he saw it. He saw the air ambulance gently land in the clearing.. It had been five minutes. Two men got out and Demetrious stood on guard. This could be a trick of the Magik/Vampire. They could have taken the air ambulance.

He used his ability to read their minds from the distance of twenty-five feet and then stood down. They were as they seemed, sent by Doctor Trippstone to get Aunt Iva to the hospital. The hospital was in Vale of Glamorgan Wales. Thank goodness for the abilities of helicopter pilot, David Lapis.

David Lapis could propel the helicopter through time and space, much faster than any helicopter should be able to travel. Demetrious knew though that Lapis' ability related only to metal objects and whatever was in them. David could move metal objects through time and space and make them appear within moments. The Vale of

Glamorgan Wales trip would take exactly twenty minutes, Lapis assured Demetrious. David was a second cousin on Demetrious' mother side and loyal to the core to Demetrious and all of the Blackstone family.

The hospital was hidden in an agriculturally rich part of the country near the coastline. Locals who saw the hospital saw only Ysbyty Preifat or Private Hospital on the front of the hospital, but felt extremely uncomfortable about staying there. It made normals feel unwanted. People of Magik, and other unnaturals however recognized it as Ysbyty Cyffredinol ar gyfer Pobl o Magik or the General Hospital for People of Magik.

Demetrious watched them load Aunt Iva onto the air ambulance.

"Eloise flew to Wales. She'll be with you soon, Aunt Iva." Demetrious promised then turning to David and the man with him he said, "Take good care of my great- aunt."

"I promise I will Lord Blackstone," David acknowledged shutting the door and starting the engine of the helicopter again.

Demetrious had to be satisfied with that he couldn't be in two places at once he thought as he watched the helicopter disappear in the distance. Now he had to find Sarah's trail. Demetrious opened up his mind and felt for Sarah's essence. He found it with difficulty and followed it further into the woods. Inexplicitly it disappeared and Demetrious was puzzled. Suddenly he was seized with a terrific headache so much so that he grasped his head in pain.

"Uncle Demetrious, this is Alexander. I boosted my message by borrowing from someone else's power. I can't sustain this very long, so I'm going to lay out what I want to tell you very quickly. Aunt Iva was taken by her sister Minnie, or Minerva, as you would know her. Minerva was told to so by the Magik/Vampire who also controls Charles Keystone. Minnie has now disappeared," he heard in his head.

"But Charles Keystone is dead. He died when Lord Eccklestone killed a number of his people," protested Demetrious.

Demetrious found suddenly that this link was now causing a massive headache.

"He's not dead. Sarah saw him."

"Sarah saw him, and you know where she is Alexander?"

"I know where she is," Alexander replied without explaining.

"You need not worry about Aunt Iva. I've found her," Demetrious explained.

"Is she okay? Sarah's ...broth wants to know if his Unc... Ink is there?"

Demetrious heard in his head Alexander's voice as the connection broke up and then seem to come back again.

"I didn't find any Ink here. But wait a minute did you say, Sarah's brother? Sarah has no brother. Who are you with Alexander? You could be in grave danger," cautioned Demetrious.

"He is Sarah's brother. I've read his mind and Sarah now remembers him. He's her twin brother. His name is Michael," Alexander explained his voice coming into Demetrious' head clearer.

"You are sure you haven't been tricked Alexander? Sarah has no Uncle either."

"He is an honorary uncle. He saved Sarah."

"This man saved Sarah? From the people who took her?"

"He took her to Dr. Tempstone,"

"Who is this person and why did he need to take her to Dr. Tempstone?"

"He isn't who you think he is Uncle Demetrious."

"Sarah's, Uncle Ink. He isn't the Magik/Vampire. His name is Mihai Du Inconue though.

"What? They lie to scheme to win you and keep Sarah. Get away from these people Alexander and take Sarah."

"He's not lying, Uncle Demetrious, and he supports you. Not only because Sarah loves you; but because he believes in the council," Alexander explained. "I'll let you speak with Michael."

Demetrious felt a buzz and then heard another voice in his head.

"Demetrious, my name is Michael Maidenstone. I am Sarah's brother," began Michael.

"If you do anything to Alexander, or Sarah, I will kill you," threatened Demetrious.

"Read my mind. I know you can even over this distance with Alexander's boost," Michael's voice came into Demetrious' head.

Demetrious opened his mind and attempted to read Michael's mind some more.

"You truly believe your Sarah's brother and that Mihai Du Inconue loves you both," Demetrious responded shocked.

"I am and Uncle Ink loves us. He would sacrifice his life for us."

Demetrious without even knowing continued to probe Michael's mind.

"You're a Magik/Weretiger? I thought weretigers were extinct."

"I am sadly the last of them."

Demetrious continued to read Michael's mind and then gasped, "Why didn't the two of you tell me sooner; that you've all been exposed to the plague? Sarah was exposed... oh no, I must go to her."

"You can't go to her Uncle Demetrious; as long as the Magik/Vampire is at large she's in danger. Doctor Tempstone will take good care of her."

"You are sure that she is okay?" Demetrious pleaded.

"She's going to be fine. She has a wonderful doctor. Sarah will be fine. you don't have to worry. You have to go after the Magik/Vampire. That is your priority," Alexander chimed.

"Sarah is fine. I must apprehend the Magik/Vampire," Demetrious repeated.

"Goodbye, Uncle Demetrious, you need to go now so you can find the real Magik/Vampire, because Mihai Du Inconue is not the leader. In fact, you suspect it is a woman."

"I need to break off this communication so I can find the Magik/Vampire. I believe it could be a woman," Demetrious responded repeating what Alexander said like a mantra.

"How did you do that Alexander?" Michael asked as he felt Demetrious consciousness leave their minds.

"It's better that you don't know Michael. I would never have used that ability if it wasn't a desperate situation."

"A desperate situation?"

"With Sarah ill, nothing would keep Demetrious from her side, but for the good of our people Demetrious needs to find the Magik/Vampire and stop them. Even Sarah would understand this and forgive me tampering with Demetrious mind."

"I think you have good intentions kid, but I'm not sure you should use these kinds of abilities. Frankly you have so much magic abilities you scare me," Michael admitted.

"Sorry?"

"It's okay kid. I'm just glad we are on the same side. Want to watch some video? I have Sleepy Hollow," Michael asked setting down two cans of coke and a bag of chips.

"It's okay kid. I'm just glad we are on the same side. Want to watch some video? I have Sleepy Hollow," Michael asked setting down two cans of coke and a bag of chips.

"You have that movie too?" Alexander asked popping open a coke and grabbing the bag of chips.

"Movie? Kid, I'm talked about the cartoon with Ichabod Crane but yes I have a movie.."

"The one where Ichabod Crane and the headless horseman? I heard there are twists and turns and Ichabod is a cop, a man of science who refuses to believe in the unnatural," Alexander cried excitedly.

"Are you sure you're old enough to watch this? It's an old movie"

"I am"

"Fine then let's watch but don't tell Sarah she'll have my head for letting you watch something too old for you."

"Really? You're not so bad Mr. Maidenstone."

"Call me Michael and pass the chips, I'd like some too."

~0~

Chapter 22 - Trust No One

"Demetrious, you need to go now so you can find the real Magik/Vampire because Mihai Du Inconue is not the leader," Demetrious heard this in his head like a mantra.

He had to find the real person. Thank goodness, Sarah was safe with Alexander and Michael. Sarah had her twin brother with her so he could keep her from going to Aunt Iva's side.

Alexander said his mother was safe, but hadn't mentioned his father. That meant only one thing to Demetrious, Alexander didn't know where his father had gone. Demetrious satellite phone rang.

"Demetrious?" began Caleb Gemstone.

"Caleb do you have a lead?"

"I have but I need a team and your help Demetrious. I should have told you my suspicion sooner; but I couldn't believe who was behind this..."

"Have you found Darius?"

"I've found Darius and the Magik/Vampire. I think we can overtake this Magik/Vampire but you won't believe who it is..."

Demetrious heard a scream then a garbled yell. Demetrious tried to call Caleb back, but there was no answer. Demetrious phoned Aristotle Bluestone.

"Demetrious, I'm glad you called. Petra's dead."

"How?"

"She's been drained, oddly enough. She died with a smile on her face."

"A smile? The Magik/Vampire cared enough to make it not hurt."

"Looks that way, boss. She left a note for you, oddly enough it didn't burn," Aristotle replied.

"Burn?"

"A fire was set to conceal the crime but we put it out before it consumed her."

"So, the note was bespelled not to burn? Read it to me," demanded Demetrious.

"Are you sure boss? It sounds personal," commented Aristotle.

"All of her feelings were manufactured in her mind. Read it to me," demanded Demetrious.

"My Darling Demetrious

I hope that you can forgive me. All I did was to protect you. We've known each other since we were children. I don't know how Sarah got between us. Was I more like one of you siblings to you? Was that the problem? I know you cared about me and you feel I betrayed you. But when you think about it, you'd realize I did what I thought was right. I never truly betrayed you. I would never give anyone that much power over you.

You may think Sarah is your destiny, but be careful she is of Eccklestone's blood. Cunning and deceptive you'll never see that in her. You think she is selfless, but she has the power to destroy you. Protect yourself well Demetrious and know that I have always been loyal to the house of Blackstone.

Know that I love you and will continue to love you even beyond death, but everyone dies and this is my time.

Dilectione mea manet in aeternum meus dilectus,, My love endures forever my beloved Vivant domus Demetrious Blackstone(Long live the house of Demetrious Blackstone) Protegere te ab illis propinquissimum ad vos (Protect yourself from those closest to you)

Vale mei dilectissimi Demi. (Goodbye my dearest Demi.)

Omnibus meis ames Petra (All my love your Petra.) This is where it ends boss."

"Damn it! Why couldn't she have told me all this. I would have protected her despite her disloyalty."

"Sorry for bringing you the bad news, boss."

"Caleb has gone missing. I think they have now."

"Boss, how did you know this?"

"That's why I called. Caleb called me to tell me he knew where my brother was then the call broke off."

"I'll get right on it boss. I'll find out where the call was routed from."

"This person is always one jump ahead of us. I don't understand it."

"There's got to be another mole," Aristotle insisted.

"But whom?"

"I've got an idea boss. If it's who I think he is, he's in your inner circle.

"My inner circle? Impossible."

"Is it? We've looked into everyone else. I think it's George Limestone."

"It can't be."

"Only way to find out is to lay a trap and then follow him to his boss."

"Fine, what do you suggest?"

"George didn't start working until we used the Leperstone trap."

"So, we use that, since he's never heard of it," Demetrious agreed.

"And in the meantime, I'm going to track down this phone call and find Caleb," insisted Aristotle.

"Thank you, Aristotle."

"Any time Lord Demetrious."

Demetrious hung up and got to work he needed to help his people he could do this. His people depended on him defeating them.

~0~

Chapter 23 - Secrets

T he man opened the office door to a

distraught looking woman.

"It wasn't my fault! It wasn't my fault!" she muttered like a mantra as another man escorted her in.

"Of course, it wasn't," soothed the man his voice like velvet.

The woman became calmer but she then she suddenly became angry like a spell broke off.

"Why are you in my office? Did I call you?"

"No, but I sensed your distress and of course I came at once."

"You do love me and worship me, don't you? I hate Demetrious. Even now I bet his name is on her lips. I know she can't love me, but do you think she has feelings for me? I tried to keep her away from him. You know I did!"

"My lady, you did!" the man agreed.

"What did I tell you about calling me lady? Only address me as Lord, or Master.

"Forgive me, master."

"I will let it pass. Best you not forget again. You must be too over familiar, just because I favor you, dear."

"No, master."

"I don't know where I went wrong. I even hired Charles to make her happy, but he couldn't deliver."

"Where is Charles now?"

"He had an unfortunate accident," she lied.

"How unlucky, for him," the man commented.

The woman stretched out their arms palms open to the man. The man took their hands in his, then put his arms around her hugging her tight. She looked deep into his eyes and said, "You'll help me, dear man. Won't you? You said I was a great leader and I always reward my loyal followers. You made a great diversion with the speed in which you skillfully distracted Demetrious. He actually thought the great leader was a man because of you. That sap, Demetrious, still hasn't guessed my identity or yours. At yet you remain an enigma Sebastian even to me."

"I must keep my counsel great lady. It is best for all that you do not know my real name," Sebastian responded.

"I could make you tell me, but I won't. I would however like to know why you want Demetrious to know of you only as Sebastian."

"Let's not speak of this."

"Did I not share all with you and make you my number one Sebastian?"

"Demetrious knows me by another name and has greatly wronged me. But he will pay."

"We will make him pay," agreed the woman. "Demetrious lords over everyone. He holds down the Magiks and forbids them use their power for gain, yet him himself benefits from the same. The vampires and the werewolves hurt no one. They just want to be their selves and he won't allow it. Our children and our children lives are censored and controlled. I took back what is rightfully ours."

"You did my lady and his control over the council will fall soon."

"The worst thing he's done? He's bespelled Sarah. She actually believes that Demetrious looks after everyone's welfare and makes all happy. Poor deluded girl. Demetrious does not deserve Sarah."

"Sarah intrigues me. The loyalty that others have for her is not because of her beauty. She shines on the inside," Sebastian replied sounding puzzled.

"I have seen such kindness shine from her. It's why I need to protect her from him. Demetrious exploits her goodness and seeks to bind her to himself. I believe he's even enlisted that witch Iva Touchstone to bind her to him. She should have free will to choose her mate."

"People have the right to choose their mate."

"Exactly Sebastian but he didn't give her that opportunity. He glamoured her with his abilities and she fell for it hook line and sinker. I hate that man. Do you know we met as children and he doesn't even remember me? Some leader! He cares nothing about others only himself. The people think he's so good. Why can't they see he's evil? He runs around gaining power for himself, yet all the fools around him think he hung the moon and the stars."

"Demetrious is able to sway the masses, but I agree especially Sarah."

"Sarah is a Moonstone; she believes there is good in all. Do you know the prophecy about a Moonstone having the ability to bring peace to all supernaturals?"

"Really? I've never heard that."

"I think it would be good to have Sarah on our side. Do you think I could I be her best friend? We were friends once."

Sebastian drew a great breath and composed himself hiding the angry outburst he wanted to say, instead he said, "Delilah, you are a gem. Sarah would be lucky to call you friend," but he really thought, "I will not allow you to harm Sarah, even if I must kill you."

"Lord Eccklestone betrayed me. He promised that my husband was alive and wanted me. Abraham did want me not anymore; he wanted me dead and he turned me. Lord Eccklestone promised my children would be safe if I tricked Demetrious into schooling them. My children don't even recognize me now and I haven't seen them in months all because of Demetrious Blackstone."

"I killed Abraham for wronging us. He made us both a vampire. I was given to him thanks to Demetrious."

"You did and I rewarded you for it. I made you my number one. You are like a brother to me," Delilah answered.

"I don't know why you don't find me desirable master. I could give you such pleasure. If you'd only let me."

Sebastian ran his fingers up her arm and she shivered with excitement. Then getting control of her emotions Delilah exclaimed, "I've seen the others that have felt your special touch and I have no desire to be dominated again,"

"If you so desire a mate, that you can dominate, I will find your true mate. I can use a spell to find him or her, it is one of my gifts," Sebastian countered.

"You would do this for me?"

"I would do anything for you. I am your captive slave. As soon as I you have Demetrious in your hands, master I will find your true mate for you."

"Agreed, but for now I must go I must find out if Sarah lives. Thanks to my great-grandmother Minerva she may die. I love Sarah, like more than my own sister. I allowed the vampire to take her to safety and now..."

"Sarah has been harmed and may die? What has happened?" Sebastian asked, his hand behind his back moving quickly under his breath he chanted in such a way Delilah didn't hear him.

"My foolish great-grandmother thought for herself without consulting me. She poisoned Sarah. Mihai Du Inconue took her somewhere, I assume to a Magik doctor. He flew her to safety and to help for her condition," answered Delilah

"And you know this how?"

"I followed when he came back for the boy."

"The boy?"

"Alexander found the place we were holding Sarah."

"I like Alexander. Seems like a fine boy. Even being raised by Lord Eccklestone didn't taint him," the man answered.

"If Sarah dies many more shall die. This I vow."

"And what of Demetrious?"

"I would have Demetrious suffer for his treatment of my babies and Sarah."

"Oh, Delilah, do you really want to continue with that lie?"

"Lie?"

"Demetrious has never threatened your children. Those kids are actually your sister's."

"So! They are still mine."

"You don't give a damn about them."

"I do too."

Sebastian raised his eyebrow and wiggled his fingers some more behind his back so Delilah didn't see what he did. He'd get the truth out of her yet.

"Oh okay, so they don't matter to me. Pesky kids! When Demetrious arranged for them to go to boarding school, I smiled. I convinced him I actually cared about them."

"And he believed they were actually your kids, how? Demetrious would have done research."

"My sister had the same middle name, as I have first name. Jacqueline Delilah is her name. Purely a simple thing to point Demetrious' people to her records and my wedding to Abraham was in Delilah my real first name so they assumed they were one and the same."

"What parent names their daughters the same names?"

"Delilah was my mother's grandmother's name."

"So, you tricked Demetrious. Bravo. But why do you sound like you hate your sister when you say her name?"

"My sister Jacqueline betrayed me every chance she got."

"And yet you took in her children."

"Someone had to my family was all gone. At least I thought it was," Delilah explained.

"You don't really hate those kids you were trying to protect them," Sebastian insisted.

"So, sue me. I also loved the power and prestige I got working with Lord Eccklestone and I didn't let him harm Sarah, or my nieces and nephew."

"No, you didn't and that makes you human Delilah.

"On your lips my name sounds beautiful," Delilah answered, her eyes looking at him with affection.

Delilah suddenly broke her gaze on his eyes shutting her eyes. When she opened them again, she looked at Sebastian with fear and suspicion.

"Why do I confide in a servant? What have you done to me, Sebastian? What have you done to your master?"

"Oh Delilah, haven't you figured out yet? I am not your lapdog, not anymore. I have escaped the compulsion you put on me. You own me no more."

"I don't understand."

"Did you think me a minor person of Magik? Did you think you could control me forever? I have finally escaped all traces of your clutches. Lord Eccklestone knew who I really was, maybe you should have found out too."

"Who you really were? You asked me not to look into your background and I agreed. Why did I agree?"

"I started getting some of my senses back and I sought to protect myself even with my abilities somewhat extinguished."

"You compelled me. Didn't you? How could you do that? No one can compel a master vampire."

"And yet I used very little of my ability to do so. If I were to use more, you do everything I wanted and more," Sebastian laughed.

Delilah gasped, then became invisible, as
Sebastian just laughed and reached for her.
He grasped her in his arms and held her
tightly even as she sought to flee.

"Your invisibility does not work with me,"
he said grabbing her.

"How do you do that?"

"I am of a powerful family, much more
powerful than yours."

"I trusted you. You were my number one,"
Delilah cried. "What will you do to me?"

"That was your mistake. You trust too
easily, but I am not you."

Delilah's eyes begged him not to hurt her
even as she pleaded, "You'll kill me?"

"No, I think I'll let Demetrious do that. He
wants to put an end to your reign against
him. I think I'll let his organization know
about George."

"George?"

"You remember George, Demetrious' right
hand man."

"But I didn't recruit George," protested Delilah.

"No, I did. Only he thought it all came from you."

"I can handle Demetrious. I have so far."

"Only by compelling me to help you and I'm not using my abilities to shield your presence anymore."

"I don't need you. I can defeat Demetrious.

"Can you? When I go you won't remember this so I can tell you my real name is Dominic Blackstone," Sebastian explained.

"You're a Blackstone?"

"Not just a Blackstone, I'm Demetrious' older brother."

Delilah paled; but composed herself smiling like she knew a secret that the man before her didn't.

"Fool! Do you think that I won't see through your lies? He's dead. He died when Demetrious was but a boy."

"You are the laughingstock, believing the lies my guardian, Grandfather Abraham told. Grandfather only cared about the boy genius, Demetrious. Everything was always Demetrious this, Demetrious that. I still remember him droning on...Do you care for your brother? Do you see that he is well? It's your job to protect him until he can be the council."

"Sounds like my family and their precious Jacqueline."

"Don't get me wrong, I loved Demetrious. He is my brother after all. I did all I could to help him. Did I get any thanks, or love from him? No! He took the job I was born to do and believed all their praise."

"You think you were born to rule the council of Le Custos?" laughed Delilah.

"Before he usurped my position, I was the chosen one. Grandfather groomed me to take over, but the minute he saw Demetrious (as a baby) all of that changed."

"What can you do with family? You can't kill them even when you want to... Oops that's not true. I killed my great-grandmother. But then she deserved it. She shouldn't have harmed Sarah," Delilah commented.

"Demetrious is my kin. I will not kill him despite the fact he tried to kill me."

Delilah pulled loose from Dominic's embrace and stared hard at him.

"But you just said he tried to kill you. He deserves payback in kind," Delilah protested.

"My brother condemned me when he came home sick and infected me with his plague, but I will not be like him. I will however have revenge. He shall suffer."

"Demetrious had the plague? But how does he still live?"

"Grandfather got the best doctor for his favoured grandchild. As I lay dying our grandfather ignored me. Only when I lay close to death did he seek out his old friend Eccklestone to come and cure me.

"Lord Eccklestone? But I thought he hated him!"

Dominic laughed and continued, "Demetrious thinks Grandfather's record so pristine. Ha! Grandfather and friends since childhood and although the council forbid contact, grandfather welcomed him into his

home, provided of course that Demetrious
never saw him. Grandfather pretended to
everyone else that he hated Eccklestone.
Archie Eccklestone..."

"You called him Archie and he didn't smite
you?"

"Once I called him Uncle Archie but that
was before he saved me..."

"Saved you? You mean he was the one
that..."

"Yes, but not on purpose. He promised
grandfather that he would save me, if he
could and make me a vampire. Grandfather
allowed him to take me without a whimper
of protest. All grandfather's thoughts were
with Demetrious. Eccklestone promised him
a life for me, that would be full, safe
amongst the vampires. Eccklestone however
had grown disenchanted with our families'
power and he decided to punish grandfather
by eliminating me. Foolish man, he didn't
realize how little grandfather cared for me.
Grandfather didn't even blink when he
thought me dead. As for Eccklestone he
threw me in a vampire pit for their food. A
woman vampire however took pity on me
and turned me."

"And you saved me from the pit," Delilah commented.

"I felt sorry for you. And how did you reward me? You bound me to you and compelled me to do your bidding," Dominic complained.

"I am sorry Dominic, I would take it back if I could," pleaded Delilah, kissing his fingers hoping to sway him.

She knelt before him.

"Get up Delilah. You make me laugh, and because of that I will let you go," Dominic replied smiling and pulling her up.

"You'll let me go? Oh, thank you, Lord Blackstone."

"I kind of like being called Lord Blackstone. Maybe I'll take that back someday soon. However. there is much for me to do. It's time Demetrious paid for his treachery and I took my rightful place."

Then leaning in, he kissed Delilah on the lips. His teeth clasped down on her lip tasting her blood with his teeth and he chanted, "I command you when I am gone it will be as if I did not exist, you remember

no Sebastian, or Dominic, then in Latin,
'Iubeo quasi post me non erit, ne memineris
et Sebastiani Dominici.'

Dominic then disappeared in a ray of light.
Delilah continued to plot against Demetrious
forgetting Dominic, or Sebastian ever
existed.

~0~

Chapter 24 – Did you miss me?

Delilah knew Demetrious would be coming soon. She'd seen the werewolf Rowen hiding in the woods beyond the village. How foolish the wolf was! Did she think Delilah didn't know she aligned herself with Demetrious?

"Hello, Delilah. Did you miss me?" a voice asked behind her.

"How did you do that?" Delilah asked turning around.

"Delilah, I've been around for a while. I am a master vampire and I'm here to offer my services."

"Who are you?"

"I am Mihai Du Inconue."

"You offer to align yourself with me, Mihai Du Inconue?"

"I do and to prove my loyalty I've brought you a gift." Ink held out a pretty wrapped bottle.

"What did you bring me?" Delilah asked eagerly.

"I don't know if you really want this gift."

"But I do," Delilah pleaded, "Now please tell me what the present is."

"Why don't you just open it?"

Delilah took the package and ripped the paper quickly.

"It's a delicious brandy from the fourteenth century. I can't believe this. What an exceptional gift. Thank you. Shall we toast to our alliance?" Delilah cried gleefully.

"Let's," Ink agreed.

Ink opened the bottle and poured it into the two glasses. Delilah sipped greedily, while Ink appeared to drink but drank none of it.

Seconds later Delilah asked "What did you put in this?"

"Just a little garlic and holy water and herb-of- the -cross," Ink answered.

"You bastard!" Delilah shouted her choking on her words.

Delilah fell to the floor screaming in agony. Just then Ink heard a noise and hid. He watched as Demetrious entered saw Delilah dissolving and smiled as he saw Demetrious chop off her head. His work was done he could go back to Sarah and so could Demetrious. Ink slipped out the back and flew away.

~0~

Chapter 25 - All the King's Horses and All the King's Men

Sarah awoke feeling tired, but she could see the sun way up in the sky. It was time she arose. It was then that it dawned at her; she wasn't in the cottage in the woods. Where was she and how had she gotten here? She tried to lift her legs to get out of the bed and realized they didn't move. She attempted to use her arms and gasped they wouldn't work either. What had happened? Had Demetrious enemy found them?

"Sarah do you remember me?" asked the man feeling her pulse and then commenting "Good, pulse is normal. Fever is down too, almost non-existent."

"Dr. Palmerstone?"

"It's me, rest easy child."

"I'm not your child. Why am I here? What occurred? Why can't I move my arms and legs? Do you hold me prisoner here? Have you betrayed Demetrious?"

"Sarah, I would never betray, Demetrious. He is like my own son. I've done nothing to you. Don't you remember how this occurred? You've been very ill, but you are get better now."

Sarah tried to recall, but all she remembered at first were fragments. She had been fighting with someone so he was told the truth.

"Do you recall how this happened, Sarah?" Doctor Palmerstone asked searching her face.

Sarah scrunched up her face concentrating trying to recall. Her head ached, but she persisted, probing the deepest regions of her memory to recall.

"I can see that this is difficult for you. What do you remember?"

"Aunt Iva and I had fled to safety... but that wasn't Aunt Iva. All those months it wasn't Aunt Iva," Sarah recalled.

"Who pretended to be Aunt Iva? Do you remember Sarah?" prompted Dr. Palmerstone.

Sarah searched her memory and recalled finding out Aunt Iva had been kidnapped and replaced by Minerva her sister. She'd captured Minerva and then someone had come along but who? Why was her memory so foggy?

"You look like you've remembered something, would you care to share?"

"I was kidnapped by this woman Minerva, or Minnie, as she called herself."

"That is true. Do you remember what occurred after that?"

"Why do I have so much trouble remembering?"

"I think that a spell may have caused some memory problems, but I think the medicines may counteract the effect. Keep working on the memories and they will come back to you."

Dr. Palmerstone was interrupted by a nurse that came in and whispered in his ear. He turned to Sarah and said, "I'll be back in a few moments I have to check on my other patient."

Sarah watched him leave wondering if the spell that someone cast...was it Minnie who had caused this paralysis? Of course, that must be it. Minerva cast a spell and the medicines and words Dr. Palmerstone were now working a cure.

Uncle Ink had come along and had reintroduced her to Michael.

She had a brother and an uncle (technically he was her honorary uncle) but she had family.

Just think about that made her smile. She had family again. But she forgot something ...But what? She had to search through what she knew. Uncle Ink had erased his presence and Michael's from her mind all these years. But she had her brother and godfather back now. This wasn't a dream. She enjoyed a reunion with her brother when Alexander came. Alexander had threatened Michael and then. Wait a minute. Alexander came before the reunion and Minerva scratched Sarah injuring Sarah.

Sarah was ill because of Minerva. Alexander had gone to find her and ...then Uncle Ink had flown her here. But where were they, in the next room? She knew they wouldn't

leave her now and where was Demetrious?
If she was sick, he would be here.

"Where is my family?"

"Family? You have no family Sarah. You're
an orphan, have you forgotten?"

"Didn't they tell you? Mihai Du Inconue is
my Uncle Ink, my godfather. And I have a
brother Michael."

"The leader of the vampires who brought
you here is your godfather? No wonder he
refused to leave."

"So, Uncle Ink is here."

As if by command, Ink swept into the room
and in an instance was beside Sarah's bed.

"Sarah, I heard you calling," Ink
commented.

"Uncle Ink, where is Demetrious?"

"Demetrious will come after he deals with
his foe, and sees that Darius is safe."

"Oh, no, how could have I forgotten does
Demetrious know about Petra?"

"He knows."

"Poor Demetrious but I think there is someone else in his office that works against him."

"Sarah dear, you need to stop worrying Demetrious has it all in hand."

"I need to stop worrying," Sarah repeated compelled.

"That's right now rest dear."

Sarah almost gave in and obeyed but then the question she feared most came to her lips, "What kind of spell is on me? I can't move."

"Sarah, honey, you've been infected with a serious disease. This disease is endocholemiaplegia."

"An endocholemiaplegia is?"

"Endocholemiaplegia a deadly disease, for all those who are of the family Magik; luckily I got you here in time."

"Then I'll get better?" Sarah asked as she turned to Doctor Palmerstone

"This is an unknown territory. We've only ever had two recoveries from this disease. I used that information to cure you."

"Two people, only two have recovered?"

Sarah gasped and tried to compose herself, but she was scared.

"Yes, but we are hopeful that you will too."

Sarah wanted to cry but she wouldn't do so now. She would do her crying in private. How she wished Demetrious was her now.

"Are you alright Sarah?" Ink asked.

"These people saved me? Who are they? I want to thank them."

Like he heard her inner plea Demetrious entered the room.

"No, thank you is needed Sarah. I am just glad you are alive. I am so sorry my enemy came after you," Demetrious stated.

Demetrious then threw his arms around Sarah.

"Demetrious I'm so glad you're here," Sarah cried, "But what about Darius?"

"Darius is safe as is Aunt Iva. Aristotle Bluestone found him and brought him back safely to us."

"Oh, thank goodness. Are all your people safe?"

"Sarah we should be talking about your worries," Demetrious chided.

Demetrious then sat down beside Sarah's bedside. Sarah continued talking of other things, she didn't want to believe she was paralyzed and she didn't want Demetrious to find out and pity her.

"What aren't you telling me? Shouldn't you be chasing the Magik Vampire? I know she seeks to destroy you."

"Funny, you should think of the Magik vampire as a woman. It took me a while to figure out that it was a woman."

"It was Delilah, wasn't it?"

"How did you guess?"

"Was it my fault?"

"No, Sarah. Your grandfather gave her to her husband, whom he turned into a vampire. Her husband turned her into a vampire and Delilah turned into a fiend."

"But her obsession with me is the reason she came after you isn't it? I did that to her the first time we met," Sarah insisted.

"She was about to kidnap you. You did what you needed to do. She is responsible for her actions, not you."

"Where is she now?"

"Someone got to her first. She drank something and dissolved right in from of my eyes."

"What could she have drunk?"

"The only thing I can think is that she drank brandy laced with holy water, garlic and the herb-of-the -cross also known as the devil's bane."

"The herb- of- the -cross? You're not speaking of the herb vervain?"

"I am. Legend has that it was used to heal Christ's wounds when he was taken down from the cross. In ancient Rome, it was used to sanitize their homes and temples. This kept out vampires and other evil entities, including werewolves."

"Not all werewolves are evil though. Correct?"

"No, of course not. Rowen Pentagan helped me find Delilah."

"I am sorry Demetrious. I know Delilah swore an oath to you, and then betrayed it.

"Why do we talking about this business?" asked Demetrious, then realizing why he begged, "Sarah, I love you. Lean on me. I know you're worried. I can see it in your eyes."

"Demetrious, you survived this when you were a child... this is the disease you had when you were a child that you were sent home with. Wasn't it?" Sarah asked afraid of the answer.

"It was."

"Then if you survived and got better, so will I," Sarah insisted.

"That's the spirit. We'll all be here for you. They can all come and see you now that you're out of quarantine."

"Quarantine? Is Michael and Alexander in danger?"

"No, Sarah there fine. They didn't contract the disease."

Demetrious waved his hand and Sarah watched as Alexander entered her room followed by Michael.

"We're fine Sarah. I've been getting to know your brother. He's a pretty wicked tiger."

"Wicked? My brother isn't wicked," protested Sarah.

"I really am," laughed Michael.

"Dad says I've spent too much time in the tomes and not enough with other kids my age, but I thought I gotten that term right. It means cool, right Uncle Demetrious?"

"That's correct Alexander."

"I'm so glad, to see you're okay. Sarah...," Michael looked like he would cry but pulled himself together.

"Hey, none of that. A big weretiger like you, crying."

"I don't know what you're talking about. I admit I worried you might not recover, but you're on the way to recovery now."

Sarah wasn't sure that was true, after all he didn't know she was paralyzed, but she didn't want to worry them. She would talk to Dr. Palmerstone later.

"Here Sarah, I brought you chocolates. The same kind I'm taking to Aunt Iva."

"I thought Aunt Iva, would be here still. She was here when I woke up before," commented Sarah.

"That's impossible Sarah. Aunt Iva has been at the hospital in the Vale of Glamorgan Wales. It's a hospital that specializes in of complicated spells."

"Uncle Demetrious is telling the truth. Dad is taking me to Wales, after we leave here," exclaimed Alexander appearing on the other side of Sarah's bed.

"Alexander you tried an invisibility spell? You're much too young for that and you shouldn't be spying." Demetrious scolded.

"Why do you say that Alexander? I know she was here."

"Sarah you must have dreamed it. She is really in Wales."

"She is Sarah. Dad's hoping, I can break the spell." Alexander cried.

Sarah couldn't believe she had dreamed Aunt Iva was here, but alexander and Demetrious wouldn't lie to her. She had to believe them. Or had it been her gift that Aunt Iva had been there when she needed her? But what of the other shadowy woman that had been there? Who had she been? It was on the edge of her memory then it seemed to slip away. That had to be a dream, because she just couldn't remember the woman clearly.

"She was spelled? By whom?"

"Aunt Iva was poisoned by her sister, Minnie, not with the plague she gave you.

The spell keeps the person suspended in a coma."

"Will she be okay?"

"We're hoping Alexander can help her. He helped another patient that we thought incurable."

"Then you should go with Darius and Alexander. I'll be alright. I want Aunt Iva to be okay."

"She will be, but I'm not leaving you."

"But what about council business won't they need you?"

"I've stepped down temporarily and my cousin, Cormac McCarthy-Peters holds down the fort."

"You can't do that," Sarah commented shocked.

Demetrious took a hold of Sarah's hands.

"Sarah, you mean more to me then the council. I'm staying there will be no more arguments," Demetrious insisted.

"May I see you in the corridor for a minute Demetrious?" Dr. Palmerstone said interrupting.

"Go Uncle Demetrious. Michael and I will keep her company."

Sarah used her ability to hear as Demetrious and Doctor Palmerstone stepped into the hall.

In the corridor, Dr. Palmerstone said, "Demetrious, I'm not going to sugar-coat this- all the King's horses and all the King's men may not be able to put Sarah back together again."

"You mean..."

"She's paralyzed and may never walk again and she may never get her abilities back again."

"You don't know Sarah she's a fighter..."

"I just want you to prepare yourself Demetrious. You won't be any good to Sarah if you can't admit it yourself."

"If and when that time comes, I will be there to help Sarah adjust but I believe she'll surprise you and walk again."

Sarah hid what she felt from Alexander and Michael; but inside she sensed a dark coldness overtaking her and fear trying to break free.

~0~

Chapter 26 - Breaking Up is hard to Do

For weeks Sarah had been participating in physical therapy. They stretched her legs and flexed out her arms until they hurt, but she still couldn't walk. As for the abilities she had found she had over the last year, telekinesis, mind control, healing and even the sparks that came out of her fingers... all of these were gone. Only the ability to overhear remained. She never thought she would miss these but she did. Somehow over the last year she had gotten used to healing people, moving things and reading people's thoughts at time. She wanted those abilities back, but most of all she wanted to walk. She felt useless to all this way.

Demetrious always there, at every turn, encouraging her and telling her that she could walk again. She wasn't the same anymore. They both had to face it. She wasn't the Sarah Dexler he had met and fallen in love with. She had to find a way to make him go and quit wasting his time with her. The Magik council needed him, not this Cormac running things. She couldn't be selfish anymore and hold him back.

"Demetrious you need to go back to work," Sarah insisted.

"I want to be here for you. You need me."

Sarah felt the need to push him away. If she would never get better then Demetrious should move on. He should have someone whole; someone who could be by his side and share his gifts and be able to protect him if necessary, someone who could be his equal. But how could she make him go? He wouldn't leave her side. She would tell him that she kissed Charles. Surely that would revolt him.

"I don't need you. In fact, you should hate me. I kissed Charles. We went on romantic walks. He worshipped the ground I walked on. You should hate me."

"You were under a spell. You couldn't help that."

"Couldn't I?"

"No, you couldn't."

"I don't love you anymore. I wish you'd
go," Sarah commanded.

"You don't mean this," Demetrious sighed.

"I do mean it. I don't love you. I thought I
did, but it was all Aunt Iva's spell. Go now!
I mean it! Take your ring and go," Sarah
screamed, throwing her engagement ring at
him.

Demetrious stooped down and picked up the
ring still holding it out to Sarah, but Sarah
refused to take it.

"Okay, I'll take the ring, but if you change
your mind let me know."

Demetrious walked towards the door.
Looking back, he exclaimed, "I'll go but I'll
be back. You can't push me away forever,
Sarah."

"You won't be back. Not if I can help it,"
shouted Sarah as the door closed.

"What's all this shouting about?" asked the
nurse coming in the room.

"I don't want Demetrious Blackstone to enter my room again."

Sarah smiled, a bitter smile, her heart breaking. She had to push him away to protect him. He deserved better and Sarah would give it to him even if it killed her.

~0~

Chapter 27 - Scotch Heals All Wounds

D emetrious sat in his office sanctuary

at his desk. His head bowed and cradled in his arms and his jacket off and over his desk chair. His sleeves were rolled up to the elbows and looked worse for the wear as his shirt showed signs of several days wear. A glass of scotch beside a half- empty bottle of Dewar's Highlander Honey was in his out stretched hand.

Demetrious' office door opened and Darius walked in. Darius took one look at Demetrious and said, "It's worse than Caleb Gemstone claimed."

"Why are you here?" slurred Demetrious, "You should be home with your pregnant wife and son."

"I would be if some stupid big brother wasn't drinking himself to death and worrying his loyal staff."

"Can't a man celebrate victories?"

"That's what you do? It looks to me you're wallow in something."

"Am not."

"Demetrious, I'm your brother. I can read you like a book now what's bothering you? Is it Petra? I'm sorry we lost her; but she was a traitor. You must blame yourself for her death," Darius consoled.

"I grieve that Petra died, but I do not blame myself she made her choices," Demetrious answered taking a swig from his glass.

"Are you keeping all that great whiskey to yourself?" Darius asked holding out a glass.

Demetrious filled the glass to the brim.

"What eats you then? Sarah's getting better, isn't she?"

"No, she's not getting better. The doctor ..."

"What did Dr. Palmerstone say?"

"Sarah will have a long time of recovery and she may never get her full strength or abilities back."

"So? You still love her, correct?"

"Of course, I love her, but she doesn't love me."

"Have you lost your mind Demetrious? The girl is crazy in love with you. Where would you get an idea like that?"

"She told me so when she threw her ring back at me."

"I can't believe they made you the head of the council, in matters of the heart you're a dolt. She tried to protect you, because she may never be the same again and instead you accept the ring and walk away. You are stupid bro."

"You really think that she pushed me away because of her illness? But I told her that didn't matter, that I loved her."

"She's loves you. You must know that. Why else would she sleep with a Neanderthal like you?" Darius replied.

Demetrious looked pained.

"You haven't slept with her? What's wrong with you? Do you need a doc? Was it that succubus we tangled with last year before we met Sarah? Did they damage the goods?"

"No, they didn't damage the goods," Demetrious exclaimed spitting out scotch and then pouring himself another glass of scotch.

Darius took it away and poured Demetrious a coffee from a coffee decanter.

"This coffee is three days old," complained Demetrious.

"Your clothing is as well, but that doesn't bother you," answered Darius.

"Fine, I'm drinking the sludge. Happy?"

"Yes, I am, now if I could get a straight answer out of you. We had some good times with the succubus' last year, before all hell broke loose; if they didn't damage the merchandise (as Aunt Iva would say) why haven't you compromised Sarah?"

"Aunt Iva wove a love potion on Sarah and me," Demetrious explained.

"She didn't," Darius stated shocked.

"She did and Sarah found out. Sarah then wondered if any of our love was real."

"Oh crap. I'm sorry Demetrious. Aunt Iva means well, but to do that…"

"That's why Sarah and I have had such a long engagement."

"Your love is real. You should have asked me. I could have told you. It's one of my seer abilities. I can see true love as long as it's not my own."

"You can?"

"I can and I'm telling you Demetrious, Sarah is the one for you. The woman that every man dreams of having by their side; you need to fight for her."

"If what you're saying is true, I need to sober up and go to her."

"I have another idea," Darius claimed,

"Let's hear it."

"Okay it goes like this…"

Demetrious listened and nodded his head. Darius made up the pullout bed and then motioned for Demetrious to use it to sleep.

"Sleep well brother. I'll go get the other person that can help with our plan and bring her back tomorrow," Darius said as he left through the office door.

Demetrious knew Darius was correct he needed to sleep, sober up and shower not necessarily in that order. Then he'd carry out their battle plan. He'd win Sarah back if it killed him; he thought closing his eyes and his last thought before he fell asleep was so that's where Alexander got the ability to compel.

~0~

Chapter 28 - The Lady of Shallot

Sarah sat in a chair starring out the

window at the forest outside her window. The sunlight filtered through the branches glinting off the droplets from the morning dew. Outside was beauty itself. She longed to walk in the forest as she once did, but that was impossible now. She had to learn to accept what she now had now.

Weeks had gone by and Sarah had gotten her wish, Demetrious hadn't come back. At least she thought he hadn't. She had left word that she didn't wish to see Demetrious. Sarah tried to convince herself she was relieved and yet she had achieved some movement back. Walking across the room with a walker had been a great achievement. Sarah wished she could have shared that news with him.

Aunt Iva was well again and Sarah felt happy about that, but she was jealous in some ways. Aunt Iva had overcome her curse, but Sarah had not. Sarah tried to resent Aunt Iva, but all she felt for the woman was love. She felt that Aunt Iva had found a place in her heart, not unlike a mother. She tried to resist the invitation it didn't seem right, but she couldn't give up the feeling of family she'd found over the last year. Aunt Iva had insisted and she'd given in. She certainly wanted to mother Sarah, so now Sarah now lived at Aunt Iva's. She missed Demetrious her heart ached with wanting to see him He was better off without her she told herself.

"There's someone here to see you," Aunt Iva said interrupting Sarah's thoughts.

Sarah looked up hopefully that it was Demetrious, but of course it wasn't. A woman with long flowing blonde hair to her waist, a thin Madonna-like presence, and tall about five feet seven entered Sarah's room.

"Who are you?" Sarah asked coldly, "And what do you want?"

"I believe you may have heard of me, I'm Demetrious' cousin, Eloise."

"But I thought..."

"That I sat by the window like the Lady of
Shallot, waiting for death to come?" Eloise
asked smiling. "Alexander, the wonder boy,
found a treatment that would help me. There
are still days when my mind sometimes
fogs, but I am much better.

Eloise then sat down on the other chair next
to the window.

"Oh. Well then go find Demetrious and
leave me alone."

"Why won't you see Demetrious? You
selfish girl. If you're worried about him
contracting the disease you have nothing to
worry about, he had it as a child, as did I."

"I'm not selfish. I already know Demetrious
had this disease, but he can walk, talk and he
has all his abilities. I don't."

"Feeling sorry for yourself? I've been there.
I was a very naughty child and strayed
where I shouldn't have and contracted the
disease. Admittedly I was also infatuated
with Demetrious (after all we are distant
cousin not first ones) and I kissed him
before I knew I was infected. Demetrious
was sent home and so was I. We both got

better though. It was decided no one would be told we had the plague that could kill people of Magik only. They didn't want to scare the people after all. It was all hushed up and the two samples that they took from our blood were stored in vaults at the council. Someone had to access that vault to infect you. No will you see Demetrious?"

"No."

"Why not?"

"I can't. If you must know Doctor Tempstone is not sure I will recover fully. The disease was very advanced when he came to me."

"So? You're not a lost cause. Demetrious loves you for yourself, not for any health you might have."

"I may never walk again. How can I ask him to marry a woman who is so weak?"

"Weak? Are you kidding me? They said you would die and maybe just part of me hoped for a moment that was true so Demetrious would forget about you..."

"Good he should forget about me. He needs to focus on the council business not me."

"You are one of the luckiest women in the entire world yet you want to throw Demetrious away out of what? Self-pity?"

"I don't feel sorry for myself."

"Don't you?"

"No, I don't," Sarah yelled.

"Don't you lie there on that bed giving up? Now you stare out the window looking for what, or should I say whom? Do you think I gave up even when I felt trapped in my mind staring out the window? I fought back! Maybe I was wrong maybe you aren't good enough for Demetrious. I should try to make him see how weak you truly are."

"Have him then, he's yours. You've recovered you are whole again," Sarah responded bitterly.

"You are a foolish woman. I would shake you if I thought that would put sense into you. Do you think that I wouldn't try to get Demetrious, if I could? Demetrious will never see me as more than a relative and I think of him as a brother now. Yet he speaks of you, as if you walked on water. If Demetrious were injured and sick would you desert him?"

"No, of course not. That would make me very shallow."

"Then why do you expect Demetrious to act that way? Demetrious loves you with a bond that cannot be broken. He is different now that he has you. He is more light-hearted. He smiles more. He has had so little love in his life. Would you take that away from him?"

"I'm not taking anything away from him. Besides he'd be better off."

"He wouldn't Sarah. I know that before Lord Eccklestone harmed me, he was unhappy. The weight of the world has always hung on his shoulders and he had no shelter from the storm. Much as I hate it, you give him shelter from that storm and a life he deserves. So as one who also loves him, I'm begging you Sarah, please don't throw Demetrious away. Accept the support you get from him and realize you can give him just as much back."

"I can't. I have to accept my limitations now."

"Don't look on them as limitations but as way to grow as a person and learn how to help other, but allow them to help you."

"I can see why Darius and Demetrious love you so much Eloise. But I just don't want to hold back Demetrious."

"You are young, so it is understandable that you don't understand all the complexities of relationships. When you truly love someone, you want the best for them to support and love them. But you also reach out to them when you need support and love. It is a two-way-street, where love blossoms and entwines. Accept your limitations... realize he also has limitations and differences. Move on together."

"Have you ever loved anyone but Demetrious?"

"The truth is I love Demetrious, now like a sister. Maybe I always did, but infatuated with being in love I leaned on him. The only man I have truly loved was Lawrence Tempstone. Handsome and brave and I thought he died saving me. When Lord Eccklestone tried to take all my abilities from me, Lawrence got in between and using his gifts, he prevented him from sucking me dry."

Eloise dabbed her eyes here.

"But Demetrious said you were a shell. I don't understand."

"He took my abilities, but he didn't get my core, the things that make me the person I am. Lawrence buried them deep inside me and Alexander that brilliant little boy found them and freed me from my prison."

"I'm sorry you lost Lawrence."

"Aw, but I didn't."

"I don't understand."

"He is alive."

"Why did you think Lawrence was dead?"

"Lord Eccklestone taunted me. He told me he had killed Lawrence, before he took my abilities."

"I'm sorry, that must have been hell."

"I thought Lawrence had died a hero and if I had one more chance with him. I would have taken it, I would have taken it, in a heartbeat."

"You would have done that, even when you were frozen, and unable to move?"

"Even then."

"Where and how did you find out Lawrence was alive?"

"Aunt Iva was poisoned by her sister Minnie. Not with the plague she gave you, but with a spell that keeps the person suspended in a coma. She was taken to the hospital for people of Magik. Demetrious asked me to go to her side while he searched for you and the Magik/Vampire. I went there and was told Aunt Iva was in room two twenty-six. I opened the door and noticed a man lying in the bed. He appeared to be sleeping and had his head turned away from me. Something about his figure made me think I knew this man. I stepped softly into the room and watched his back when he turned over.

At first, I refused to believe my eyes. Then I cried tears of joy. I kissed him tenderly on the lips and his eyes opened. He smiled at me and kissed me back. Then reaching out, Lawrence held me tight in his arms. It seemed hours that we lay stretched out on the bed just revelling in our togetherness. His doctor came in some time later and was amazed. He thought Lawrence would never awake. They didn't even know whom he was.

It seemed until I kissed him, they had given up hope of him ever coming out of his coma. He had to learn to talk again and he still can't get around except in his wheelchair, but Lawrence is better and is now in my home with therapists at his call. I have the love of my life back. You can't imagine how good that feels, or maybe you can?"

"That seems unreal like a fairy-tale. Are you sure you didn't make this up?" Sarah commented.

"It's all true. At first after he found out he might never walk again, he tried to shove me away. He believed that I was better off without him," Eloise explained.

"How could he think that? You love him," Sarah commented.

"I do love him as Demetrious loves you. As I explained to him and now, I tell you if you have a person who loves you more than you do yourself, you want that person in your life. No storm is too hard to weather when you have arms that shelter you from the tempest."

"It's not the same," Sarah protested.

"Isn't it? Demetrious would lay his life down for you and you would do the same for him. So how can you ask him to walk away?"

"I'm being selfish, aren't I?" Sarah admitted.

"We are all selfish, but sometimes we have to set that pride aside and except the help we need. Especially when it comes from someone who loves us."

"She's right you know," a tall thin man on crutches said from the door.

"Lawrence? You're walking?"

"Yes, my darling Eloise, I am thanks to you and our love. You see Sarah, Eloise and I are the lucky ones. We share a bond that cannot be broken. No curse can break the connection between us, it can only make us stronger."

"I'm glad you two found each other again," Sarah responded.

"You have a chance to retain the union that has made Demetrious and you stronger and happier. Don't give up on Demetrious. Don't throw that love away. He is one of the finest men I have ever met and he loves you enough to stand by you as you would he. Eloise thought she had lost me and it nearly killed her. But Eloise still continued fighting against the curse. She fought hard to come back so my death wouldn't be in vain."

"You look very happy together," Sarah commented.

"And so, could you and Demetrious," Lawrence insisted.

"He probably doesn't want to see me again. I've been so cruel to him."

"If you give him a chance, I'll bet he'd surprise you," Eloise commented, "But you'd better not hurt him, or I'll scratch your eyes out."

Lawrence opened the bedroom door and Demetrious strolled in.

"That's where you're wrong. I love you Sarah. Nothing you could ever do would ever chase me away," Demetrious cried holding out her engagement ring she'd thrown at him. "Sarah will you marry me?"

"Will you take me as I am with or without gifts and hobbled unable to walk far?"

"Sarah, none of that matters. You are my life. Without you I am sad, broken and a much darker person. You have opened up the world to me. With you by my side I feel there is good in the world. I see all the good in people instead of all the bad. I smile all the time and people notice and comment. You make me a better person. I need you in my life to make me whole. Please say you'll marry me."

"I will, but only if Eloise will be one of my bridesmaids," Sarah agreed looking at Demetrious then turning to Eloise.

"Of course, I will. If you'll do the same for me," Eloise agreed showing off the engagement ring on her finger.

"Oh good, then it's all fixed now I have two weddings to plan." Aunt Iva cried coming into the room, "Now you boys go into the kitchen. I just made some molasses cookies."

"Yum, my favorite. Thank you, Aunt Iva," Demetrious commented and kissing Aunt Iva on the cheek.

"Don't let him eat them all the cookies, Lawrence. Demetrious has to fit in his tux in a month."

"A month? How can we plan a wedding so fast?" Sarah asked.

"This is Aunt Iva. She's a master planner; she always gets things done on time," Eloise cried, but looked disappointed that Aunt Iva had mentioned her wedding.

"Your wedding is in two weeks time, Eloise. That boy could use some fattening up. See that you get him ready for your big day."

"I love you Aunt Iva," Eloise cried hugging her, followed by Sarah.

"I'm just so happy. I'll have all my chicks under my roof this month. Darius, Janelle and Alexander arrive this evening. They'll stay for a month, while their house is renovated. But for now, we've got some work to do," Aunt Iva said pulling out a scrapbook.

"What's this book?" Sarah asked.

"It's some suggestions for your weddings. You too can tell me what you want and I'll arrange it all."

"She is prepared for anything," Sarah commented.

"I told you."

Sarah started looking through the wedding books. Soon Eloise, Sarah and Aunt Iva were laughing. Lawrence and Demetrious decided to take a walk in the woods and leave the ladies to the wedding plans. They felt their duty was to agree to whatever plans were made and that would come later.

~0~

Chapter 29 - A Reception and Insurrection

"**E**loise and Lawrence's wedding

was incredibly beautiful," Sarah commented sitting at a table.

"Our wedding will be lovelier," Demetrious exclaimed taking Sarah in his arms.

Sarah looked around the room and saw lots of people sitting drinking and watching the happy couple's first dance. She envied them. She could walk now but dancing would be beyond her at her wedding.

"And now please join the happy couple on the dance floor," the best man exclaimed over a microphone.

"I wish I could dance," Sarah cried watching the couples take the dance floor.

"Your wish is my command," Demetrious exclaimed.

Demetrious then proceeded to wiggle his fingers and took Sarah in his arms. Sarah's leg felt weightless and she found herself hovering above the floor as they whirled around the room.

"I love you Sarah Maidenstone -Dexler."

"I love you too Demetrious."

Demetrious then kissed Sarah.

"Save some of that for the wedding," Lawrence cried.

Eloise and Sarah then went to the bathroom to touch up their make-up.

"You look so beautiful and happy," Sarah commented to Eloise as she put her lipstick on.

"As you will in a few weeks," Eloise admitted.

"We better get back before they send out a search party."

Sarah and Eloise left the bathroom and went
down the long hall to the reception.

"Why is Cormac here?" Eloise asked.

"Didn't you invite him?"

"Of course, I invited him but he refused to
come. He said he had to watch over the
council until Demetrious got back from his
honeymoon with you."

"I want to know what they discuss. Cormac
looks very worried."

Eloise and Sarah crept closer to hear
Cormac say, "Demetrious, I have to tell you
Damocles Scourby is on the move."

"On the move?"

"He's taken Rowen and her husband
Dragomir prisoner."

"What do you want me to do Cormac? Do
you want me to come back now instead after
my wedding?"

"Can you come back just for a couple of
days and help me with this?"

"Go, Demetrious just be back in time for our wedding," Sarah insisted, "You told me how dangerous this werewolf is."

"I'll be back in time for our wedding."

"You'd better be buster or I'll come and find you and it won't be pretty," Sarah commented.

"I'll be here with bells on," Demetrious promised.

"Lose the bells. Just wear a tux," Sarah answered.

Demetrious then left with Cormac and Sarah went back to Aunt Iva's. They had a clinic tomorrow. Sarah would keep busy until Demetrious came back doing her therapy and trying to access her abilities in the clinic once more.

~0~

Chapter 30 - The Wedding of Sarah and Demetrious

Sarah looked down at her wedding dress. It shimmered and shone with all the intricate beading on the skirt of the dress. The bust modest and form fitting, a bustier of lace layered with see through lace covered her top half. Sweetheart sleeves completed the look.

Sarah felt beautiful. The full layered skirt covered the limp still left from her bout with illness. Demetrious had given her a gold cane that he confided held a sword to complete her look and assist her in walking down the aisle. Sarah hoped she never have to use it. But since her illness her powers had been sadly extinguished and Dr. Palmerstone said they might take a year to come back. Demetrious worried about her safety.

Sarah looked around and wondered where
Janelle had gotten to. Janelle had opted out
of being the matron of honour because she
was so pregnant. Eight months pregnancy
made it difficult to stand for long periods of
time. Just before Sarah had come down the
aisle she breezed by with Alexander in tow,
headed for the washroom. Alexander didn't
want to leave her unattended as he was sure
she could go into labor at any time. The fact
that she wouldn't register with him, no
amount of reassurance from his father would
sway him so.

Darius humoured him and so did the rest of
the family as long as it made Alexander
happy it was worth it. Sarah smiled think
about it. She was sure Janelle was in good
hands with Alexander they'd be out soon.
They might miss a few minutes of the
wedding, but filming would cover what she
missed. She saw Demetrious waiting for her
at the end of the aisle and smiled even
wider. As he reached the end of the aisle
Demetrious took her hand in his.

"My dear friends and council members we come together to celebrate a wedding today which gives me great joy," begins Father Trippstone. "I will conduct most of the ceremony in Latin for those who do not understand we will repeat the English. We begin... Nupitas celebrare Demetrious Aloysius Blackstone, Seraphina Marie Dexler-Maidenstone. We come together to celebrate the wedding of Demetrious Aloysius Blackstone and Seraphina Marie Dexler-Maidenstone. Does anyone have just cause why these couple should not be joined let them speak now or forever hold your peace?"

Father Trippstone looked around and then stated, "Very well then, please begin Demetrious."

"Seraphina my love we have been through so much. My pillar of strength in my life and a source of undying support. That is why I promise you, from this day forward, that I am yours for all eternity. With faithfulness love conquers all. Heart speaks to heart. I offer to you Seraphina my heart sincere, in the presence of these people. Everything is said stronger in Latin so I repeat this in Latin."

Omnia dicta fortiora si dicta Latina. Mi amor ,multa superavimus discrimina Tu mea es fortitudo ac fons praesidii perennis Haec est causa quod tibi promitto me dehinc tuam fore in aeternum omnia De fideli vincit amor. Cor ad cor loquitur cor meum tibi offero Demetrious prompte et sincere cor populo"

"Demetrious my love we have been through so much. There was no easy way. You bring me home and love is sweeter with you despite difficulties. My pillar of strength in my life and a source of undying support. I couldn't have come back from my illness without you. That is why I promise you, from this day forward, that I am yours for all eternity. With faithfulness, love conquers all. Heart speaks to heart. I offer to you Demetrious my heart sincere, in the presence of these people. Everything is said stronger in Latin so I repeat this in Latin.

Omnia dicta fortiora si dicta Latina. Demetrious, mi amor ,multa superavimus discrimina Cum fors fortis amisi, tu me domum reduxisti amor dulcius ex asperis Tu mea es fortitudo ac fons praesidii perennis Haec est causa quod tibi promitto me dehinc tuam fore in aeternum omnia De

fideli vincit amor . Cor ad cor loquitur cor
meum tibi offero Demetrious prompte et
sincere cor populo"

"I Demetrious, take thee Seraphina to be my
lawfully wedded wife, to have and hold
from this day forward ,for better or for
worse, for richer or for poorer, in sickness
and in health ,to love and to cherish, till
death do us part, according to God's holy
ordinance, and there to I pledge thee my
troth."

"I Seraphina, take thee Demetrious to be my
wedded husband ,to have and to hold from
this day forward, for better or for worse, for
richer or for poorer, in sickness and in
health, to love and to cherish, till death do us
part, according to God's holy ordinance, and
there to I pledge thee my troth."

Demetrious placed the ring on Sarah's finger
and stated, "With this ring I thee wed, with
my body I thee worship, and with all my
worldly goods I thee endow. In the name of
the Father, the Son, and of the Holy Ghost.
Amen."

Seraphina placed the ring on Demetrious'
finger and stated, "With this ring I thee wed,
with my body I thee worship, and with all

my worldly goods I thee endow. In the name
of the Father, the Son, and of the Holy
Ghost. Amen."

"What God has brought together and joined
let no man put asunder. I now pronounce
you husband and wife. You may kiss the
bride. Come on Demetrious you better do it
before I do."

Father Trippstone then laughed.

Everyone clapped as Sarah and Demetrious
kissed a long drawn out kiss. As Demetrious
accepted congratulations from Darius, Sarah
looked around for Janelle and Alexander.

"Demetrious, I haven't seen Janelle since
before the ceremony someone should go
check on her," Sarah insisted.

"Janelle and Alexander can't be found?"
Darius asked.

"Maybe Alexander was right and she went
into labor. I'll come with you and we can
check on her," Demetrious offered.

"No, you stay here. Enjoy this, it only comes once. I'll go look."

Just then a fight broke out at the front door of the church. Michael had taken down an intruder into the church. Underneath Michael, a man as tall as Demetrious and Darius. When he lifted his head of raven coloured hair, his eyes blue and piercing meet Demetrious' eyes with a smile.

"Hello brother. My invitation must have gone astray. Long-time no see. I guess I missed the wedding."

"This is your brother?" Sarah asked but was ignored.

"Dominic? But that's impossible you're dead."

"Rumors of my demise have been greatly exaggerated," Dominic stated a huge grin on his face.

A man entered shortly after his hair the same color as Demetrious as well. Demetrious' face became ashen and his voice barely registered, "Dad?"

"No, I'm older than him. I'm a grandfather to you. My name is Aengus Blackstone," the man said and then turning to Dominic he asked, "Did you tell Demetrious?"

"Besides the fact that you are somehow related to me Tell me what and why should I trust you," asked Demetrious.

"Damocles Scourby has taken Janelle and Alexander," Aengus announced.

"Cormac held him prisoner. How did he escape? And where is Cormac? Why didn't he tell me this?" Demetrious asked.

"What? How do you know this?" Darius barked.

"Alexander sent me a message and then was cut off as they drugged him," Aengus explained then turning to Demetrious he said "He has Cormac and a number of the other council members."

"What that's impossible Cormac can't be taken and Alexander would have contacted one of us. He doesn't even know you. Why would he contact you? Why should I believe any of this?"

"Demetrious, I know you don't want to believe all of this. I met Alexander when Sarah was afflicted with Endocholemiaplegia and he saw whom I was."

"Saw who you were?"

"Demetrious you don't have time for this bickering. We all must find and fight for Alexander and Janelle. You need to contact Rowan," Sarah commented.

"Don't tell me what to do Sarah," Demetrious sniped.

"What do I know? I'm only your wife," Sarah said under her breath.

"I'm sorry Sarah. I know you're right, but I don't know that we should trust this stranger. It could be a trap," Demetrious apologised sending a psychic apology to Sarah.

Sarah frowned and then acknowledged the apology by putting her hand in Demetrious'.

"I don't want any more talk we need to leave now," Darius insisted.

Turning to Darius, Demetrious said aloud, "We will get them back Darius."

"From your lips to God's ears," Aengus commented.

"But you're a vampire, why would you believe in God?" asked Sarah.

"He is?" Demetrious said surprised.

"Can't you see that Demetrious?" Sarah asked surprised, then turning to Aengus, she demanded to know, "Do you glamour him?"

"No, it wasn't me," Aengus admitted then turning he commanded, "Ink, cut it out."

Ink stepped out of the shadows and Sarah glared at him.

"It was necessary Sarah. We have to hurry Alexander and Janelle are in grave danger," Ink explained.

"I have a long story but it's one for Demetrious' ears first. The main point is that we need to go rescue Alexander and I need Darius and Demetrious to help me do so."

"I will go nowhere with you. You're a vampire and you're glamouring yourself to look like my father. So why should I trust you?" Demetrious insisted, "If my nephew is missing, my brother and I will find him."

"I do not project an image. This is the way I look. My grandson looked like me."

"Grandson? What lies do you tell?"

Aengus held out a ring on his finger the ring had a stone of ruby and engraved above and around the stone in gold, 'Circumspice tecum cor et anima pro fide conservantur ditet familia", and in small letter almost invisible Familia Praevalebit Blackstone below the stone.

"Where did you get that ring? It has our family crest," Demetrious cried, his face an ashen color Sarah had never seen before.

"It's mine. I told you I am a grandfather to you."

"You are a vampire."

"I am."

"Then how can you be grandfather to me?"

"It's a long story that we don't have time for today. Please Darius, I know you have the talent to look into souls. Please use it on me and tell Demetrious that I only have

Alexander and his mother's welfare in my heart.'

"Is this true Darius you have this ability?" Demetrious enquired.

"I do. I don't know how he knows that."

"And you never told me?" Demetrious complained sounding hurt.

"Demetrious, I don't like using the ability. You have abilities that you have that you don't like using either," Darius said pointedly.

"I understand but can you break the rule just this once?"

"I already did Demetrious. He's telling the truth. We're wasting time."

"I'm sorry Sarah. I have to go. Not much of a honeymoon, but we will have one once Alexander and Janelle are safe," Demetrious stated.

"We're all going. You might need my abilities," Sarah insisted.

"I'm sorry Sarah. You can't come. You aren't able to protect yourself," Demetrious said.

One of Demetrious guards moved his hands
in a circular movement near Sarah and she
found herself closing her eyes and knowing
no more.

~0~

Thank-you for reading this story; if you
enjoyed this story please think about leaving
a few words for me at your favourite retailer

~Sincerely S.G. Lee

Please continue reading an excerpt from the
next book in the series ~ The Hazard of the
Die.

SNEAK PEAKS – Excerpts~1-4

Excerpt from The Hazard of the Die - Chapter 1- Fight or Flight

Sarah awoke angry and locked in a

room. She thought about seeking a divorce, she was so angry. What was this the middle ages? Did Demetrious actually think he could keep her a prisoner until he came back? He had signalled one of his guards and now she found herself a prisoner.

Unlucky for him, some of her abilities had come back with her anger. She would escape and then help Demetrious save Janelle and Alexander. She needed to take her life back and not let people think of her as the victim that needed protecting. She tried to think of the door opening and waved her arms as she seen Demetrious do. Drat it didn't work. If

at first you don't succeed try, try, again.
Drat another failure.

What did she do wrong? Why couldn't she
do this teensy weensy little magic spell?
Was it stress? Did she stress out to much?
Sarah knew she'd had some trouble with her
abilities since her illness, but she thought it
had been coming back. This seemed like
such a small thing to do. After all before her
illness she'd lifted people and had fire shoot
out of her fingers. Now it seemed she could
barely lift her arms to say the spell and then
they didn't work.

She had to get out of here. Demetrious
thought he protected her by locking her in
here, but it reinforced her vulnerability to his
enemies, didn't he understand that? She had
to get out of here and help them find
Alexander and Janelle.

She'd try levitating the door. Crap it
wouldn't move. Maybe she could trick them
into opening the door and then run out when
they answered?

She hammered on the door for some time
with no corresponding answer. Did they
really think she'd put up with this? Focus,

Sarah, focus, on the task at hand. She needed to get past the locked door but how?

Sarah looked around there were no tools small enough to pick the lock so that was impossible. She looked around and spotted a small tool box under a table. They thought she was locked in here and couldn't get out she show them. She use one of the tools to take apart the door screws that didn't require the Magik that had so far alluded her when she needed it.

She opened the tool box and spotted a multi tool screwdriver with all the heads, even the star head that the door screw required. She would be out of here in a jiffy.

The bolt was rusty and didn't want to move after two hours by her watch Sarah had moved it not one inch. Ha, they left her the sword cane she'd use it maybe that would work. No, it wouldn't budge hinges or the lock. Sarah decided it wasn't worth it to continue. Sarah had grown fatigued and knew her illness weighed on her. Doctor Palmstone and warned her to find rest immediately after suffering these symptoms or have a relapse. She lay down on the bed and fall asleep.

Sarah dreamt of Janelle, at least at first she thought it was a dream. She saw Janelle ashen and lying on a bed, blood surrounded her. Beside her were two babies, a boy baby who lay gray and lifeless beside her and a small girl baby with lips and cheeks of rosy pink. The small girl baby breathed softly in and out, and whimpered everyone once in a while as if dreaming.

"Sarah?"

"Janelle? This isn't a dream?"

"No you're not truly dreaming. At last I've reached you. This is a projection into your dream state."

"I want to help you Janelle."

"Good because we need your help. You can do nothing for me and my baby son David but you can save Alexander and my baby daughter, Davinia."

"I thought you were pregnant with only a son, but you've had twins?"

"Here let me tell you all that has happened by showing you."

Sarah suddenly felt like she was in Janelle's body. She stood within Janelle shoes as she went to the washroom during the ceremony. Alexander waited obediently outside the room, when all of sudden Sarah felt Janelle's water break. As Janelle, Sarah shouted for Alexander who came in and that's when she was grabbed along with Alexander.

Alexander didn't fight back since they threatened his mother and his sibling. They bound her eyes and transported them somewhere nearby. Alexander torn from her side and forced to drink something which rendered him unconscious; Janelle could only watch as they dragged him into another room as labour pains rocked her.

Janelle begged them to tell her Alexander was all right and the man in charge told her that Alexander was drugged and spelled so he wouldn't be able to access his abilities. He would sleep until morning and if she were good they would be united. It was then that her kidnapper realized Janelle was in labour and they hustled her to a bed. A woman was called in to assist her in her labour. A tiny baby girl was born first, her size not a match for her boisterous lungs with their lusty cry. A short time later Janelle felt the need to push again and a seven pound boy came into the world. He was quiet and didn't make a sound despite the tap on his buttocks by the woman. His skin was blue and translucent and all the tiny veins and organs could be seen in his body. Janelle knew just looking at the small baby that it was too late. Janelle wept for her son and wondered if she had been attended by a doctor if he would have lived.

The bleeding began then, torrents poured from Janelle's body and she knew she hadn't long and Sarah felt her reach out to the only woman she trusted to raise her children, her sister-in-law Sarah.

"Find us Sarah and save my children. I trust you to help Darius and Demetrious raise them. I bequeath you my abilities. Take them now."

"I don't understand. How can you give me your abilities?"

"Sarah just open up your mind and allow my energy to flow into you."

"Okay," Sarah answered and did what Janelle asked.

"It is done. Tell Darius I always loved him and take good care of my children and thank you Sarah. You have been the best sister and friend, I have ever had."

"I'll do my best Janelle. I promise you I'll tell Darius what you said but you can tell him yourself."

"I know you will Sarah. Hurry now," Janelle cried.

The connection between them abruptly broke and Sarah knew without being told that Janelle had died. Sarah gulped back tears and tried hard to wake up hoping that she was wrong and it was all a dream but she knew in her heart of hearts, that it was not and she needed to seek out and save Davinia and Alexander. She felt stronger than she had in weeks and knew it was the power and the strength that Janelle had given her. She felt odd though, like Sarah herself had given birth and when she looked down at her shirt she saw a wet spot forming as her breast now leaked milk. She went to the mirror, and looked at it. Sarah still appeared in the mirror, but it seemed that Janelle had given her the ability to feed Davinia when she rescued her. Or maybe the wedding present she had thought to give Demetrious allowed her to do so? Sarah thought back to the day that created the present she knew Demetrious and she would cherish.

A month ago when Demetrious had convinced Sarah to marry him, Eloise and Lawrence had quietly left and Sarah and Demetrious had given into the passion they had felt for so long.

Sarah had never felt so alive, every nerve ending tingled and she had revelled in touching every part of Demetrious and he had done the same for her. They were finally one. They had been intimate right up until two days before the wedding when Aunt Iva had divided them saying it would make the wedding night more special.

Sarah had felt sick to her stomach that day. Worried she'd scheduled an appointment with Doctor Palmerstone and he had run a pregnancy test telling her that it was positive. Sarah had been thrilled she now had the best wedding gift in the world for Demetrious, his child. Then Sarah and Demetrious needed to talk about his behaviour. He couldn't be allowed to imprison her to protect her. One thing was sure though life would never be dull as Demetrious' wife. But first she had work to do she had free herself and go find two little babies and Alexander. They needed her until she could get them to their father.

Look for Hazard of the Die in e-book and paperback coming soon

Excerpt from ~Dreams Can Kill
Chapter 1-Survival

The rain pelted down on me, as I struggled to come to my senses. My head felt like it had split in two, as if little lumberjacks had taken up residence. I opened one eye. The world spun sideways like a ride at the fair. I tried shutting one eye, then the other. I nearly fell back to sleep. I opened my eyes again, fighting the sleep which wanted to overtake me. I shuttered my eyes again, as my stomach protested. My whole body manipulated, bruised, bent and broken like some old rag doll discarded.

Sleep...sleep would solve my problems, my brain protested. No! I had a reason I needed to stay awake and alert...A little sleep, a part of me protested again. No, I must stay conscious. But I remained so tired. I dragged myself across the pebbled ground. My right leg stuck out at an impossible angle, obviously broken. I saw by lifting my head slightly and turning it that there appeared to be a road up ahead. I had to get to the road. If I dragged myself that far, surely I would be rescued?

But it was oh so hard, to drag yourself backwards, when you couldn't perceive where you were going. Oh no, what if he came back. He would finish me off...finish what he had started.

He who? Who was this person, who left me to die? Why couldn't I remember? Don't panic… the thing to do is right now is to reach help; then and only then would I be safe. I caressed large pieces of gravel which cut into the back of my head. I sensed I was close to the road. I reached out with my good hand and touched a paved surface. I knew I didn't have much strength left. I experienced the energy drain quickly leaving my body. I tried to fight the drain, but the world faded to black.

~0~

Chapter 2 - Time flies when you're having fun

I opened my eyes slowly. A tube appeared to have been inserted in my arm, feeding me intravenously, another tube down my throat as well. The lumberjacks in my head had been replaced by a dull achy sensation, as if I wasn't quite there. I suffered from weakness all over, but my body didn't have the same sensation, as when I had blacked out on the road. My leg felt whole again and yet my leg didn't appear to be in a cast, or slung up on a tripod. How much time had passed? This definitely looked like a hospital room. The walls were pale white and I lay in a single bed. I rested in a private room how about that?

A nurse in a white cap entered the room. She grabbed my wrist and she proceeded to take my pulse. Alarmed, she stared straight into my face, "Well! Look who is awake. Welcome back to the real world," she proclaimed.

I tried to speak and realized the tube in my throat prevented that. Why was a tube in my throat I wondered? How long I been here? I assumed I looked scared because the nurse explained in a soft voice, "There, there honey, you take deep breaths, easy now."

"Why don't I go get the doctor? He can come and have a look at you and remove the tube from your throat."

I tried to nod my head in agreement but my head moved like lead. It seemed like eons before a man in a white doctor's coat appeared at my bedside. He appeared tall and lanky; with dark curly brown hair and warm deep blue eyes. Without any preamble he announced, "We will now remove this tube. Take a big breath now."

The tube came out as I gagged. Now I could ask the questions which plagued me.

"How did I get here? And where am I?" I tried to ask, croaking out the words, as if my voice hadn't been used in a while.

"Speak slowly. Here, have sips of water," answered the doctor.

"How did I get here?" I repeated, sure that I had been speaking clearer because I had taken a sip of water.

"I don't know who found you, but an ambulance brought you here in critical condition. You had a broken leg, some broken ribs, and a fractured skull."

"I came here in critical condition? So, I've been here awhile?" I asked shocked.

"Yes, you've been here awhile. You were at a different hospital first. You are in Andrews' clinic now."

"Your condition appeared to be perilous there for some time. They lost you twice. We had placed you in a coma to let your brain swelling go away. Then we didn't know if you would ever come out of the coma."

He continued to explain like he couldn't quite find the words. But why would a doctor have trouble explaining a medical condition?

"I guess time flies when you have fun," I stated flippantly, hiding fear I didn't quite understand and becoming puzzled.

Why did he say first they then we? Hadn't he been there?

"I would like to examine you to see how you're doing now and get an update on your condition."

"I'm good. As you can see," I answered in response.

"I don't know if you even realize, but your speech isn't as clear as you think. You're slurring your words," he stated. "I'm sure the words will come easier in time, but I'd like to check your reaction time and some other physical reactions."

What could he be talking about? I wasn't slurring my words. Was I?

The doctor began his examination. A flashlight flashed deep into my eyes. I blinked in response, as the light, so bright, made my eyes hurt. His response seemed to be to write down something on the chart, and pick up my wrist to take my pulse and blood pressure. He then listened to my chest with his stethoscope.

I moved my head and tried to sit up, but the effort zapped all my remaining strength. I surprised myself at how I felt like a newborn baby. He continued his examination. I grew tired but fought the sensation. If I closed my eyes for a moment, would the feeling would go away? I closed my eyelids and fell fast asleep.

~0~

I ran over hills. The night appeared so

dark, and ink black; I could barely view two feet in front of me. My feet stumbled, as I tried to see the uneven ground in front of me. My palms clenched with sweat, as my heart pounded like the organ would jump out of my chest. I turned around, my eyes darting from side to side searching for my pursuer. No sign, but I knew he wasn't far behind.

My hair in a high ponytail, whipped at my face, as I picked up the pace in my flight. He seemed close enough, that I had the sensation of his breath on my neck… so close he might reach out and touch me. I turned again to see if I could glimpse him near, and I saw a man. But what puzzled me was what materialized in the man's face. Where his face should be, a gaping black hole yawned.

How could this be? The thought plagued me only for moment, as fear gripped me and survival instinct kicked in. Realizing if he caught me I would be killed, I ran stumbling over rock and uneven ground. When the inevitable happened, I tripped falling to my knees. He had me. There was no escape from my fate. I would die now. I struggled as he grabbed my left wrist twisting my arm.

This appeared no dream, I might awake from; he had me now and he would kill me.

I twisted slightly trying to free my wrist but he grabbed my other wrist and shook me slightly saying…, "Quite a dream you were having, but a dream none the less. Nothing can harm you now."

I stared into his face and slowly his look changed, from the faceless man, to another face entirely. This wasn't the man in my visions; the demon in my nightmare. I knew in my heart this remained an altogether different kind of man

This face with smiling blue eyes radiated warmth, and kindness. His face stayed gentle, not violent. I had been dreaming and had mistaken his touch for the man in my dreams. I flushed with embarrassment.

"You are quite awake now? I won't harm you. Now, do remember me?"

I stared at him, slowly waking up, and realizing where I was.

"I'm your Doctor, Doctor Andrews, at your service, my lady. We met before when you awoke from your coma," he continued speaking softly, and gently, bowing at the waist and smiling.

Shouldn't I have recognized him immediately? Heat rushed to my cheeks, as I turned red in embarrassment.

I was a fish out of water. I didn't like the way I reacted; like something had happened and all was a secret to me. I liked to be in charge of my life every aspect, and right now it seemed like I appeared in charge of nothing.

"How long have I been here?" I whispered, trying to speak louder.

"I would have said it's a lot longer, than you think," he replied cryptically.

"Do you always answer a question with a question? I want an answer for my query," I demanded angrily.

"What do you remember?"

"I believe I asked you to stop making this an interrogation. If you must know, I remember waking up a little while ago the nurse came in and then you came a little later," I answered exasperated, wondering what could be wrong with me. I didn't get angry so easily. Did I? Why did I behave this way? Everything he said seemed to make me angry.

"Your little while ago was two days ago...," he explained, breaking off as if afraid to say more.

"But that's impossible..."

"You fell into a restorative sleep. It is not uncommon for patients who have been in a coma to do so."

"Two days? I slept for two days?" I commented incredulously.

"Yes," Doctor. Andrews stated.

"How long was I in a coma?" I asked worried to hear what he might say.

"What month do you remember?"

"You have to be in charge, don't you? Questions! Questions!" I replied, delaying the answer. I was suddenly afraid that I'd been in this coma far longer than I realized, and grew angrier.

"I know you're scared. Are you sure you want to know? The information can wait," he insisted.

"I'm not scared," I lied with false bravado, "I remember quite clearly the month is March."

"It is the eleventh of September nineteen hundred and seventy-one. Do you remember what happened the day of the accident?" he asked.

"That's not possible. I can't have been in a coma for six months. Why do you lie to me?" I spat at him.

"I know it's hard to assimilate but time has passed and it is September," he insisted softly, but firmly.

"Why do you persist in a lie? What do you have to gain with this preposterous story?" I demanded; still not ready to believe this.

"Exactly! What do I have to gain? Sharron, I'm not lying to you," he stated sadly.

Until that moment I hadn't given any thought to my name, but as Doctor Andrews called me Sharron, I realized I wasn't even sure if that was my name. I didn't have a clue what my name was. My name might be Sharron, but I didn't recall the name. My name could be Mary, or Angela, or any other name in the world. If I had a surname, I couldn't remember it either. A huge blank spot stood where any recollection should be.

How could my last memory be of March, but I still had no recollection of my name, er names? This was normal after a long coma. I decided. Perhaps my memory had been so underused, and only had temporary gaps? Or I was hungry? Yes, it had to be one of those things. A temporary aberration of the mind... No need for me to worry. No, need to share any such information.

My memory was only hiatus. That had to be the answer. Give it a few days and my memory would all come back. There was no need to tell the doctor, especially since my recollections would all come back. Absolutely not, I reasoned.

After all what good would it do to tell him? He'd look at me either with sympathy, or call in a shrink. I wanted none of the sympathy, and whispered glances which would follow. So, I had a few memory gaps, nothing to worry about. It was perfectly normal after a coma, I reassured myself.

"What will you do with all this information Sharron?" asked Doctor Andrews suddenly concerned.

"I must admit the information was a bit of a shock to find the month was September and not March, but I'm over the surprise. "I'm hungry what does it take to get food around here?'' I demanded, quickly changing the subject. Besides I was ravenous.

"I think you can start some light foods, some soft foods, Jell-O soup etc.," Doctor Andrews spouted. Turning to the nurse he commanded, "Nurse get a light meal for my patient."

"Certainly Doctor," the nurse replied, coming into the room rather quickly, at his summons.

Just when I thought I had successfully gotten rid of the doctor, he turned around and said..., "I know you are rather tired and hungry right now, but I'm sure you to want to discuss these revelations later today."

How could I get him to change his track? I didn't want to discuss my memory loss with anyone. I wasn't ready for anyone to find out I didn't know who I was. If I told him, would he treat me like a mental patient?

No, I wasn't going to tell him, or anyone. I needed to fake what I remembered. They'd never know, I couldn't remember. I would then have the time to accept this myself, and hopefully everything would come back. No one would ever have to know.

Wait a minute, did he know that I didn't remember? He talked about the fact I'd been in a coma, but had he given me any knowing glances? I gave him a sideways glance. Deciding he didn't have a clue about my memory problem. I plotted to keep it that way.

"There is not a lot to talk about; but if you want to we can discuss my medical condition we can get to that later," I replied, hoping he would take my response as an agreement and leave.

Luckily for me he took the hint. Maybe he would even forget to come back and discuss this later? No, I hoped for too much, but he did look convinced that I'd talk to him later. Good then he'd go away.

"I will return later, Sharron."

He then left taking his questions with him. I breathed a sigh of relief. Now alone with my thoughts, surely, I'd conjure up a memory or two. First, I would eat and refuel. That would help the memories, as well as my stomach. I stared at the food the nurse had brought in. I'm starving to death and the nurse gave me not enough food to feed a rabbit? I tried to pick up the spoon and found my hand wouldn't cooperate.

"Would you like some help?" the nurse asked kindly.

"I can do it myself," I responded stubbornly.

Although I had found it difficult to raise my hand to my mouth, that soon became easier. I found by clamping my hand around the spoon I could manage to feed myself. It was then I realized how much work I had ahead of me. The nurse watched, so I smiled at her like everything was fine. She smiled back and left.

I soon made short work of the food and wanted to move on to the therapy I recognized I needed. I would set the memories, or lack of them aside, and working on building up the muscle tone and abilities I'd lost. When the body restored itself, I would begin to remember. I understood without being told, that I had to begin like a baby to exercise my limbs and I wanted to start immediately. Let's be honest. I realized I could remember something. I grasped now that I was an impatient person, at least when it came to doing things I had to be doing. I called the nurse on the call bell to ask about therapy and exercises.

"Yes?" I heard a disembodied voice somewhere over my head say. Momentarily puzzled, I then realized the voice came from an intercom.

"Sorry to bother you but when can I start therapy? I need to get my limbs moving," I explained.

"Dear, you are barely out of coma. I'm sure your doctor would want you to build up your energy first. Or wait at least until you started solid foods."

She sounded surprised and had a hint of censor in her voice. No support there. I wanted those six months back, but clearly that wasn't going to happen. Move on, I told myself. I'd wasted six months sleeping, time to fight back and get back into fighting form as they said. But who had said that?

I somehow knew I was a fighter. I'd have to do everything myself; something I knew I always did. But how did I know that? I thought about what would work, and what limbs need to work. My hands needed to a work out. Okay, they need to grip. How do you make hands stronger?

You give them something to grip. Squeezing something soft, medium soft, would work. Where to get something to work my grasp? I couldn't even get out of bed. My limbs were useless, absolutely useless. My hand shook in weakness, from forcing the stupid thing, to do its job and feed me.

All of this began to feel hopeless. No, I wasn't some stupid helpless female. I had to figure out a plan. You're on your own, I told myself, nothing new. You can overcome any odds. Think, Sharron, think!

How about some finger exercises? Slowly working each finger, and then in tandem, I would get back movement. I began the exercise I devised. It sounded so simple when I had thought of how to exercise the hand, but painful and tiring. Work through the pain, I told myself. Isn't that what you've always heard?

I forced myself to do the exercises for what seemed like hours, until I couldn't take the pain any more. Then I decided to exercise my arms. Gripping well enough to pull myself up to the bar over my bed, I reached I'm with my right hand to grab the pole. My fingers won't cooperate. My fingers are weakened and my grip slipped. Damn it! Even simple exercise was impossible.

"Nothing is impossible," a voice spoke loudly in my head. But whose voice did I hear? My memory had fled, if it was ever there. I only comprehended the voice had been someone I loved, and respected. Was this a father, or a father figure? I knew I was bone weary, and a great sea of lethargy stole over me. It would be counterproductive not to take a nap, I reasoned. Surely a short nap would restore my energy and I would begin again.

I closed my eyes soon I began dreaming. At first the dream appeared happy. I viewed myself in a beautiful home and grinning at someone I couldn't see.

I smiled and felt great joy, but the sky grew dark and I found myself outside on a field. The moon overhead slowly covered by clouds, and I grew terrified. Something was wrong. The faceless man chased me once more. I ran over rocks and streams and more rocks. He kept coming and coming. I knew he'd soon be on me. He nearly had me when I willed myself to wake up saying... This is a dream and I want to wake up now!!!

I awoke gasping for air like I had been running a marathon. A strange man sat by my bed. His hair appeared dark, practically black, greasy, and slicked back. He had black thick glasses that he peered over like they were a prop.

An oversized suit coat in plaid and matching pants completed the picture. Despite his harmless appearance, he struck terror to my heart. What gave me the idea he put on this persona, like a piece of new clothing? I think it was his face which seemed to give it all away, like he tried too hard to portray someone he wasn't.

As I gazed at him, he jumped from the chair he sat and exclaimed..., "About damn time you woke up out of the coma Sharron. I thought you laze there forever."

He then continued, as if choosing his words carefully, "Oh Sharron, this is the most wonderful day of my life." Then he pulled me to him, fiercely.

"Let go of me, this instance. Who do you think you are? I said don't touch me! And quit acting and looking around there's no audience for your play," I blurted out, before I stop myself.

"Sharron that's not funny. Quit joking. You always had a wicked sense of humour, but I'm not laughing." the man stated, sounding annoyed and grabbing my wrist.

"I said let me go, and I meant every word. Now kindly take your hands off me," I demanded at the top of my lungs, struggling unsuccessfully to free myself of the grip, he now had on my wrist.

Taken back by my yelling, he let me go, but he still continued to treat me, like a bug under a microscope. Suddenly switching gears, his face changed. It was if a curtain went down over his face. He took on a concerned look and then a hurt look. I admit he nearly had me fooled.

I started thinking I had forgotten a
boyfriend, but surely, I wouldn't suffer from
such bad taste.

He wasn't my type. He seemed quite violent
too. I wouldn't have been so foolish to get
mixed up with a weirdo like him! Would I?

"Sharron quit staring at me that way you're
making me uncomfortable. I'm not amused
here...Wait a minute you're not kidding!
You don't recognize me at all! You don't
recognize your fiancé?"

I recognized somehow that he was put on an
act. No, I wasn't engaged to him. If I had
been it would boggle my mind. He had to be
lying, I decided. Why I didn't know, but I
knew he lied.

I had no sparks with him. In fact, something
about him gave me the creeps. He repulsed
me and made my stomach hurt. He certainly
didn't sound sincere. He put on an act ... but
why? He grabbed my wrists again, once
again in a vice grip. I struggled valiantly, but
his grip tightened and I couldn't handle his
fierce clutch in my weakened stated.

"Let me go you, caveman. I don't know you and what is more, I don't ever want to know you," screamed at him fighting frantically.

"Sharron you cut me to the quick. Why do you say such things to me?" he whined, letting go of my wrist, but gripping my arms even tighter.

Maybe it was because of my dream, but suddenly I was terrified. Why did they leave me all alone with this crazy man? Where was everyone else? Couldn't they hear me shouting?

"Let me go. Let me go.... don't touch me," I yelled at the top of my lungs, and then screamed, hysterically "Help me someone help me."

As I started to pull harder frantically to be free, he stilled held fast. What kind of evil demon had me in his grasp? I tried to bite him, but that was impossible; finally, in the answer to my screams were footsteps running. Seconds later a nurse and Doctor Andrews entered.

"Let my patient go immediately. I said let her go," Doctor Andrews growled, pulling the man's arms behind his back.

I breathed a sigh of relief. I was safe. Doctor Andrews had saved me.

"I wasn't hurting her! What kind of a man do you think I am? Gee, I have more bruises than her. She acted crazy, so I grabbed both her arms to calm her," the man explained, sounding plausible.

Surely Doctor Andrews and the nurse who followed him in, didn't believe his act?

"Your technique doesn't seem to have calmed her, but it certainly frightened her," Doctor Andrews said, checking my blood pressure and heart rate.

"You can't tell me what to do. She's my fiancée I can speak to her anyway I want," complained the man, loudly.

"You've upset my patient. Her blood pressure and heart rate is elevated as well. This is not good for my patient, so I can tell you what to do. What is your name?" demanded Doctor Andrews.

"Titus Brown is my name and Sharron is my fiancée," the man replied a little too quickly.

Doctor Andrews consulted his clipboard. He pointed to it and then announced, "This is the approved register and you're not on the list. Leave now, Mr. Brown, or I'll have security escort you out of the facility."

"I'm not going anywhere. Who do you think you are?"

Mr. Brown showed his true colours, I thought. They would trounce him faster than you could say Jack Robinson.

"Mr. Brown, so far I've been pleasant. The nurse has already called for a security guard. I suggest you leave now and don't come back, or you will find yourself with a trespassing charge and jail time," Doctor Andrews said through his teeth.

"I'll be back with my lawyer and you'll be sorry," Mr. Brown menaced.

Two security guards entered and forcefully removed Mr. Brown from my room. I began to shake like a leaf. I tried to stop, but I grew frightened. Someone had tried to kill me and that is why I was in the hospital. What if it was *Him*, Mr. Brown?

They wouldn't let him take me when he talked to his lawyer? Would they? Words I hadn't want to share, spilled out of my mouth, first in torments, and then at a screeching level.

"I don't know who the heck he is, but I do know I don't know him. I'm not his fiancée. Don't let him come back lawyer, or no lawyer. I don't want to see him. Someone did this to me! I wouldn't be surprised if the person was him!" I guess I appeared a little too hysterically and forcefully, because the next thing that occurred was Doctor Andrews plunged a needle into me.

"Please, please don't. It's not necessary, really. I'll be good," I pleaded too late.

"It's a little sedative. I don't like your colour, your blood pressure, or your heart rate. You've had a nasty scare and your body isn't able to cope with this right now. Calm down now," he said comforting "Go to sleep."

"I think I hate you," I replied vehemently.

"That's okay, you can hate me if you need to," he answered, smiling.

Damn him and his handsome smile! Something about the grin, made me want to smile back and tell him all my secrets.

"Don't leave me alone. He might come back," I pleaded as I drifted into a deep drugged sleep.

~0~

If you'd like to read more of this book please buy it at Amazon.

Excerpt from Jack Be Nimble

Sucker

It all started Monday morning and boy, I
hated Monday mornings. As I climbed the
steps to my tiny office, I could feel the
waves of heat; already seeping through my
cheap suit. It was hot enough to fry an egg
out there and it was only eight a.m. The door
was stiff in the heat and I noted that
someone had tried to break in. There were
scratches by the door. Everything looked in
its place. The cabinet with my files was still
locked as was my desk, obviously an
attempt to break in, but not a success on
their behalf. My half- empty bottle of cheap
hooch was still there.

I threw my hat up on the coat rack in the
corner and peeled off my suit coat jacket
hoping that my window fan would kick in
soon. Then I took the bag, I carried with my
breakfast, over to the coffee cup on the
shelf. I cracked the two eggs into it and then
poured orange juice over them. Oops, almost
forgot the chaser a little Tabasco sauce.
Good for what ailed me, as my head ached
from the cocktails, I'd imbibed last night. I
then sat in my desk chair, blessing the fact
that I had been gifted by a client with a chair
which had swivel wheels. I swiveled for a
bit, then turned and faced my door; wishing
for a client to breeze in to end my boredom.

I read my etched name Jack Daniel Forbes
private investigator, on the door for the
fifteenth time. I twirled in my chair once
again, to look at it and found a woman
standing there. And not just any woman, this
woman was a knock-out. She had blonde
hair in fashionable chignon. A real looker
with her bright blue eyes and come-hither
smile, and gams that want on and on. Her
skirt was split up to the knee. She had the
look of that movie star... you know the one I
mean. Carol Lombard now she was classy,

not like that Mae West who you couldn't
bring home to your mother. Except the dame
wasn't smiling, but grimacing, as if to keep
from crying. As she pulled out a tear stained
handkerchief and walked over closer to me;
I could see her eyes were red and puffy as
well.

"Are you Mr. Forbes?" she asked her voice
musical even when trembling.

"Yah, I'm Jack Daniel Forbes like the sign
says," I answered, intrigued by whatever she
wants to tell me.

"Can I trust you?" she asked.

"I'm very trustworthy ma'am, unless you've
committed a crime, there are no worries on
that score," I reassured her.

"I have to trust someone. I'm going out of
my mind," she stated hesitating "Maybe if I
knew a little bit more about you?"

"Well you know the skinny on me. My
name is Jack Daniel Forbes. I was copper
for ten years, until the heat got a little too
hot when I turned in some flatfeet, for being

on the take. That old blue wall went up and this detective was down for the count, until I opened up my own private investigation office three years ago."

"That's all very interesting I suppose, but I still don't know that I should trust you. If word should get back...."

"I was named after the whiskey bottle my mother finished the night I was conceived. Hey why do I tell you that? That's a little bit too personal sorry." I blurted out knowing that I was lying but hey I couldn't help myself. Didn't I tell you she was a looker? She looked at me like I had two heads

Surprising myself I continued making an effort. I felt that I fumbled a little there something about this dame made me want to reveal everything about myself, to her. Of course, I did the dance, a little charm and schmooze that I was famous for and I felt she'd be putty in my hands. She wasn't. She seemed immune to my charisma.

I rarely brought up my childhood even to lie about it. What had I been thinking? I had been a cop for ten years and I did turn in a flatfoot on the take break the code of blue;

but I had escaped my criminal childhood
years before that. My real moniker was
Giovanni Fabbrizzo Junior, better known as
little Johnny or Jack Giovanni in the
neighborhood where I grown up and I used
to run numbers for my daddy's best friend.
Until I had my ears boxed. Wait a minute;
forget what I said and forget you heard that
name, I'm Jack Daniel Forbes now that's my
moniker and don't forget it.

"No, I appreciate your candor; I'm not much
for banter anyway. I suppose I can reveal
things about myself as well. My name is
Mrs. Grace-Ellen Parks and someone is
trying to kill me," she blurted out and then
began sobbing all over the place.

Now am I sucker when a woman cries? I
can't stand the wallowing. It does something
to me. My insides turn to Jell-O and all I
want to do was take her in my arms, but she
said she was a Mrs., and I respect the bonds
of matrimony. So, I just patted her arm
saying there, there and handed her the
handkerchief out of my suit coat jacket.

"You are a gentleman, aren't you?" she said glancing at me in surprise and wiping her eyes gently patting them.

"I try ma'am, "I replied thinking she had all the ear markings of a vulnerable woman that I could sashay into my bed when this had been wrapped up.

"My husband is trying to kill me!" she stated, in a stage whisper as if she was afraid to say it.

"No, you have to be mistaken. He'd have to be crazy to get rid of a knock-out of a broad like you," I replied.

"I am not mistaken. Maybe you weren't the right man for the job, after all," she exclaimed rising in a graceful way.

"No wait, Mrs. Grace-Ellen Parks. If your ball and chain really tried to do away with you, then you need someone like me to prevent it."

"I don't know what to do what if I'm wrong? I wouldn't want it getting back to my ex-husband," she retorted.

"Ex, but you just said he was your husband." I protested.

"A slip of the tongue, he divorced me a few months ago, but my Daddy, Judge Banks got me alimony. I'm not poor, I can pay your fee," she explained.

"Oh, so that's it, your ex wants to rid himself of you to stop letting out his pockets. We can fix that."

"Do you think that's it?" she asked excited.

"Yes," I replied proudly.

"Come to my house at six p.m. so we can plan some more. Here's the address. Don't be late," she demanded then added with a kiss she blew at me, "Goodbye, Sir Launcelot."

I stewed most of the afternoon wondering what she expected me to do at six p.m. Am I just the muscle to her? I'm not in the business just to be a fathead. That's the way a guy gets hurt or possibly killed in this job. But the dame needed help as long as he wasn't a trigger man. I was safe. But just to be safe I'd bring my shooter.

At five twenty-five p.m. I went to my desk
drawer to get my gun a Remington .41
caliber Double Derringer. My only purchase
when becoming a private detective, this
baby was my pride and joy. I had my throw
away strapped to my ankle calf. It would
certainly defend the dame from her
murderous ex. I turned the key and to my
surprise no gun. Damn someone had gotten
in here after all and they had my gun. Why
hadn't I noticed its absence earlier? I would
have to report it missing later to some of my
buddies, ones I still had left on the force. I'd
be late if I didn't hurry. Thank goodness I
had my trusty back-up. It wasn't as nice or
even as accurate in my opinion, but it would
do in a pinch.

I arrived at the address a few minutes before
six p.m. to see the door a jar. Had he gotten
in ahead of me? I bounded up the stairs to
hear a gunshot. Was I too late? I ran into the
house hoping to find her and save her. I
heard yet another gunshot coming from the
upstairs bedroom. I bounded up the stairs,
opened the door, to find her holding the gun
over a man bloodied on the floor. He had a
huge wound in his chest, he bled heavily

from. She had shot him straight through the forehead the second time. That was not a pretty picture, as the blow back disgusted me to say the least. She stood frozen as if in shock and then the shivering began. I went to the bedroom next door and grabbed a blanket, throwing it around her shoulders. Poor woman! She'd defended herself and this was the result; then I noticed my missing gun lying beside his body.

"He tried to kill me. I shot him," she croaked.

"Yah, you're all wet, muffin. You took my shooter and you plugged him Clearly it was premeditated," I complained loudly.

"I had to, I was so scared," she answered, tears pooling in her eyes again,

What could a man do? I could only stand those tears so long; I took her in my arms and comforted her, only to have her push me into the bedroom next door. I let matters get out of hand and the next thing I know the cops break in, guns a blaze to find us in flagrante delicto. She's crying rape and saying I killed her husband. She's shaking like a leaf and they're buying her every word. I was toast. You look at me and you look at her and who would you believe?

We were both arrested her sticking to her story that I killed her husband and had tried to rape her. (Yes he was her husband, not her ex as she claimed.) She claimed I stalked her and her husband had spoken severely to me. Then I had plotted to kill him to have her.

It seemed I was in a fix. I used my one phone call to reach out to my buddy on the force, Pat O'Malley. I hadn't seen Pat in a few years, but Pat was eager to prove that Grace-Ellen was a fraud and a murderess.

I was in jail nearly a week, before the key came to breaking Grace-Ellen's story came out. I stored the gun in my desk drawer but the bullets? The bullets were stored in my room under the floorboards. Grace-Ellen had to buy bullets so she could plug her husband. Pat O'Malley canvassed many stores and finally tracked down the gun shop Grace-Ellen bought the bullets at.

Grace-Ellen screamed and ranted and raved that it wasn't her, but the guy that sold her the bullets. It seemed like a she said he said moment yet again; until the Bruno's wife stepped up and said that she had seen that woman Grace-Ellen in their shop.

Grace-Ellen decided to give them the lowdown; at least her version of the truth. She still continued to claim she was a battered wife and she had enough she took my gun for protection and bought the bullets only to protect herself. She almost had them believing it but the first guy she tried to hire to knock off her husband came forward and put the kibosh on that. She'd promised him herself and a lot of money but he was playing for the other team and he wasn't interested. Grace-Ellen ranted and raved about that one and threatened to reveal his sexuality. She kept calling the man a poof.

He told them her that he didn't care what she said, he didn't liked, the opposite sex and people would just have to accept him. He then confessed that Grace-Ellen had been plotting all this for a while and I was just the patsy she picked. Seemed like nice enough fellow. Maybe people should live and live.

What happens behind closed doors ain't no business of mine or yours, I'm thinking. Of course, the man had just saved my hiney and I was grateful.

When Pat started searching the system from state to state a minor miracle occurred Pat reached the right ears and eyes.

Mrs. Grace-Ellen Parks had done this before in three different states, each time picking out a patsy for the fall guy. She was a black widow, getting rich of the proceeds of each of her husbands' demise. One of those men she had conned had been hung for her crime; the other two awaited their execution in the electric chair. The cops who had convicted the men drove to our town and when they saw Grace-Ellen they were able to identify her under several different names. Turns out the one flatfoot said Grace-Ellen wasn't even her real name. Her name was really Eunice Perkins from Arley Alabama. Seems they wanted her there too. She'd killed her whole family there and took every penny they had. As for me, I'm very grateful to Pat O'Malley for saving my bacon.

Pat is a gem. She loves being a cop; despite the fact that they don't respect her. She is better than most those cops at her precinct

but they stick her with typing jobs and
traffic patrol. All those jobs that none of
them want to do. Pat wasn't just a police
administrator I could banter with; she was a
woman and a darn good investigator. She
was the one that tracked down all the
information on that woman. Damn those
other flatfeet. I hated that they didn't respect
her. I wore Pat down and we started seeing
each other quite a bit. What can I say I'm a
sucker for tears and when she cried because
I was free, I saw Pat in a new light. She
didn't even throw my fumble in my face and
when I glanced at her, I saw true beauty and
grit.

Pat and I began a dance. I'd soirée her
around from time to time and sometimes
she'd pretend that is what she wanted. Other
times she would date a fellow cop. A
mistake of I ever saw one but you can't tell
someone you're the guy for them. I'd wear
her down, I vowed.

Summer turned into autumn and I took her
to the Harvest dance. We danced the night
away and I was convinced I had her in the
palm of my hand when he walked in... one
Sergeant Ray Walters. He told Pat he'd been

looking forward to meeting one of his fellow
flatfeet. Who pointed Patty out I don't
know; but they didn't do either of us any
favors.

I hated him from the minute I met him. Most
of all I hated the way he brought a smile to
Pat. She was my Patty not his except she
wasn't. She thought Ray After that every
word out of Patty's mouth was Ray did this
Ray said this.... RAY, RAY, RAY!!!

What a fire extinguisher. How I hated that
name. He was a cake-eater, making a play
for every woman near him but did Pat see
that? She did not! She cast a kitten when I
brought it up and accused me of lying and
being jealous. Hell yes, I was jealous but I
didn't lie.

I was dizzy for the dame, but Sergeant Ray
Walters wormed his way into Pat's heart.
She forgot all about me. Some say I should
have been more forgiving and thought only
of her happiness; but I really believed I was
he was a crumb bum. I knew he was; the
world just didn't know it and was my turn to
prove it. Ray might have the bulge, but I had
the muscles and Ray would go down if he
was who I thought he was and if he was a
good guy then he'd have my blessing and I

back off. Patsy deserved happiness even if it wasn't with me.

I started investigating the guy. Scouting him wasn't easy. I had to dress up like a sweet patootie. Even my own dearly departed mom wouldn't have recognized me. I was a looker, a hot mama, if those wolf whistles I got walking down the street were anything to go by. I sought my quarry and watched him pretending to be a good time girl hoping he wouldn't run me in. It wouldn't look good on my rap sheet.

I watched like a hawk as he patrolled the street. I saw him rough up a couple of no good torpedoes. a hustle them off to some cells. He gave some jaywalking tickets to some very pissed off citizens. My surveillance was not paying off.

This should have made me back off, but it made me more determined. Ray was dirty I knew it. I watched him for another week; toning down the costume I wore I dressed as an older woman, a bum off the street. I looked hideous with blackened teeth and a smell that would chase a dog away. He'd never recognize me and neither would Patty if I came across her.

I spotted the asshole taking bribes and pulling out my camera. I clicked off a few shots got some he didn't notice but the last one I took where the dame we all knew as the Mayor's wife kissed him and gave him the cash his eyes opened in shock. The flash alerted him though and he ran after me I barely made it into a building where I had hidden my real clothes. There I dispensed with my get-up and hid out until the goombah left. I went to my rooms developed the shots and I then took my pictures to the district attorney and internal affairs. They put the pinch on him. Ha, ha!

 I had to testify and for awhile Pat was mad at me. My abundant charm however won her over that and the fourteen-carat diamond she wore on her finger as a promise that come, we'd marry. (I'd had to work day and night for some bigwig to earn the dough for six months but it was worth it)

A short time later and I showed her my wedding present to her. They'll be no more women tricking this P.I. I've got a partner now and the name on the door in gold lettering is Jack and Pat Forbes Private Investigators.

~0~

If you enjoyed this story read on for more of Jack's adventures in Jack be Nimble on sale at Amazon story

~0~

Excerpt from Stray Bullet
Preface:

In the small town of Driftwood, Colorado, under starry skies, residents went about their business. The town was now ready for the arrival of the new sheriff having gussied up the urban decay with a few coats of paint. The new sheriff would see the bad parts of town soon enough the mayor thought and turned over in his bed and went to sleep. The hospital looking after a few patients was unusually quiet under the full moon; other people in the settlement getting ready for bed and then turning on late night programs or setting alarms and climbing into bed.

Across town a man getting ready for bed after a long hard day at work completed his paperwork, stripped naked and stepped into the shower. As the water ran down in torrents the shower glass doors shattered, the man fell to the floor and rivets of blood ran into the drain. He was the first to die that night.

A few doors over gunman entered killing the husband and wife in their beds and the children as they slept. Blood covered the floor and ceilings in those rooms. None of the neighbours heard a peep they simply slumbered on. Other homes across the town were entered and the residents, husband wife and children were also shot and killed. No one had time to shout out or call 911. It was all over in a few minutes with no time for whimpers only the muzzle of silencers doing their jobs and hitman scurrying into the night.

"It's done, boss. The teams are leaving the state. Yes, I'll do that now. He's coming in the morning. I'll check in after I meet him. His name? All I got is G. Bullet not sure of his first name, it's not on any paperwork. See you, tomorrow… okay Friday," the man said into his prepaid cell phone and then took out sim card breaking it into pieces. Then he discarded it in a nearby bin at the now decrepit old pulp and paper mill. He had to go to work soon. A new sheriff was coming to town and he wanted to be there to greet him.

Chapter 1 - Friendship Trumps Bullet

My name is G and I'm on my way to a new life to become a sheriff in a town called Driftwood. Sounds boring, doesn't it. If you'd asked me five year ago, I would have told you of course it was; but now this is what I need and my daughter needs…a nice quiet life, in a quiet town, where I could raise my daughter without whispers and rumors. You want to more about that statement? I'll get back to that, but I'm told people will want to know about me a subject I'm not really comfortable talking about.

Asked to describe myself I would say I'm tall over six feet…okay six feet five inches. I am muscular, as I lift weights. I'm not overly muscular, just enough to take down the bad guys. Some people think I look like Tom Selleck in his youth, personally I don't see the resemblance.

G. is a short form for my first name, but I don't like to talk about my real first name. Let's just say my parents grew up in the happy-go-lucky seventies and were heavily influenced by the weird names that people

gave their children. What you still won't
give up? You demand that I tell you my first
name? You want to play the guessing game?

My first name is unmentionable I don't talk
about it ever!! My last name is wait for
it...Bullet...I know a clichéd name if you
ever heard one. Honestly, it's my name. It
has been mine my whole life.

My last name had raised a few eyebrows.
Can you imagine how many chuckles I've
gotten when I tell anyone my full name?
Still can't guess? Some of you have
deducted correctly. So now you know why I
usually don't divulge my first name.

In order for you to understand the relevance
of my last name I'll have to explain more
about my family and their origins.

My grandfather when escaping persecution
in Russia came through at Ellis Island and
decided to Anglicize his name to Bullet; so
my dad used that and now I do.

What's that you like to know grandpa's
original name? Well so would I,
unfortunately he took that name to his grave
leaving no clues behind. But he was great
man, a hard-working cop. I come from a

long line of cops. With a last name like Bullet it tends to earn respect being a cop.

Grandpa was killed on the job by some backward gangsters bent on destroying one another. My dad swore he never be a cop and went to San Francisco were he promptly fell in love with my mother went to the police academy there and then impregnated my mother.

After I turned one, he decided he needed more family and got a job as a cop in the city where his father had served and brothers now served as cops. When he worked there for six months he had planned to send for mom and me and marry her. Unfortunately, the first day on the job he ran into a domestic situation and was killed in the line of duty. He hadn't told his family about my mother or me so we came as a surprise when mother showed up with me in tow for the funeral. They soon adapted however and accepted her and with her me.

When I was four years old, my mother learned she was dying of breast cancer. My dad's three brothers, James, Bennie, and Alfred also cops, stepped up to raise me. They were a demanding bunch always pushing me to be strong and tough. I had to

be resilient and learn all the fighting
techniques that they taught. Let's just say I
am proficient in a number of fighting
techniques.

Their younger sister, my Aunt Louisa was a
teacher and just starting her career when
they took me in; however, Aunt Louise
found plenty of time for me. She made my
childhood more normal though my uncles
would often say she shouldn't coddle me.
My uncles drove her away with their
constant beratement and by the time I was in
my teens she moved to teach in Colorado to
save her sanity. She still managed to chide
the uncles into letting me visit her in Denver
in the summer for two months; the best two
months of the year for me.

Getting back to my uncles they hated my
first name as much as I did (though I think
they liked me even less; but did their duty).
They also felt that I had come out of
nowhere so they nicknamed me Stray and it
stuck; that's what most of the cops on the
force called me. Aunt Louise was the only
one who ever called me; by my first name.

Why do I speak of my Aunt Louise? Aunt
Louise had recently retired to a small town
called Driftwood, Colorado and I often

wished she had been closer, especially when I had run into the wall of blue at my job. Cut to today as I told you earlier, I'd taken a new job as the sheriff in the same town, Driftwood, Colorado.

As I drove to the Sheriff station; I saw that the downtown area was newly painted but other parts were decrepit and rundown. Stores had been closed and signs had been posted that said for rent but the places looked like they hadn't been rented in a long time. The back alleys showed signs, of hookers working their wares with discarded condoms, beer bottles and other paraphernalia.

The town was surrounded by trees; but the main source of jobs in the past had been lumber and the company had pulled up stakes and moved away. Factories and brickyards were closed.

Some of the homes have seen better days and the downtown core was eerily quiet, with vacant storefronts lining the streets. Crime which in the past hadn't been a problem was suddenly up and maybe that's why the Sheriff had quit? But that was the reason I was here. I'd shape this town into a town we could all be proud of again if the re-elected mayor could do as he promised and bring in the jobs. I wanted to be happy here.

I'd just dropped off my three-year-old daughter with my Aunt Louise. Stella Marie, my daughter seemed okay with the new place and Aunt Louise; but was I? Aunt Louise was sixty years old and a retired school teacher. Why was I so worried? First day jitters obviously. Aunt Louise had my back. She knew what idiots her brothers really were and how they valued their friendships even more than family. Being a single father, I needed her more than ever.

Aunt Louise had urged me to apply for the vacant job of Sheriff after hearing about my troubles as a cop in a suburb of Halton, Illinois. I don't want to get into those troubles right now. Today was a new day and I decided it was going to be great even if it killed me. Just kidding! I was not going to get killed like my dad had on the first day of the job. Nerves were getting to me.

Sure, it was hard settling into a new place for a child. A little voice worried that I had made a mistake; but this was a new start for both of us we should be happy. A month ago, I had been offered my dream job,

Sheriff of a small municipality in Driftwood, Colorado. Driftwood looked to me like a small town of three hundred people where I'd be happy raising Stella-Marie.

The streets were tree-lined; the cookie cutter houses had beautiful floral displays out front. The lawns were immaculate green and lush. Children rode their bikes up and down the streets with no fear of predators or gunplay. The people had seemed friendly and warm when I came for my interview for the job. What more could we want? I'd thought.

I'd done my research; but nothing had prepared me for the men all walking out on me. I stepped into the Sheriff's car.

This blue flu wouldn't do! I knew from the dispatcher that the other cops were not happy with my appointment because I was an outside hire; but damn it was my first day on the job and they had a duty to serve and protect the citizens of Driftwood.

How could the four deputies just not show up for the day? Calls to their residences had gone to voice mail so they were even avoiding talking to me. I had to put my foot down hard or the men would never respect my leadership. I'd already faced a wall of blue in my old job; people pulling out the old politics line and drawing in ranks on the thin blue line. I'd wanted a new start to change the harassment I'd faced in my not so fair city over the last three years.

A bit of a long story which we'll get into later but suffice to say the line in blue was put up against me; simply because I stood up to another cop who committed a crime.

Driving down the road to go to my new deputy's home I grew angry. Hadn't I been through enough of this crap from the guys in Halton? I had been harassed day and night by those assholes.

Parking the squad car and mounted the wooden steps on the house. I knocked lightly on Deputy Gregory Barnes door. No answer. I gave it my best thundering police knock and the door swung open of its own accord. I pulled my service revolver and entered the residence wily. A smell of dead berries and apples entered my nostrils. I felt in my pocket and then taking it out swished my menthol medicated lip balm under my nose. My adrenaline kicked in and suddenly I felt exhilarated and hyper aware.

I followed the putrid odor to a bedroom and found the late Greg Barnes with two bullet wounds to the heart surrounded by a dried rusty brown pool of blood. He'd been there at least two days. Nothing was disturbed in the home. No overturned furniture, nothing seemed out of place. He lived alone; so, no help there. Was it a rogue girlfriend? Why was he dead?

What the hell? The first day on the job and my deputy is murdered? I needed those other cops that hadn't come to work today to help me solve this murder. Damn them and their blue flu.

I made the call to the coroner who was on call for autopsies. Then I secured the scene and called in the neighboring counties police force on loan until I could find my police force.

Less than an hour later, I had two officers, Alfred Jones and Paulo Scarlatti, I sent to the two of them to retrieve the first officer Joseph Paciocco on my list. Imagine my surprise when he called back to tell me that my other officer, Joseph Paciocco was dead too. Two shots to the heart and it looked like the same felon. Was I going to find all my missing officers dead?

A quick search of the other residences found all of the bachelor cops dead shot the same way. The family men with their families at home were dead too; but so were all their family members. They had all been shot with one shot to the head in their beds. They had not stood a chance. This was a professional job as each scene had been carefully scanned and nothing was left to find in the way of evidence other than the blood and bullets.

All in all the dead were Gregory Barnes, Joseph Paciocco, Jack Abrahams, Paul Jones, his brother and fellow officer, Harold Jones and Harold's wife Cheryl, and their two children, Gail, and Fred, Vincent Vecchio and his wife Paula Antrim (both cops on the force), their baby, Adrian a newborn was alive in his crib and was taken into custody of the Children's Aid until a relative could be reached. Also dead were Robert Di Salvio and his wife Rebecca and their fifteen-year-old son William and their daughter Helen eight years old, Kas Mahmoud his wife Dayita, and their three sons, Aaban, Aahil, and Aatif ages five seven and nine.

What in the hell was going on? Someone had killed whole families. Why? Did they know something someone didn't want them to know? Was it retaliation?

This meant looking into backgrounds and finding out things people didn't want you to know. Being the sheriff didn't make for a popularity contest in any case but this would have to be handled very delicately. The police officers on loan couldn't continue to investigate this after all I only had a temporary loan of their services for today. Even if I wanted to investigate, I had to have help. I needed to call the FBI pronto and I knew just the guy my former partner, Gordon Chum.

I dialed Gordon's number by heart. He answered on the first ring asking me about the new job and then said he'd speak to his boss and get the okay to bring a team down as soon as possible.

Meanwhile I was trying to comfort the staff left at station and ducking calls from reporters from all over the country and residents of Driftwood who were demanding to know what had happened. I took deep soothing breaths...Gordon would be here soon we'd get to the bottom of this. Penny

Ambercrombie the office dogsbody and police dispatcher took charge and hustled the troops off to their stations to work on the tasks I'd given them.

Penny was tall and lean possibly one hundred and ten pounds though it was hard to tell for her clothes hung on her in non-descript browns that did nothing to enhance her looks and she stood at least six feet tall. Her hair was a rich chestnut and was wound tightly at the nap of her neck into a bun. Her eyes were her most striking feature that not even her terrible clothes sense could hide as they were a glittering emerald green that showed immense interest and intelligence. She appeared to be in her late twenties though her skin was leathered with the weathering an outdoors enthusiast had.

I could see that Penny was be an asset to me and the sheriff's station in my job. But first I needed to call Aunt Louise and Stella- Marie and hope my daughter wouldn't get too upset that daddy would not see her until tomorrow at the earliest.

I picked up the phone and called the number by heart. There was no answer. Where could she be, I wondered? My question was answered in the next few seconds by my office door swinging open. There my Aunt Louise stood with Stella Marie. Aunt Louise demanded, "Gunner is it true? Are they all dead?"

The next thing that happened was three-year-old Stella-Marie jumping in my arms and saying "Daddy, I missed you."

I closed my office door no sense in putting on a show to the remaining troops and I hoped no one had heard my aunt utter my first name. Stella-Marie took the chair nearest me.

"I want an answer Gunner."

"Not in front of the c.h.i.l.d."

"Ch. i.ld, child, that's me," my precocious daughter answered.

"Stella-Marie already knows all about this. She turned on the television while I was in the bathroom and she heard about all your deputies and their families being found dead. She insisted I bring her here."

"Then you both know what I know. I'm investigating and I've called in the FBI."

"Daddy, are you safe? In that movie with the Kung Fu guy they tried to kill him and then killed his family," Stella-Marie answered.

"What have you been watching?"

"I remember his name, now. I love Jean Claude van Damme movies," Stella-Marie stated.

"Me too, pumpkin and we're safe. I haven't been here long enough to be mixed up in whatever is going on here," I reassured.

"You'll find the bad guys?"

"Daddy will find them. That's what daddy used to do before he had you," I answered.

"Be careful," Stella-Marie said with adult wisdom beyond her years.

"Stella-Marie is correct. You need to stay safe."

"I promise both of you, I will stay safe."

"We'll trust you."

"Can we have dinner together, daddy?"

"Of course, we can my apple dumpling."

"I'm not an apple dumpling."

"No, you're my little pumpkin."

"You're silly, daddy."

"What would you like for dinner? Pizza? Chinese food?"

"Pizza! I want pizza!!" Stella-Marie chimed.

I ordered her favourite Hawaiian pizza and we forgot work for a few minutes as we ate. Stella-Marie told me about her day between bites. Stella-Marie sounded happy and was adjusting well to living in this new place. She didn't seem too worried about my job anymore. She kissed me goodbye and said, "Get'em, daddy. See you tomorrow, nighty, night."

I breathed a sigh of relief my daughter seemed happy despite all that was happening. I was the new sheriff so the danger to me from who ever committed these murders must be minimal if any, so my family was safe. Still I told Aunt Louise to keep Stella-Marie indoors and keep the doors locked reporting any suspicious activity to me.

Gordon arrived a few minutes later, "I'm Special Agent Gordon Chum FBI," he said showing his badge then continuing he said, "I'm here to take over this case."

"No. You're not you're here to assist me and the good people of Driftwood."

"I am here to serve the people yes, and if that means taking over the investigation in a town that has seen fit to kill all its police officers save one..."

"How dare you? This town is peaceable. There is a perpetrator or perpetrators who have committed a heinous crime but we will get to the bottom of this."

"You should have recused yourself Sheriff."

I heard Penny Ambercrombie gasp and then mutter under her breath, "What a maniacal idiot and a kook to boot."

"No, shouldn't! This was my first day on the job. I was to begin tomorrow but I thought I'd get in and do a little paperwork first. I am imminently qualified to investigate this. I hadn't even met these men or their families; but I care very much about what has happened to them. They are police officers and my squad. Every one of them is mine so this crime was committed against me and my family. Do you understand?"

"I understand the feeling and I promise not to step on your toes, Sheriff. My men and I are at your disposal in this investigation. You are in charge. Perhaps we could discuss the particulars before my colleagues get here?" Gordon stated.

"Please follow me this way to my office, Special Agent Chum," I answered.

"Call me Gordon," my pal offered.

"People call me Stray, or G," I stated.

Gordon pretended to be shocked and lifted an eyebrow at me. Penny looked at Gordon with disgust but went back to the front desk of the station.

Gordon entered my office and shut the door, loudly. Spotting the pizza, he said, "That went well."

"Yes, it did. Did you see the dispatcher, Penny Abercrombie craning her head and her ears to listen to you?"

"I saw her when I came into the station. She was frowning at you and giving you dirty looks when you weren't looking like she didn't believe you belonged here, Gee."

"I noticed those looks all day," I answered.

"That should be the end of that you can thank me now. She is directing those looks to me now and I'll wager she'll spread all over town how you defended the honor of the dead."

"Thanks, Gordon for the assist; but how will we can we keep up the lie?"

"We begin a new friendship," Gordon said calmly then continued, "I hope you saved me a few slices of that pizza, I'm starved and my team is checking into the No-Tell Motel down the street within the hour."

I smiled and nodded handing him a couple of slices. It was good to see my old partner again.

"You are staying with me and Aunt Louise aren't you?" I asked.

"Lucky for you or is it me they are limited space in this town to stay and of course this allows me to begin a new friendship with you. All my agents have taken up the last rooms in the motel so I'm grateful your aunt will put me up. You did ask her, didn't you?"

"Didn't think I had to; you know Aunt Louise loves you."

Gordon raised another eyebrow.

"Fine I'll call her now."

I dialed and Aunt Louise answered her cell phone on the first ring. Aunt Louise said of course, Gordon was staying here. I told her not to tell anyone we knew her and she agreed after I told her why. Then she said she had to go as she had pulled over to answer the cell phone.

"So, it's settled?" Gordon asked.

I nodded.

"What a terrible first day on the job for you pal," Gordon commented, "Especially after what happened to you more than three and half years ago."

I thought back to what I had been through the last three and half years and I found myself reliving that chaotic time in my mind.

I'd been about eight years on the job in the city of Halton, Illinois, a cop, just like my dad and grandfather and uncles before me. The city had gone to the gangs. It was two steps and one step forward. Every time we turned around; another shooting another victim of a drive-by. Just the other day the victim was a seven-year-old kid innocently riding their bike! Luckily the kid lived; but we actively hunted for the shooter or shooters. I should have taken that as an omen seeing as my grandfather and my dad lost their lives in the police service, but I went merrily on my way doing my job not expecting my life to come crumbling all around me.

A routine call to a richer neighborhood for a disturbance started it all. The dispatcher didn't think to tell me it was a domestic disturbance and the man had a gun. I'm always careful in those situations; more careful then the average cop, but if you don't know you can't take precautions.

I knocked on the door and announced myself and shots barreled through the front door grazing my forehead and tearing my knee apart. I burst through the door grabbed the shooter and he shot me again.

That should have got me accolades and medals right? After all I was shot doing my job, but no, all of those rightly went to my partner, Gordon Chum. The third shot resulted in a thigh wound that almost made me bleed out on the spot if it wasn't for the quick work of my partner Gordon Chum securing the prisoner and belting my thigh. Okay, so I got a medal or two, but Gordon was the real hero. See why he was the first man I called when my force had been gunned down.

Gordon is a second generation Asian American. A good looking fellow and kinder than most men, he speaks softly and carries a big stick. People underestimating him rather walk away unscathed. Gordon standing at five foot six weighed roughly two hundred and ten pounds of pure muscle. He knew every fight technique I knew and more. He saved my life a time or two.

Gordon was arguably one of the best partners I've ever had. Gordon saved my life after I was shot on duty and secured the scene until back-up could get there. He also called for an ambulance for me. I was carted off to a hospital where I spent the next three weeks in intensive car being prayed over by my fellow cops, and the rest of the city.

Whatever chits they called in with the big guy upstairs it worked, I survived and I should have been happy about that; but all I could think was I missed my moment I was supposed to die like my dad and my grandfather before me on the job. It wasn't that I was that different when I came out of the coma.

Okay, so I had a few scars inside and out. My forehead now sported a scar that I could cover with bangs and temporarily bum leg. The leg didn't seem to want heal in fact at one point they threatened to take off my leg; but good old Gordon helped me fight them on that and the knee healed to the point I could walk on it. But it wasn't good enough for work, at least not then.

Suffering from self-loathing (and yes, a little post-traumatic stress disorder, if I truly admit it); I began to be curt with everyone closing myself off from everyone and everything. My wife, Gina took the brunt of all of this. I was cruel to her at every turn. When she came to visit, I'd ignore her.

I knew I needed help from the police shrink but I couldn't accept or admit that I, the wonder boy actually had a problem. Gordon begged me to quit loathing myself so much and making everyone else around me miserable but I didn't listen. I was content to wallow in my anger and self-loathing.

Weeks went by and Gina seemed unhappy despite her forced saccharine with me. She gave me an ultimatum get help; or she would leave me. I decided I wanted Gina so I found a shrink of my own choosing Doctor Collins for his add in the Yellow Pages.

Doctor Collins turned out to be a woman. Don't get me wrong she wasn't a fantasy (that blonde fantasy with legs up to here and hiding behind glasses); no she was more like your grandmother. Non-descript, her silver hair short and curled tight to her head. Her voice was soft and she always offered me milk and cookies before a session. I kind of felt weird at first like she was family and I'd never been all that chatty with family anyway. I had so much trouble talking at first that I'd just sit there and stare at the walls; but after a few sessions she got me to open up about my childhood and then finally about the shooting. I began to feel better and worked on getting my knee back in shape so I could return to work.

I had a routine and I followed it. Therapy followed by afternoon sessions of psychotherapy. With the drugs Doctor Collins prescribed, and all our talks I began to almost feel normal again. Okay, so I'm lying; I still had a few stray thoughts that I was a failure and that I should have died; but I labored hard to overcome them and worked on being nicer to my ball and chain. I even began to buy her flowers. As for my leg it was almost good enough to return to work.

Doctor Collins had scheduled my appointment for two p.m. on a Friday and I had looked forward to getting it over with and going home to surprise Gina. A cop buddy had offered me his family cottage and I planned a trip to the Poconos for the next week. I'd already called Gina's work and got her the next week off. It would be a fantastic surprise for her and a chance for us to just lay back and enjoy our weekend. I could even cook all the meals that I caught from the lake as it was loaded with fish.

I decided to change my appointment and let Gina know that it would now be at noon instead of two p.m... Surely, I could charm my shrink into seeing me earlier and if not well then I see her next week after my trip. I arrived at the doctor's office to find a note on the door. It seemed my shrink. Doctor Teresa Collins had died suddenly this morning and they were rescheduling. A number to call followed the announcement.

Died! And all they thought about was their schedule? Devastating and only then realizing how close I had gotten with my shrink. I fell to the floor crying and took about a half- an -hour to recover enough just to pull myself together. I told myself over and over everything would be okay but I didn't really believe it.

Enough of this shit!! A little therapy and I turned into a wimp; who cried at the drop of a hat. I was a Bullet and we were strong manly types; made of steel not mush!! People died!! Get over yourself I admonished myself. I had a life... a wife who loved me despite myself. It was time to man up and be the husband she deserved. I just had to get away with Gina. I'd go home and surprise her now.

Stopping at the gas station to fill-up and walking into pay I spotted roses. I picked some up and thought how pleased Gina would be. She deserved this after all I'd put her through the last two months. She'd surprised me two weeks ago, telling me that she was pregnant. I was overjoyed looking forward to our baby coming in six months.

We had a new beginning and I would make her as happy as Gina had made me. I thought about the look on her face; her joy at our baby and decided to book her favourite restaurant before we left town. We could then leave at nine p.m. I'd drive all night and we reach there by morning. It could be done despite my gimpy leg. Okay so I lied, I wasn't fully recovered; but soon I would be. My physical therapist was pleased and said I might even be able to go back to work in a month.

I went home opening the front door with my key and... You know what happened? It was that other old cliché...husband comes home and finds his wife naked doing the tango with another naked man.

I didn't recognize him from the back as he jumped out the window, naked clothes in hand. She could tell me who he was in her own good time. And I had plenty of time as I seethed and wanted to kill him but not her. I didn't want to hurt her at all I just wanted to take her in my arms and make this go away.

I took huge breaths and then realized it takes two to tango. I had brought this on with neglect and coolness towards her when all she did was support and love me. I took deep breaths to calm myself and rationalized. I was sure this was just a one-time thing.

I'd heard women could get quite horny in pregnancy I obviously had let her down. I had been a terrible husband moody brooding, distant and angry. Gina deserved better and I could forgive her this. Couldn't I? Sure, I was angry, but I would never harm Gina despite my thinking for her lapse in judgement. I had stared at her five-foot nine naked figure with its well-endowed breasts and tiny waist and wondered how she hid our baby in it. Her curly black hair fell in ringlets to her waist.

I realized I loved her. I loved our baby. It
had been my neglect that had driven her to
this; I was prepared to forgive her and take
her on my planned trip. We'd been married
fifteen glorious years, okay so not glorious,
fiery; but she was also pregnant and I
wanted my child to have a stable home with
two parents one of them me. I'd been spared
so my kid could grow up with a dad it was
as simple as that.

I told Gina all of this and she laughed. It
seems that she and her paramour had been
carrying on since day one of our marriage.
Once more she had an amniocentesis last
week and received the results this morning
the baby was his not mine. I was devastated
all those dreams of playing catch with my
daughter. Taking her to daughter and daddy
dances. Having her look up to me, with hero
worship came crashing down. Yes, I know it
could have been a boy; but I had my heart
set on a girl.

I admit it I went against all my principles
and begged her to stay and claim the baby
was mine. We were married so the baby was
legally mine. She laughed that twinkly laugh
that I knew so well and I had to restrain
myself from retaliating as she told me she

already left me I just hadn't noticed. Gina said she was tired of living a lie. Now that I knew it was all out in the open and she file for divorce and move in with him. She lunged at me slapping me and asked why could I be like him?

I want to hit back at her but I couldn't if I it back I wouldn't be any better than the men I arrested who abused their wives.

Why couldn't I be like him? The man that she slept with, she raged. I was stupefied and getting angrier by the moment I knew I needed to leave before I regretted losing my temper; but I needed to know who had replaced me.

She laughed again and said I find out soon. I begged her to tell me and she did.

HIM?

I fell to my knees. How could it be him? No, it wasn't Gordon Chum; but someone else I considered a friend and brother. Gordon wouldn't do that to me. The dirty dog who had betrayed me had been a partner, a mentor and good grief the man was old...fifty-five if he was a day and close to retirement.

Why had she cheated on me with my former
partner Derek? He'd broken the cop code
you didn't sleep with another cop's wife.
He'd slept around I heard how many women
he'd been with had she? I told her and she
laughed telling me it was his cover story.
She continued snickering and said at least
every woman didn't try to pick him up in
front of her. She packed her bags and then
trounced out the front door to join him at his
house.

I thought I could handle it all and maybe I
could have if she hadn't come back a half an
hour later saying she'd changed her mind.
She stripped to her skivvies and begged me
to change her mind. What's a hot-blooded
male to do? I wanted to prove I was the
better man, the better lover, so I turned my
back and began stripping too.

That's the last thing I remember before
waking up in hospital. How I got there and
what happened after that I couldn't recall
until much later.

The doctor kept speaking to me but it
sounded like gibberish. My brain didn't
want to understand. I don't know why. I
closed my eyes, but before I drift under, I
hear them talking.

"Will he be okay now, doctor?" Gina asked.

"We'll know better when he answers my questions," I perceive the doctor say far away.

I recalled hearing footsteps as someone left. A voice I recognized as Gina whispered in my ear, "You stupid son of a bitch. Why didn't you die? You'll wish you had now."

I struggled to wake before she could harm me; but I remember it was like moving under quicksand. I heard an alarm sound and footsteps run into the room.

"What did you do you now, you evil bitch?" I heard Gordon yell as I feel myself falling through layers of unconsciousness into nothingness.

~0~

Excerpt from ~ **A** Penny Saved A
Murder Earned

Chapter 1 – Bloody Shoes

"A penny saved is a penny earned" ~ Benjamin
Franklin

T he blood streaked across the floor, but

he had carefully sidestepped it. Stupid bitch!
She got what she deserved. How dare she
defile his Angel's property? He hadn't left a
trace...had he? No, he was too clever by
half.

A voice he didn't recognize interrupted his
thoughts, "I didn't spot you entering.
Working late, dear? Of course, I forgot; you
have an early opening tomorrow."

The man strode closer to the killer and the
body lying on the floor, "Wait a minute, you
aren't the lady. Who are you? You shouldn't
be here," the man continued clearly alarmed.

"You shouldn't be here either," the murderer insisted.

"You, you killed Megan. I'm telling."

"Really? You know this was something you shouldn't be allowed to see."

"I'm leaving. I didn't notice anything," the man lied, witnessing the blood.

"I'm sorry pal. Wrong place, wrong time!" the killer answered.

The homeless man ran dodging racks, finally deciding to hide behind some shelving. The killer ran after him, puzzled for a moment because he could see no trace of the homeless person. The murderer then laughed, as he realized how foolish the vagrant was being, his stench gave him away. He subdued the man with a Taser gun. Waiting seconds. he then pulled the man from his hiding place. Taking ties from within his pocket; he fastened the man's arms and feet. Satisfied that the homeless person was now trussed up like a turkey, he smiled.

"P...P....P...Please! I don't want to die!" the man cried, visibly sweating and starting to shake.

The man tried to kick out his legs and arms but failed.

"You've heard about fate? Well sorry but this is your fate, buddy!" the murderer explained.

"P...P...P...Please, I'm begging you! Couldn't you let me go? I won't tell! I'll move to another city. Besides who would listen to a homeless man?"

"Someone would. My Angel would."

The homeless man then smiled as if to gain trust from this killer, "You won't hurt the lady who owns the store, will you?" he asked.

"I would never harm my Angel. How dare you?" the killer responded outraged.

"S...S...S...Sorry! I didn't mean to insult you! Please just let me go. I'm harmless ask anyone...."

"What is your name?"

"Why do you need my name?" He asked looking puzzled then reconsidering he answered, "My name is Al."

The killer put his gloves back on and
smoothed them and then turned his back on
his victim.

"You're going to kill me now. Aren't you?
Just don't harm the sweet lady who owns
this store. Will it hurt?" the man asked
resigned.

"I would never hurt my Angel. She is sweet,
isn't she? Unfortunately, that also makes
unscrupulous people take advantage of her."

"I promise I would never take advantage of
her kindness. I wouldn't!!! She's the best
part of my day and this city, Happy Valley,
Ontario. She picked me up from the gutter
and helped me."

"I know you wouldn't and it hurts me to do
this. Tell you what though, I'll make your
death painless because I like you, Al," the
killer offered, feeling suddenly sorry for the
man. Then he checked himself. Living on
the streets was hell; maybe he was doing the
guy a favour? Yes, of course he was. Taking
a pill bottle out of his pocket and opening
the dispenser, he placed some in a coffee
cup he took from the sideboard. He filled the
cup with the tepid coffee from the coffee
pot, stirring the pills in rapidly.

"C...c...c...couldn't you let me go? I won't tell and I'll watch over her when you're not here."

"Sorry, times up, Al. Here now, drink this coffee," the assassin commanded placing the mug at Al's lips.

Al tried not to drink and spit some of the coffee out, but the assassin plugged his nose and the cup was soon empty.

"Admit it Al, you had a crappy life. Just give in and go to the light. I hear good things wait there for people like you," the killer stated.

Al tried to fight some more, but he soon found it was losing battle. Al's breathing slowed as he slipped into a deep sleep and stopped breathing altogether. His age and living on the streets made the pills work fast.

Now what to do with the body? The killer thought. His Angel must not find this man's remains here, bad enough he left Megan's body here for his Angel to find. He couldn't hide Megan though she needed to be found.

Every needed to know she suffered for her crime. Maybe even his Angel would see Megan's evil and protect herself from people like that. This man, Al however knew his Angel and she cared about him. It was so like her to look after the homeless. He could let her cry over Al. Where could he put the man so he wouldn't be found?

The dumpster of course...the perfect place for Al! The day after tomorrow was garbage day. Covered in garbage no one would find Al.

~0~

The next day

Lily

Ominous clouds replaced the

morning's sunlight turning the skies to shades of deep purple and navy blue, streaked with gray. Lily Kelly stared at the sky for moment, and then departed the

courthouse doors in Happy Valley, Ontario,
Canada, skipping down the steps. The city
looked its age of over a hundred as the
buildings downtown looked old and
decrepit. If only the town could find some
money to fix downtown Lily thought.

Then her mind turned to Amelia, her cousin
and best friend. Amelia needed Lily to
support her in her grief. Lily had a fight with
her husband Horace again this morning
about how much time he was spending at the
office and how much time she spent
supporting Amelia. Lily was always
working, and so was Horace, so how much
time was Rose their fourteen-year-old
daughter really getting?

Lily had won in court, but all she could
think about was her family. Everyone
needed her and she felt like she was being
pulled in three different directions.
Something had to give and it looked like it
was her job. She would have to cut back on
some of her work. Her family had to come
first.

Lily stumbled some more over the steps
only stopping from hurrying across the
courtyard to her office, when her heel broke
on her shoe. Today was supposed to be

about her victory after her win in court; but it appeared with her expensive shoe's heel breaking, she was mistaken. They ought to get the ruts in the paving stones fixed; that was her reflection as she cursed her bad break. What did they say about omens? Maybe she should have taken a hint from the heavens' darkening? She noted as her bad luck had seemed to get worse with the arrival of some reporters.

"Ms. Kelly, give us a statement about the Rockwood case?" yelled one reporter.

"Ms. Kelly, how does the Sulimani family feel about your victory?" yelled another.

One bold reporter stepped forward, "Crown Attorney Kelly, congratulations on your win. Was it hard to try a case which involved a council member?" asked Paul Knight from the local television station, thrusting a microphone in Lily's face.

"Anyone who commits a crime in Happy Valley will be tried by the Crown with the full force of the law, despite their office. So no, I did not find it difficult to do my job," Lily replied testily.

"Thank you, Ms. Kelly. What does the Sulimani family think about the judgement?"

"Amani Sulimani was five-years old, when Zebadiah Rockwood's truck went through a red light. His truck struck the back of the Sulimani's SUV killing her. He then left the scene pursued by good Samaritans, who wished to stop Mr. Rockwood from continuing driving drunk: a pursuit caused by Mr. Rockwood's actions, which put a number of lives in danger."

"Will the family be comforted with this conviction?" queried another reporter.

"Amani Sulimani existed as their only child. Mr. Rockwood's conviction will not bring her back, but hopefully will bring some peace of mind to her family knowing he will be behind bars." Lily answered.

"Do you sense, given your own personal tragedies that you'll be able to get a sentence fitting the crime?"

"My family's history does not come into my trial cases, only the person's guilt."

"And when will sentencing take place?" asked another reporter.

"Sentencing will take place next month."

"Thank you, Ms. Kelly. This is Paul Knight reporting, with an update on the Zebadiah Rockwood's drunken driving case. Zebadiah Rockwood was a long-time council member here in Happy Valley. He took a leave of absence to deal with his legal issues. Mr. Rockwood was charged with impaired driving causing death, two counts of failing to remain at the scene of an accident and dangerous driving last December. When asked about the conviction today Mr. Rockwood and his lawyer issued a no comment. We will have the complete story for you at six pm. Paul Knight reporting for CHPV-TV."

Lily hated speaking on camera, even though it was part of her job as the Crown attorney, so she was glad the scrum had been completed.

She hated sounding tough and unyielding but it was all in the description of her job title. She had fought difficult challenges to get this job and she had to work hard and fight hard to keep it. After all there were aspects of her job she loved like putting the bad people that would harm others away. The press was gone and she was now free to go to her office to file her reports and leave early. She crossed the street, entered her building and went straight up to her office.

"Victory is mine!" Lily Kelly cried triumphantly as she walked into her office.

"So, you won?" asked Colleen Finn, her administrative assistant.

"Yes, I bested that idiot, Michael Taylor. He thought he would beat me in court. He actually believed his client would win."

"Good for you, boss, I knew you would nail his lily-white ass to the wall. He's such a scumbag lawyer all his clients seem to be as guilty as hell."

"Colleen! Language! But thank-you," Lily answered, showing pearly white teeth.

Colleen looked expectantly at Lily and she felt stupid did she miss something? Oh, the joke! Lily hadn't laughed at Colleen's wit.

"Funny, I got it. Zebadiah Rockwood's sentencing takes place next month, but he will be held until then; no bail, no goodbyes to his favourite watering hole. As the Crown, I'll recommend the longest sentence

I can get that he can serve. It's victories like these which make my job worthwhile. I don't know how much satisfaction this will give that little girl's family, but at least they'll know her killer remains in jail. He can't take another life again, because he will be incarcerated."

Lily went over to her desk and sat down.

"Can you imagine Michael Taylor, tried to use the defence that Rockwood was not drunk. Just tired? He claimed Rockwood drank only after the accident, while driving his company's truck; so, the company couldn't possibly be responsible,"

"I believe you told me that before," Colleen commented, "However I'm glad you proved he'd drank so much before getting in the truck. That proved he was legally under the influence when the accident occurred. I hope I was some help in that aspect."

"Yes, you were invaluable."

"Thanks, Lily."

"It's still early; only nine forty-five, and my day's clear until what, two-thirty?"

"That's correct." Colleen replied.

Colleen checked a day planner, frowning, "Is everything okay, Lily? You seem a little down."

"Everything is fine. Amelia's grand opening starts at noon, but I promised to be there sooner if possible. If I go right now, I'll surprise her," Lily grabbed her coat to leave.

"I'm glad she's doing so well. Although after what happened, Amelia needs the encouragement. Please tell her, I'll try to get to her store another day. I hope her store has great success."

"Thank-you, I will tell Amelia. Hold all my calls Colleen. Unless it's urgent then call my cell."

"I'll do that. What time should I say you'll be back?" Colleen responded to a departing Lily.

"Tell whoever asks that I'll be back after two p.m..."

"And if they ask where you are?" Colleen questioned.

"Tell them I'm meeting with a witness," Lily replied with a wink.

"If there's cake bring me back a piece. Please, boss?" Colleen begged.

"I ordered a cake, but it's not supposed to arrive until one thirty so we'll see. I'm leaving now. Remember only urgent calls to my cell phone." Lily cautioned, leaving through the front door.

She twisted her shimmering brown hair back up into its traditional bun. Pulling out her cell phone, she dialled Amelia's store. There was no answer. How odd! Amelia must be busy putting out last minute stock.

~0~

A few minutes ago

A lone male walked into the store. His left hand held a gun while his right hand steadied it. He strode in with caution. His dark brown eyes dart from corner to corner, searching for an assailant. His well over six-foot tall frame slouched. Ruggedly handsome, with dark brown hair clipped short to his head; he was dressed in a dark blue jacket and dress pants; a badge is also clipped to his belt buckle. Finding the scene secure he putting his gun away and pulled a pair of gloves out of his suit coat pocket and a pair of booties, which he slipped on his shoes.

He checked the victim. No pulse. Advancing forward, he bent down to check the second woman; her phone still in her hand, her head bloody. He noted the second victim was still breathing, though unconscious. He looked around, as if waiting for someone. Deciding they weren't coming yet; he took out a mini recorder. He started scanning the scene and speaking aloud.

"This is Sergeant Detective Emmett Rogers. I am at the scene of a homicide, at Quirks, one forty-five Maple Street. A woman lays sprawled out across the floor. The woman's arms are positioned underneath her, as if to break her fall.

The back of her head and her long blonde hair are streaked in rusty-brown blood, as well as her clothing below the hair. Blood pools across the floor spiralling out in two long streams. Footprints are noticeable, as if someone stepped through the drying blood. The weapon appears to be a pair of scissors, found beneath the victim. I have marked both of these."

The man spoke aloud as he walked around, carefully avoiding contaminating the evidence, by stepping over a paper cup.

"A coffee cup... possibly one of those lattes is overturned. I'm sure the forensics team can determine this if necessary. Its contents are also spilled on the floor and countertop. Coffee is spilled at the front door and possibly on the shoes. The second victim's shoes are not on the bruised victim, but on the floor. The shoes can be found near an overturned ladder, at the front door. It appears the woman, who appears unconscious, may have been carrying a ladder and toy stock to place on the shelves, when she slipped in the blood.

The man paused to think.

"This might be a setup by the second victim to cover the actual crime. The woman, however, seems to have the victim's blood all over her clothes and hands like she crawled through the blood. I believe there are two possible scenarios here. One the owner of the shop, one Amelia Kelly (the unconscious person), murdered her employee or unknown victim and set this up to appear a perpetrator broke in and killed her accidentally hurting herself in the process. Or two... it is at it now seems that she stumbled on the crime scene and harmed herself."

He pulled out a notebook again and examined the room taking some more taking notes.

"Is it a robbery gone wrong? It is too soon to tell. The store owner will be en-route to hospital as soon as the EMTs have arrived. Interview to follow. The time is now ten twenty a.m.," he concluded turning off his recorder.

He examined the room scribbling on his notepad.

~0~

Now

Lily and Detective Emmett Rogers

The man's eyes turn and his vision focused completely. A woman entered the store. His eyes took in her tall and slender form and her long shimmering brown hair, pulled into a tight roll. He noted she was closely followed by the Emergency technicians and gave a sigh of relief. The woman entering the store had brilliant blue eyes. He had a feeling she often turned heads, even dressed as she was, in her business attire. But he noted something about the way she walked screamed money and upper class.

"Oh no, Amelia!" she screamed and tried to rush to Amelia, but was stopped by the man's arm.

"This is a crime scene ma'am. We don't want you disrupting our evidence. Let the EMTs and detectives do their job. Then you can go to ...you're er...friend?" Sergeant Detective Rogers commanded.

"Crime scene? What has happened?" Lily asked politely, wanting to be cooperative.

"Ma'am, I'll know better after I assess the scene. Until then, please remain near the front door." ordered Detective Rogers briskly.

"I promise I'll stay out of the way; but at least can I get her Adrienne Changs?"

"What or who, are Adrienne Changs?" said Detective Rogers looking totally perplexed.

"Shoes, those shoes right there!" Lily pointed to a pair of heels lying behind the yellow tape.

"You're worried about shoes? Woman! Do you have any idea of what's going on here?" Detective Rogers snapped, shaking his head.

"You sexist pig!" countered Lily under her breath, "Men!" Losing her temper now and louder she continued, "Those shoes are worth five hundred dollars! And she probably wore them for what a half an hour? And you want me to walk away and leave them to be destroyed in some kind of liquid!"

"Liquid that's blood! And five hundred dollars for shoes? Is she crazy?" Detective Rogers asked dumfounded.

"No! She's not crazy. How dare you?" Lily asked suddenly outraged.

He was smug, wasn't he? Handsome yes, but oh so smug, she questioned herself. That wasn't important. Amelia was injured on the floor and he questioned her? Instead of letting her go to her cousin! What was wrong with Lily? Why was she so worried and focused on the shoes? They were only shoes. Amelia was injured; who cared about footwear?

"Sorry, ma'am, the shoes are evidence now. Name? Occupation? Address?" Detective Rogers barked, ignoring her statement.

"I want to see your identification first, and then you'll get the information," insisted Lily.

"I am Sergeant Detective Emmett Rogers," the man revealed, showing his police badge.

"Oh, that's funny," Lily uttered laughing, "If you and Amelia were introduced it would be Aem and Em."

Lily followed this up by hysterically laughing and then alternatively crying. What was wrong with her? She never lost it like this. She always appeared a professional.

She had seen crime scenes. She could handle this. Couldn't she? Amelia would be okay. Wouldn't she?!

"Get a hold of yourself Lily. You have embarrassed yourself," Lily heard this voice in her head, she recognized as her father's. Odd, how her Dad's voice, came back to her now, she rarely saw him, since he lived in Prague and he only called about twice a year.

"Ma'am, what you are saying is not remotely funny. Are you all right? Put your head between your knees if you feel lightheaded. I think your friend's relatively fine. She might have a head injury and possibly a broken leg, but she'll be okay." Sergeant Detective Rogers then turned to the Emergency technicians (EMTs) to seek confirmation demanded, "Right?"

"Should be. But head injuries can be serious," the one EMT replied.

Sergeant Detective Rogers shot him a disapproving look.

"Yes, the Sergeant Detective is right. She'll be fine. She'll be taken to the hospital for treatment," the Emergency Technician agreed, finally.

"See...what did I tell you? Now that we have that out of the way; I need to see some identification and then get some answers to my questions. Name? Address? Occupation? The reason you are here?" Detective Rogers barked at Lily.

"Amelia's my best friend and more. This should have been the greatest day of her life, her opening of her new store; a one of kind toy and collectibles retailer. A grand opening and now it's ruined. Who did this to her?" Lily asked, uncharacteristically wringing her hands and still trying to regain her calm, as thoughts of Amelia's demise threatened to enter her mind.

"Ma'am, she slipped in blood. She hit her head on the floor and on the ladder. No one harmed her. She did this to herself," explained Sergeant Detective Rogers.

"I realize she's clumsy, but she didn't put blood there to trip in," defended Lily angrily.

"No, the blood was spilled by whoever killed the woman behind the counter."

"Someone is dead behind the counter?" Lily responded shocked and surprised.

"No comment; as I explained Ma'am this is an active crime scene. Now as I asked before what is your name?" Detective Rogers insisted forcefully again.

"Lily Kelly-Brooksfield. My husband is Horace Brooksfield, the mayor. We live down the street on Beaconfield. Do you want the number? It's nine hundred and sixty-two." she replied condescendingly.

"If you're Mayor Brooksfield's wife... then you're the Crown Attorney." Coming to this realization, Sergeant Detective Rogers hid a sigh.

"Please update me on this active crime scene, now," commanded Lily pulling back her shoulders.

Emmett Rogers put on his professional face and smiled. The smile was just so warm and inviting that Lily felt warm all over. Lily frowned back at him; she was just felt so angry. This cop who grinned back at her was the biggest reason. She was a married woman. She shouldn't be attracted to a cop who apparently existed to give her grief and solve a murder. She threw back her shoulders again. It was okay to look at someone attractive, she excused herself.

Everyone looks, and most of the time it meant nothing. It's only if you acted on any attraction it became wrong. She would never act on the temptation. Besides he appeared to be the most annoying man she'd ever met.

"Ma'am, you know I can't fill you in on any of this case. You'll have to recuse yourself from this case, as you're familiar with the crime scene." Detective Rogers emphasized, once again interrupting Lily's thoughts.

"Why don't you just come out and say what you think. You consider me a suspect," Lily uttered.

"A lot of people are suspects in my book. I have to make a case for them committing the crime or I have to eliminate them as suspects. And don't attempt to solve this yourself; amateurs just get in the way." Detective Rogers explained, his eyes wandering.

Lily was slightly amused. Detective Rogers thought she wanted to insinuate herself into this murder investigation? She might not have before that comment, but she did now. He seemed to be focusing on Amelia or Lily as his prime suspect. Lily knew neither of them had committed this murder, so that meant she had no choice but to find out for herself who had committed this crime. She would pretend she wanted nothing to do with this situation, even as far as passing it off to her underling Barbara. After all she could always investigate behind the scenes.

Spotting the emergency technicians Detective Rogers exclaimed "Oh good, the ambulance has arrived to take the victim to the hospital. Now can we can get down to brass tacks; you can fill me in on these people and anything else you know or have held back from me."

"I want to go with her," Lily protested.

Lily pulled herself back taking several steps back putting distance between herself and this cop. It was odd, how alive she felt when she jousted with him. He was a cop investigating a murder and she was married.

"Stop this now Lily!" She told herself.

"Ma'am, I realize you want to go see your friend. Before I could release you from the scene, I need something from you. We need you to identify the other victim. Maybe you'll recognize her when I turn over the body." Detective Rogers explained,

softening a little, as he slipped on another
pair of gloves.

"Only if you'll stop calling me Ma'am. Call
me Lily or Crown Attorney Kelly, but not
Ma'am. It makes me feel eighty years old."

"If it will get you to identify the
victim...thank-you Crown Attorney Kelly."

"Let's look, shall we?" Lily agreed.

Lily took a breath as she gathered herself to
observe who lay there dead. She gasped as
she stared over the counter to see the back of
the woman's head. She covered her mouth
in horror.

"Good grief! I never realized they appear so
alike from the back," replied Lily shocked.

"Who do you think she looks like ma'am?"
demanded Detective Rogers.

"What did I say about ma'am? Don't they
give you sensitivity training at Police
College? You want to know who this is?
This is Megan, Megan Fowler. She's an
employee of Amelia's. But she works
evenings she's...is.... was a college student. I
can't believe this is Megan. Megan is such a
sweet girl and worked part-time to be able to

422
S. G. Lee

go to school and support her mother. Why would someone kill her? Do you think it's possible someone mistook her for Amelia?" Lily rambled, tears slipping from her eyes.

"That's a possibility, ma'am. We will explore all aspects."

"I know the drill, Sergeant Detective Rogers." Lily gave the detective a mock salute, "Why can't you admit that they mistook Megan for Amelia?"

"We don't have any of the facts yet, Ms. Kelly," replied Detective Rogers.

"What about Amelia? Is she in any danger?" asked Lily. "If I were to speculate, I suppose that could be a possibility," Detective Rogers answered non-committally.

They both watched as the technicians gathered the evidence and blood samples and took pictures before the body was taken away.

"Will someone be assigned to guard her and keep her safe?" Lily asked getting exasperated.

"That's in motion, Crown Attorney Kelly," Detective Rogers explained, trying not to sound annoyed that she's telling him how to do his job.

Detective Rogers and Lily turned as another cop swaggered into the store. Burly and well over six feet tall, his hair was dark like Detective Rogers. Unlike Detective Rogers, this man preened like a peacock; Lily was aware of the type. Guys like him smiled with their mouths and not their eyes. They thought all women should admire them and only them. She noted his smile went as far as his lips.

"What have you got here, Emmett?"

"Nothing you need to be concerned about, Brad," Detective Rogers replied, obvious tension showing between the two.

"You should be able to get some great publicity out of this one," Brad said loudly to Detective Rogers.

Brad then strutted over to the murder scene.

"It's my case, Brad," Detective Rogers insisted.

"I'm not trying to interfere," Brad persisted walking around, "I just thought if you needed some help, I would lend a hand. It doesn't look like something you could handle on your own."

"I don't need help, thanks, Brad. I don't need you messing up my crime scene." Detective Rogers declared "I've got it all under control.

"It doesn't look that way to me. I would solve this case quickly. You could use me in your corner," Brad continued.

"We don't need you. Now the Crown attorney is here, so I have it all in hand. Goodbye, Brad." Detective Rogers practically spat.

"Ah, the lovely Crown attorney Kelly is here. Can't go now," Brad exclaimed trying to sound charming but failing miserably.

"And you are?" asked Lily putting her full aristocratic chill in to her voice.

"I'm Brad Owens, at your service, Attorney Kelly. Sergeant Detective Brad Owens. I use to be Emmett's partner," Brad explained smiling and pointing to Detective Rogers.

Detective Rogers rolled his eyes. "Thank God, you're not anymore," He stated under his breath loud enough for only he and Lily to hear.

"So. what do you think, Crown Attorney? Was it a robbery gone wrong?" asked Brad.

"I'm not sure. Why do I bother to tell you this? This isn't your case," Lily commented suddenly not willing to share with Brad.

She didn't know why. Something about his smile, and the way Emmett Rogers had reacted to him made her dislike him. Brad's smile was phony, like a used car salesman. It was slick and slimy. That wasn't fair to used car sales people. Lily was sure they were more honest than this phoney, Brad Owens. Lily had come across a lot of people in her job. She certainly felt she was a good judge of character. In fact, she could spot a phoney a mile away. Detective Emmett Rogers, unlike Brad Owens, appeared like he knew his job. She'd heard of him many times, but had never run into him on the job until today. Thank goodness for the Internet on her phone. He was a dedicated cop. He had done his time and had come up through the ranks, strictly on merit. Detective Rogers didn't seem to like Brad Owens and that was reason enough for Lily not to trust him.

Emmett Rogers had an exemplary record as a police officer; she trusted his instincts and knowledge over this smarmy, Detective Brad Owens. He'd get to the bottom of this. Lily wished he would let her leave soon and check on Amelia. They had spent their teen years together and were as close as sisters. She'd always felt responsible for Amelia, being two years older. She wanted to make sure Amelia was okay.

"Okay. Well if you don't need my help, I'm leaving because I have work to do. There are other crimes to investigate." Brad answered leaving, "See you around Emmett."

"Not if I see you first," muttered Emmett under his breath.

"So, am I free to go?" Lily demanded.

Emmett then offered her his pen.

"I have your address, so as long as you sign here in my notebook. "You are free to go," he said gesturing.

Lily glanced over at Detective Owens and watched him leave before reaching for the book. She then signed her signature with a flourish. Detective Rogers scanned the signature, thinking momentarily, it was just as elegant as Lily. He shook his head, reminding himself to stay connected to reality.

"So, I am free to go, Detective?" Lily repeated.

"I'll be checking in on your friend, of course, and I may need to follow-up with you later, but as of now, you are free to go." he smiled, already exhausted.

"I would expect nothing else from you, Detective Rogers."

As she got into her car, Lily breathed a sigh of relief she had finally been able to leave the store. She buckled up her seatbelt and put her car in gear.

Backing the car up, Lily pulled out into the street and narrowly missed getting hit by a car, she didn't view. Luckily the other driver slammed on his brakes. She noticed the male driver shouting, "Stupid woman driver" as she read his lips in her rear-view mirror. He was justified in his anger. It had been her fault, but she didn't have time to dwell.

She headed down the road toward the hospital; despite her resolve her mind wandered. She thought about poor Megan's mother getting the news of her daughter's death. It would kill Lily to get news like that about her adopted daughter, Rose.

What kind of monster kills a young woman? Why did, whomever it was, have to kill Megan? It wasn't a robbery, she'd read in Detective Rogers' notes, when he gave his notebook to her to sign her statement. As Lily drove, more questions flooded into her head. Was Amelia the real target? Megan certainly appeared like Amelia from the back.

Amelia didn't appear too hurt. Maybe she suffered a concussion? Concussions could be serious; she knew from her readings. The EMT hadn't said Amelia was in serious condition though. Not that the EMT could explain before Emmett Rogers got on his case. Revving the engine, she waited impatiently for the light to go green. Once Lily reached the hospital, she could reassure herself, Amelia was all right.

If you enjoyed this book and or/first partial chapter from A Penny Saved A Murder Earned-Book 1 of the Kelly Murder Mysteries or any of the other excerpts (look for them in e-book and paperback at Amazon) please also look for my other e-

books and paperbacks listed on the next page and available now at Amazon and consider leaving me a few words at your Amazon .

Sincerely S. G. Lee.

List of Books by S. G. Lee

Murder Mysteries

Dreams Can Kill

The Kelly Murder Mysteries

1~A Penny Saved A Murder Earned-

2~ A Diller A Dollar A Really Dead Scholar

3~Betty Blue Lost Her Holiday Shoe

4~What Will Poor Robin Do?

5~This Little Piggy Had None

The Kelly Murder Mysteries-Book 1-3

A Stitch in Time-Prequel to the Kelly Murder Mysteries

The Sheriff Bullet Murder Mysteries

1-Stray Bullet

2~Untraceable

Coming soon~ 3~Dead Center

Paranormal:

Love's Labour's Won

A Tiger's Heart Wrapped in a Player's Hide

Reborn – a novella~ prequel

Short Story Books

Murder Most Fowl

Jack be Nimble

Day of the Dead

Legends, Folktales and other Stories

The Stuff of Nightmares

ObsessionX2

Christmas

Christmas is Calling

The Christmas Card

The Christmas Angel

Visions of Sugarplums

Poetry

A Poetic Touch - The Human Condition

Poetry in Motion ~ A Forest of Feelings

Children's Books

Mare the Hare

Henrietta and the Donor Egg

The Magical Life of Me

www.ingramcontent.com/pod-product-compliance
Lightning Source LLC
Chambersburg PA
CBHW022239020726
47496CB00004B/982